ANGELA
HENRY

ANGELA HENRY

was once told that her past-life careers included spy, researcher and investigator. She stuck with what she knew because today she's a mystery-writing library reference specialist who loves to people-watch and eavesdrop on conversations.

She's the author of four mysteries featuring the equally nosy amateur sleuth Kendra Clayton, and she's also the founder of the award-winning MystNoir website, which promotes African-American mystery writers, and was named a "Hot Site" by USATODAY.com. When she's not working, writing or practicing her stealth, she loves to travel, watch B horror movies and is an admitted anime addict. She lives in Ohio and is currently hard at work trying to meet her next deadline.

The Paris Secret

ANGELA HENRY

CARINA
PRESS™

CARINA PRESS™

ISBN-13: 978-0-373-06248-5

THE PARIS SECRET

Recycling programs
for this product may
not exist in your area.

www.CarinaPress.com

Printed in U.S.A.

The
Paris
Secret

Author Note

In the fall of 2007,
much like my heroine Maya Sinclair,
I took a solo trip to Paris, France. And just like Maya
I also toured the Palace of Versailles and heard a tale
about a French queen who gave birth at the palace to
a child fathered by her African lover. I was instantly
fascinated by this story and started researching it
as soon as I got home. What I discovered was that
though this child, Louise-Marie Therese, aka the
Black Nun of Moret, did in fact exist, and was
financially supported by King Louis XIV throughout
her life, her true origins and the circumstances
surrounding her birth remain a mystery
as well as a topic of debate.

Acknowledgments

I would like to thank my editor, Jessica Schulte,
for seeing the potential in this book. Her guidance,
patience and expertise helped me to make it shine
and her humor made it a fun and painless process. I
would also like to thank the fine folks at Carina Press
for giving this quirky cross-genre book a home and
for being such a great team to work with.

UN

"WHAT KIND OF an idiot goes to the most romantic city on earth all by herself to get over a broken heart?"

That would be me. And the slightly nasal voice in my head asking that question belonged to my best friend, Kelly. That voice continued to nag me about how dangerous it was to be in a foreign country with a broken heart as I stood in the long line at Customs at Charles de Gaulle airport. It even had the nerve to follow me when I boarded the tram to baggage claim. She wouldn't shut up. I wanted to scream that I wasn't an idiot and my heart wasn't *that* broken. But shrieking like a crazy person in the middle of the airport? Not such a good idea, mainly because handcuffs and a straitjacket wouldn't go with my outfit.

By the time I'd arrived in Paris that morning my emotions were bouncing from one extreme to the next. I was extremely tired from my sleepless overnight flight, extremely excited to finally be in Paris and extremely scared because I had come all alone to a foreign country—where I barely knew the language. Maybe Kelly was right. Maybe I was an idiot. But it was too late now. I was already here. And I was going to enjoy myself if it killed me. I just needed a little sleep and then Kelly's voice would disappear just like my last boyfriend.

"Ah, Madame Sinclair, our solo traveler has arrived," exclaimed a dapper Frenchman holding a clipboard when I finally managed to locate my tour group in terminal 2C.

The man's badge read Sebastian Marcel, TransEuro Tours. He was dressed in a neat blue three-piece suit with a striped shirt and red bow tie. A white handkerchief poked out of his jacket pocket. He sported a headful of thick snow-white hair and wire-rimmed glasses perched on the end of his narrow nose.

"Bonjour," I said to Monsieur Marcel and the group. Curious stares and a few friendly nods returned my greeting. My gray eyes, honey-colored skin and long, thick dark hair are always a source of speculation. I could see the unasked questions frozen in every furrowed brow and narrowed eye. But they'd be stunned to know that I was just as curious as they were about my origins. My mother had been African-American. I have no idea about my father. The answer to that mystery died with my adoptive parents.

"I trust your flight was pleasant?" the tour guide inquired.

"Yes. Thank you."

A quick perusal of the twenty or so people gathered confirmed my worst fears. The tour was entirely made up of couples. And I wasn't just the only solo traveler. I was also the youngest and the only one with a permanent tan. Thankfully, the tour was semi-escorted, which meant after we were escorted to our hotel and given info on optional group excursions, we would be left on our own to do as we pleased, meaning I wouldn't have to stick out like a sore thumb for much longer.

"So you're on your own?" asked a middle-aged woman with glasses and short brown hair. Her accent was Australian.

"Yep, just me. Couldn't find a friend to bring," I replied with as much cheerfulness as my exhaustion would allow.

Actually, I was supposed to be on this trip with Ben, my boyfriend of a year. However, since he'd recently gone back to his ex-wife, he was no longer in the picture. Apparently, much like a pair of cheap magnets, Ben and his ex just couldn't stay together or apart for any great length of time and reconciled and split up every few years. Ben had felt so guilty about dumping me that he'd attached the e-tickets for the trip—paid in full—in my "Dear Maya" email as a lovely parting gift. More than likely he just wanted to avoid me coming to his dental practice and acting a damned fool if he tried to take his ex on *my* trip. Either way, I still felt like a losing game-show contestant who'd wanted the grand prize and instead ended up with the set of Ginsu steak knives—plunged into my heart. I'd actually thought Ben was going to propose to me in Paris. He'd proposed alright, just not to me.

Since no one I knew was able to go with me, I cashed in Ben's ticket and bought a new wardrobe for the trip. A free trip and new clothes hardly made up for the two months' worth of tears I'd cried. But they were certainly a step in the right direction. And besides, who am I to stand in the way of two idiots in love? Heavy emphasis on the *idiots* part.

"Well, good for you! Don't think *I* could go it all alone, though. Be too scared. I'm Meryl Berman, by the way, and this is me husband, Ted. We're from Brisbane. This is our first trip abroad." She held out her hand. Ted Berman smiled and nodded wearily though I couldn't tell if he looked tired due to the flight or to his wife's babbling.

"Nice to meet you. I'm Maya Sinclair from Columbus, Ohio. This is my first time overseas, too." I shook her hand.

Monsieur Marcel quickly gathered us together and escorted us through the crowded airport and down to the lower level parking lot where the air-conditioned bus that would take us to our hotel sat waiting.

"So what do you do in Columbus?" asked Meryl as we stood in line waiting to board the bus.

"I'm a reference librarian at Capital College."

"Oh, a librarian. How lovely. You must be awfully smart."

Not when it comes to men, I wanted to say but didn't.

Ten minutes later, we were boarded and on our way. I was happy to be sitting by myself so I wouldn't have to make small talk. I could just stare out the window and keep an eye out for Paris landmarks.

And then after what seemed like miles of factories belching smoke and corporate-looking office buildings, there it was. Off in the distance, coming up on the right side of the bus, was the Eiffel Tower in all its glory. Of course, I'd seen replicas of it in Vegas and at Kings Island. I never dreamed I'd see the real thing in person and it took my breath away. I pulled out my digital camera and started snapping pictures. I could feel myself relaxing. A smile tugged at the corners of my mouth. I was *really* in Paris. Maybe this would be okay after all.

Something hit my foot. A tube of hair gel.

"Sorry," came a voice next to me. One of my tour

mates leaned across the aisle. His artfully spiked blond hair indicated that the gel was his.

"No problem." I smiled and handed him the gel.

"I can't believe you found room for all your damned hair care products but forgot to pack the camera. Our first view ever of Paris and no pictures to show for it," said the older man sitting next to him. He was pissed. The blond just rolled his eyes.

"I told you the camera is in my suitcase under the bus. Quit being so melodramatic. Frowning makes those wrinkles in your forehead look like trenches."

"I'm happy to share my pictures," I blurted. "I can send you a digital file if you give me your email address."

"Oh, that would be great! Thank you," exclaimed the older man. "I'm Brian Mitchner," he said, reaching past the blond to give my hand a firm shake. "And this gel junkie is my partner—"

"Jarrod Perlman. Nice to meet you," interrupted Jarrod.

I introduced myself. And there was an awkward silence while Jarrod stared straight ahead with his arms crossed against his chest. It wasn't any of my business but if I was traveling to Paris with my boyfriend, I'd hate for our trip to start out on the wrong foot just because of a mispacked camera.

"Well, you know what they say?" I said, making an attempt to lighten the mood.

"What?" they asked.

"Paris is for lovers." We all laughed.

And then Jarrod had to go there. "Babe, if Paris is for lovers, why are you here by yourself?"

"Because I'm an idiot."

OUR TOUR GROUP WAS staying at Bienvenue Hotel located in the 7th *arrondissement,* within walking distance of the Eiffel Tower. I could see the tower peeking over the rooftops of the buildings, teasing me, as the bus navigated the traffic. We finally stopped on the corner of a busy street right next to the elevated metro tracks. The bus was unable to make it down the narrow backstreets to get to our hotel, so the driver unloaded our luggage on the sidewalk. Some of my tour mates weren't happy about carrying their bags to the hotel, but I was too happy to finally be in Paris to care about a short walk.

The area was more residential than touristy. Numerous small shops and ethnic restaurants lined the streets. Sidewalks were cluttered with small tables where people lingered, enjoying wine and cigarettes. A *boulangerie* displayed long dark loaves of crusty bread next to stacked jars of jewel bright preserves. Fresh produce of every variety and color was displayed in baskets in front of the corner shop. Another enticed passersby with whole chickens roasting on spits. It was a feast for the eyes as well as the stomach and mine growled loudly.

I did my best to ignore the sighs and mutterings of the locals as I maneuvered my large suitcase through the crowds, around the corner and past a tiny store no bigger than my living room to a small doorway marked by a gold-and-black awning. The smell of garlic from the Italian restaurant directly across the street filled the air. I could have passed out from hunger.

I pulled out a candy bar from my purse while I waited to check in. The hotel's dimly lit lobby was small but around the corner a dining area and courtyard out back were visible. It was still fairly early, not quite noon, and some of my group had gone out back to sit and wait for their rooms to be available. Lucky for me, I did pre check-in online at home. My room was ready.

"I show a Dr. Julius Price also on your reservation, *madame*. Will he be joining you later?" asked the pretty dark-haired desk clerk as she handed me my key card.

I completely blanked for a few seconds before I remembered Julius was Ben's much-hated first name. He always went by his middle name, Benjamin. Ugh! I couldn't believe I'd forgotten to let the hotel know I was arriving solo. I'd just assumed Monsieur Marcel would inform them.

"Uh, yeah," I said quickly. "In a few days." I shouldn't have lied. Maybe it was denial, embarrassment or simply wishful thinking, but I couldn't bring myself to cancel Ben's reservation.

AFTER SHUNNING THE rickety-looking, closet-sized elevator, I dragged my suitcase up four winding flights of stairs and down an unbelievably narrow hallway to room 5B. I leaned panting and sweating against the door for a minute or so before I was able to open it. Once I was inside, it was as if I'd stepped back in time to my college days. This was no hotel room—it was a small, neat and clean room the size of my freshman dorm. A large bed dominated one wall. But on closer inspection the large comfy-looking bed was actually just two twin beds pushed together.

Pastel stripes of pink, purple and blue decorated the curtains and bedspread. A small wooden desk with a chair and a phone sat by the door. No closet but a nook behind the door held a metal bar for hanging clothes and a shelf overhead with an extra pillow and blanket. A small TV was mounted on the wall opposite the bed. A small desk was positioned underneath. The tiny bathroom consisted of a narrow shower stall, toilet and pedestal sink.

The room's one large window overlooked the hotel's courtyard. I opened it to let some fresh air in. Conversation and laughter floated up from the courtyard below. I unpacked and sat on the bed. Big mistake. The plan had been for me stay awake until later that afternoon and then take a short nap before having a late dinner. I had every intention of walking over to the Eiffel Tower and finding someplace to eat lunch. But I was just too tired. I'd been up for 24 hours. Instead, I lay back on the bed and closed my eyes. I told myself it was only going to be for a few minutes. I was fast asleep in no time.

A SHARP POKE TO MY shoulder woke me. When I opened my eyes a woman was staring down at me. She must have been in her mid-fifties with hard blue eyes that flashed with anger. Her frosted blond hair was pulled into a messy bun and her thin scarlet-coated lips wore a frown. Being jolted from a deep sleep made me instantly cranky. According to my watch, it was a little after one o'clock. I'd been asleep for less than an hour.

"Are you housekeeping?" I sat up and rubbed my eyes.

"Certainly not!" the woman replied. She might have been pretty but I couldn't tell since she now looked like she was trying to smell her upper lip.

"Then what are you doing in my room?" I was now awake enough to get a better look at her. She was wearing a stylish tan-and-burgundy-checked suit and black flats, not a uniform. Still, I was very confused.

"Your room?" she spat out. "What are you talking about? Check out was at eleven o'clock this morning. This is my room now. You need to leave immediately or I'm calling the manager!"

"Manager?" What the hell was she talking about?

"You heard me. You've got two seconds to clear out of here or I'm calling the manager."

"Look, lady—" I grabbed my key card from the desk and waved it in front of her face "—I checked in *this* morning. This is *my* room."

"Like hell it is!" She pulled her own key card from her blazer pocket and flashed it at me. "If this isn't my room, then how could I have gotten in here?" Two red suitcases sat just outside the open door.

"Okay," I said slowly. "Obviously they've put us in the same room by mistake. There's been some kind of mix-up. I'm sure they can straighten this out at the front—"

She turned and charged out of the room before I had a chance to finish my sentence, leaving her suitcases in the hallway for me to trip over. She must have run down the steps as though her tail was on fire because she was already giving the desk clerk hell by the time I got down there.

"Madame. Madame," repeated the poor desk clerk, a different person than the woman who'd checked me in. This clerk was a man who couldn't have been much out of his teens and was completely terrified. He was holding his hands up as if he were trying to stop the flood of words spilling from her mouth. He couldn't get a word in.

"It's 'Doctor' to you," she said haughtily. "Dr. Juliet Rice! I reserved a single and you've put me in a room with a stranger!" She gestured toward me. "I demand to speak to the manager!"

The clerk typed furiously on the computer's keyboard as he stared intently at the screen. However, after hearing her name, I knew exactly what had happened. And from the way the clerk's face turned bright red, he'd just realized it as well.

"Pardonnez-moi, madame," mumbled the clerk. Then he turned and called, "Zalima!" followed by a flood of rapid-fire French. I only understood a couple of words, the most recognizable one being *probleme.*

The woman who had checked me into my room emerged from the small office behind the front desk. The clerk and Dr. Rice started talking at the same time. It took three tries to get them calmed down. Once she looked at the reservation, my suspicion was confirmed. The young clerk, whose name was Georges, was new and his understanding of English was limited. He'd mixed up Dr. Juliet Rice's reservation with Dr. Julius Price's reservation and had mistakenly put Dr. Rice in the room with me.

Unfortunately, checking Dr. Rice into my room had somehow canceled her own reservation. In the meantime, her room had been given to someone else. The hotel was now full and there would be no more rooms available until the next morning.

"You've got to be kidding me! This is completely unacceptable!" Dr. Rice threw up her hands in disgust. "I'm calling your corporate office to let them know what I think of your customer service!" She started fumbling in her purse for her cell phone, as though she had the number on speed dial.

I tried to take some of the heat off the situation. "The names are so similar. It was an easy mistake to make. There are two beds in the room. I don't mind sharing if it's only for one night." Actually, I hoped Dr. Juliet Rice would be so pissed off she'd go stay at another hotel. No such luck. Zalima quickly went into damage control mode, refuting everything I'd heard about Paris's lack of customer service. Lucky me.

"Ladies, please accept my sincerest apology of behalf of the Bienvenue Hotel. I will give each of you a complimentary night stay for tonight as well as a meal at our restaurant," said Zalima, looking directly at Juliet. Smart girl.

Apparently, *free* was a word that appealed to Dr. Juliet Rice. My new roommate didn't hesitate before asking, "And you're sure there'll be a room available in the morning?"

"Yes, Dr. Rice. I am showing there will be several rooms available," Zalima said, consulting the computer. "Just come down after breakfast tomorrow and we'll get you all settled into your new room."

"Oh, you can count on it." She tossed her phone back into her purse and headed back up the steps without a backward glance.

"Merde!" exclaimed Georges, leaning against the counter in relief after she was gone, earning him a scowl from Zalima.

My understanding of French must have been improving because *shit* was exactly the word I'd have used, too.

BY THE TIME I GOT BACK upstairs, Juliet had dragged her luggage into the small room and was attempting to pull the beds apart.

"Don't just stand there. Come help me," she commanded.

Only I wasn't Zalima or Georges. And I wasn't having it.

"Come help you, what?"

"Move the damn beds apart, of course. I agreed to share a room not a bed."

"Help you move the damn beds apart, *what?*" I asked again, not budging from the doorway. She stared at me a moment in confusion before the lightbulb went off in her head.

"Please," she said, letting out a breath. "Will you *please* help me?"

After we moved the beds as far apart as the tiny room would allow, Juliet pulled a red sleeveless dress with a Christian Dior label out of one of her suitcases and hung it on the back of the bathroom door.

"What type of medicine do you practice?" I asked, attempting to make small talk.

"I'm not a medical doctor. I have a Ph.D. in art history. I teach at Stanford." She said it like it was something I should have already known.

And since I work at a university myself, I *should* have recognized her attitude of arrogant entitlement immediately. It was one I dealt with regularly. Professors who thought they walked on water and treated anyone without a doctorate degree as an inferior being were the bane of my workday existence. Dr. Rice pulled black three-inch pumps with a peep toe from her bag. The red soles identified them as Christian Louboutin. At least the woman had good taste in clothes.

"Wow. Must be some hot date if you're martyring the Christians," I commented since it appeared she wasn't going to ask me anything about myself. She sighed and rolled her eyes.

"Not that it's any of your business, but I can afford quality so I only wear the best. I'm an important woman. My clothes reflect that. She eyed my very wrinkled jeans with distaste. "I don't do jeans. It sends the wrong message."

"Well excuse the hell out of me." Why was I even bothering to talk to her? And just why was Ms. Quality staying at a budget hotel?

"I'm sorry," she said quickly, shocking me. She was sitting on the side of her bed. Her face was drawn and pale. "I'm just on edge. I've got a lot on my mind. I'm not usually so abrasive." She nervously fingered a chunky rectangular-shaped sterling pendant around her neck. It had a large letter *J* engraved on the front. Like the rest of her stuff, it looked very expensive.

"No harm done," I said, not believing her. I'd bet my left eyebrow that *abrasive* was this woman's middle name.

She gave me a thin, tight smile and headed into the bathroom. Once Juliet was finished, I quickly showered and changed into black pants and a tan sleeveless V-neck sweater. Though we didn't have much else to say to each other, we remained cautiously polite even as we left the hotel.

"Enjoy your first day in Paris. It's an amazing city," Juliet told me before disappearing into a waiting cab.

I wondered where she was going but deduced that any woman wearing a show-stopping red dress and fuck-me pumps in the middle of the day wasn't planning to go have tea. I assumed I wouldn't be seeing her again until very late, or, if I was lucky, not until tomorrow morning when she moved her things to her new room. Of course, I should have known I'm not that lucky.

DEUX

SINCE IT WAS time for lunch, I bought food from the open-air market set up under the elevated metro tracks around the corner from my hotel. I decided on a picnic at the Eiffel Tower. I found a spot on a grassy area and devoured a baguette, some wonderfully runny Camembert cheese, roasted chicken, olives, a raspberry tart and pretty much an entire bottle of red wine. Drinking so much wine hadn't been in the plan but seeing so many people in love, and being constantly reminded that I was alone, gave me an excuse to keep my glass filled.

There had been a couple lying on a blanket practically screwing a mere ten feet away from me, so I just kept my back turned to them. But then another couple walked by. Their heads were bent together and they were laughing at a private joke. Their arms were wrapped around each other's waists as though they'd never let go. On a nearby bench, an elderly married couple held hands. By the time a beaming bride and groom arrived to take photos for their wedding, my bottle was more than half-empty and I was a pitiful, weepy wreck.

I knew wandering half-wasted and crying around Paris wasn't such a great idea. I figured I'd be nice and safe on a cruise until my buzz wore off and I headed across the street for the docks along the Seine. Fifteen minutes later, I was sitting on the top deck of a Bateaux-

Mouches tour boat, well away from the large groups of German, Italian and Japanese tourists vying for the best vantage points to take pictures from. I left my digital camera in the canvas day bag slung across my torso. I just wanted to savor the sights for now. There would be plenty of time for picture taking once I was sober. The bright sunlight made my eyes water. I reached inside my bag for my sunglasses and—ouch! I pricked my finger. I had thrown in a kitschy brass corkscrew I'd bought from the market to uncork my wine. Its handle was a miniature replica of the Eiffel Tower. Carefully reaching past the corkscrew, I located my sunglasses and put them on.

The boat had already passed under the gorgeous Pont Alexandre III with its tall pillars topped with golden gilded statues, and was heading toward the Pont de la Concorde, which, according to the boat's recorded multilingual commentary, spanned the Seine between the Quai des Tuileries on the Right Bank and the Quai d'Orsay on the Left Bank. As I was looking off into the distance at the Obelisk of Luxor in the Place de la Concorde, a flash of red on the bridge caught my attention. I took off my sunglasses and leaned forward slightly in my seat to get a better look.

It was a blonde woman in a red dress. It was Juliet Rice! She was talking to a man but as the boat inched closer their body language and expressions revealed they were in the middle of a heated argument. He kept circling her and shoving something that looked like a picture in her face. She kept trying to get away from him but he kept jumping in front of her, blocking her path. Juliet was scared. I tried to stand but my bag got caught and I was pinned to my seat.

"Juliet!" I waved my arms, trying to get her attention. She didn't hear me. Other people on the boat turned to stare at me. I could only blame what happened next on the wine. I extricated myself from my bag, leaving it wedged between my seat and the empty one next to me, and ran toward the front of the top deck, pushing my way through a crowd of tourists.

"Juliet! Juliet!" I called out again.

This time Juliet turned to look and so did her companion. Juliet spotted me and frowned. She used the momentary distraction to turn and hurry away from the persistent man. He sprinted after her and grabbed her by the elbow.

"Hey! Leave her alone! Let her go!" I yelled.

Juliet hardly needed my help. She swung around and slapped the man hard across the face. The crack of her hand on his flesh was so loud I heard it clearly. The boat passed under the bridge and I lost sight of them. I ran to the back of the boat and looked up as we emerged from the other side. Juliet was gone. But her companion was not only still there, he was leaning forward looking right at me.

He was gorgeous—muscular with a medium build and at least a good decade younger than Juliet. His dark hair was close-cropped. He had sensual lips and something my friend Kelly calls sexy scruff—a five o'clock shadow that would be a full-grown beard if he didn't shave soon. He was wearing faded jeans and a navy T-shirt that was just tight enough to emphasize his well-defined chest without showing off. Our eyes met and I could see his were a vivid, startling shade of green. I couldn't tear my gaze from his and continued to gawk at him until he finally walked away.

Was he the one Juliet had gotten dressed up for? Had I witnessed a mere lovers' spat? People were whispering and pointing at me like I was crazy. Feeling really stupid, I headed back to my seat. I reached between the seats for my bag. It was gone.

"Has anyone seen a brown canvas bag with a long strap?" I asked. No one answered.

I sat and tried to calm down. While I'd unnecessarily involved myself in Juliet's business, someone had stolen my bag. And it was my fault. I'd practically given my bag away. I resisted the urge to cry as I mentally inventoried the contents of my bag. Thankfully, my passport was back in my hotel room, safely locked up in my suitcase. But I'd had two hundred euros, an ATM card, an expensive digital camera and my cell phone in my bag.

"Did you get your purse nicked?" asked a young woman with an English accent sitting two rows ahead of me. All I could do was nod as hot tears spilled down my face.

"Oh, that's a shame. You should go file a report with the crew," she suggested and the older woman with her nodded in agreement.

"Thanks. I will." I got up and quickly headed downstairs to the first deck.

I was really too embarrassed to go talk to the crew. What could they do? There must have been a least hundred passengers on board. It would have been so easy for someone to take my money and valuables and drop the bag over the side of the boat. But I guess it would be better than doing nothing. I spotted a young crew member in an enclosed booth near the front of boat and knocked on the glass, startling him.

"Parlez-vous Anglais?" I asked when he opened the door.

"Non," he replied dismissively and began picking at a zit on his chin. I struggled to think of the French word for *stolen*. My French/English dictionary had also been in my bag.

"Uh, ma bag...ah...volee?" I said uncertainly.

That did the trick. He rolled his eyes and pointed to a sign in French with multiple translations underneath. It read: *Bateaux-Mouches is not responsible for lost or stolen property.* I was officially S.O.L. Then he closed the door and sat back down.

"Asshole," I mumbled under my breath.

I headed into the bathroom to pull myself together. I splashed my face with cold water. When I lifted the lid of the trashcan to throw away my paper towel, relief washed over me like a tidal wave. Because there, sitting on top of a pile of wet paper towels, pop cans, candy wrappers and lots of newspapers, was my bag. I sat on the toilet to examine it. Every pocket and compartment had been unzipped and unsnapped.

Oddly, only my souvenir corkscrew and hotel key card were missing. My money, ATM card, camera and cell phone were all there. The corkscrew was meaningless, but a stolen key card was bad news. I began to pick through the garbage hoping to find it, but once I encountered a fragrant crap-filled diaper, I gave up.

IT WAS AFTER SIX WHEN I got back to the hotel. The desk clerk assured me that it was impossible to know which room the key card unlocked and that it would be useless to the thief. But he checked the room for me anyway.

Juliet walked in just as I had my new card in hand and headed past me without speaking.

"Juliet, are you okay?" I caught up to her at the bottom of the steps.

"What are you talking about?" She glared at me.

"You were on that bridge earlier with a man. It looked like he was harassing you. Are you okay?"

"I have no idea what you're talking about."

"But I saw you. And I know you saw me. You looked right at me. I was on a cruise. You slapped him." I knew what I'd seen. Why was she lying?

"Are you drunk?" She backed away from me. I put my hand over my mouth in embarrassment and took a step back.

"No," I said.

"Yes, you are. You reek of alcohol! I don't know who you saw but I can assure you it wasn't me. I was in meetings all afternoon. And how dare you address me by my first name. Only my close friends call me Juliet, and you are certainly no friend of mine. Now, leave me alone!" She hurried up the steps.

Stunned and embarrassed, I headed up after her. Her sobbing could be heard loud and clear through the closed door. She was crying so loudly that she startled from the fetal position on her bed when she finally realized I was in the room with her. Whatever had happened had left her completely devastated.

"Just pretend I'm not here and I'll do the same. Clearly I made a big mistake in being concerned about you."

"Well, I made a mistake, too." She turned onto her back, letting big sloppy tears fall down the sides of her face. "A big, big mistake. I don't know how I could have been so wrong."

"Welcome to the club, honey. It happens to the best of us. You'll get over it." I refused to be drawn into her man problems when I had problems of my own.

"No, I won't," she replied cryptically in a flat voice.

"Why?"

"I broke my promise. I broke it for nothing. I thought I was finally doing the right thing. But it was all a lie. Now, I'll never be trusted again. I gave up everything! Everything!"

"Look, Dr. Rice, I got my bag stolen earlier and had to get a new key card. If you're not going back out, deadbolt the door after I leave just to be on the safe side, okay?"

Her response was to turn toward the wall and start crying again. I went into the bathroom and quickly brushed my teeth and freshened up. It didn't take long for my anger to evaporate, especially since Juliet might be going through similar man problems as me. Sitting on the side of her bed, I gently touched her shoulder. She tensed but didn't turn over.

"Are you going to be okay? Would you like me to bring you anything? Some food or maybe—"

"Please," she said without an ounce of emotion, "just leave me alone." I left Dr. Juliet Rice to her tears and headed out of the hotel. I had gone half a block when someone called to me from outside a Lebanese restaurant. Jarrod and his partner, Brian, waved to me. I crossed the street to join them.

"We saw what happened in the lobby and were just wondering if you'd like to join us for dinner. No one should eat alone in Paris," proclaimed Brian. It looked like Jarrod had been at the hair gel again.

"Come on. We're not taking no for an answer." Jarrod pulled me into the restaurant with them.

I allowed myself to be pulled. Truth be told, I was lonely and needed the company. I was also hungry again. Drama has a way of doing that to me. Once we were settled at a table and our orders were placed, our waiter uncorked a bottle of red wine. I covered my glass with my hand. I'd be sticking to Perrier. While we nibbled on complimentary olives and pickled vegetables, they told me a little about themselves. They'd been together for twelve years and had come to Paris to celebrate their anniversary.

"What about you, Maya? Do you have someone special?" asked Brian. I filled them in on my pathetic love life.

"Well it's his loss, babe," replied Jarrod. "Don't even sweat it. Men like that aren't worth the energy it takes to fart. I ought to know 'cause I've been with my share of them."

"She doesn't want to hear about your sordid past," Brian teased as he pushed his horn-rimmed glasses up on his nose.

Jarrod rolled his eyes. "Brian just doesn't want people to know the love of his life is a felon. Before I met him, I was strung out like a junkie on a car thief who looked just like Brad Pitt from Cali. It was exciting as hell until I ended up in jail. But this man here," he said, reaching over and squeezing Brian's hand, "set me on the path to the straight and narrow."

"Narrow, maybe. Straight, hardly," exclaimed Brian, making us all laugh.

"So, what's the sitch with the bitch?" Jarrod didn't even attempt to hide his nosiness.

"Please excuse him, Maya," said Brian, cutting his partner an embarrassed look. "He's as addicted to gossip as he is to hair gel."

"Don't pay him any attention." Jarrod dismissed his partner with a wave of his hand. "He won't admit it but he wants to know, too. So, spill it girlfriend. What's that woman's deal?"

"You mean Dr. Juliet Rice?" I strung her name out for full effect. "She's an important woman. She teaches at Stanford and you'd damned well better remember it or she'll remind you…repeatedly!" We laughed again. Our food arrived and I dug into my lamb and rice.

"You mean that hussy's a professor?" asked Brian, with his mouth half-full of couscous.

"Yeah, with that counterfeit couture and bad high-lighting job we thought she was an old hooker," said Jarrod.

Water almost squirted out of my nose. "You mean her clothes are fake? How can you tell?" I was truly impressed.

"Oh, don't look at us like that. It's not some kind of gay man's intuition. We own a dry cleaners in Portland. We can spot bootleg designer duds a mile away," concluded Brian.

"It's all in the cut, the fit and the detailing," explained Jarrod. "Real designer clothing shouldn't be ill fitting, especially as much as they cost, and the stitching should be seamless. The hem on that red Dior knock-off was lopsided. It looked like someone high on crack sewed it." Brian nodded his head in agreement.

I hadn't even noticed the hem of her dress.

"Well, what about the shoes? Are they fake, too?"

"Now they might actually be real. We do minor shoe repairs occasionally. One of our wealthier clients owns about two dozen pairs of Louboutin pumps and loves them more than her children. She has a pair something like that prof was wearing. But then again, if the dress is bootleg then the shoes probably are, too," said Jarrod.

"Why lie about something so stupid?" I asked.

"If people think you don't know any better they'll tell you anything, especially if it makes them feel better about themselves," concluded Brian.

By the time we finished up our meals and ordered dessert, Brian had detailed all the ins and outs of the dry-cleaning business.

"Do you come from a family of librarians?" asked Jarrod.

I hesitated before answering. Since I'd grown up in foster care, questions about my family always made me uncomfortable. I honestly had no idea what kind of family I'd come from. I went into foster care when I was two, after my adoptive parents were killed in a car crash. There wasn't a family member who was willing to take me.

"Nope. I'm the only one," I said simply.

It was dark and chilly when we left the restaurant two hours later. Brian and Jarrod talked me into walking over to the Eiffel Tower with them to watch it light up. They waited in front of the restaurant for me while I ran back to the hotel to get a jacket. I headed up to my room and ran smack into Meryl Berman on her way down.

"Oh, Maya, you gave me a fright. Are you having a nice time?"

"Pretty much. How about you?"

Her face fell. "Haven't had a chance to see much yet. Ted slept all afternoon and I was too afraid to go out on me own. Then we went out to get a bite and he had too much wine and argued with the waiter. Now he doesn't want to go anywhere. He gets so mean and stubborn when he drinks. Maybe tomorrow I'll get a chance to see the sights." She was miserable.

"I'm walking over to the Eiffel Tower with another couple from our tour. Why don't you come with us? It'll be fun."

"Are you sure?" Her face brightened.

"I just need to get a jacket and I'll be right down. Just wait for me in the lobby."

I had my key card out and ready when I got to my room, but the door was already open a crack. I pushed it open all the way and flipped on the light. The room was wrecked. The contents of both of our suitcases were strewn all over the room. The desk drawers had been pulled out and dumped on the floor. The mattresses were askew as if someone thought something might be hidden underneath them. And the room reeked of cigarette smoke. Damn it! Either Juliet must have left and neglected to pull the door completely shut behind her, or someone broke into our room. Either way, it looked like we'd been robbed.

My open suitcase was on Juliet's bed. As I rushed over to check the hidden compartment in the bottom where I kept my passport, my feet got tangled in the straps of a black bikini top that must have been Juliet's, and I tripped, almost knocking my head against the desk. I angrily kicked the top across the room and then searched my suitcase. My passport was still there.

"Thank God."

In fact, I couldn't find anything missing, making me wonder if Juliet trashed the room. She'd been pretty upset when I'd left. But why trash the room? And where did she go? The bathroom door was closed. Was she in there? I walked over and pressed my ear to the door. I couldn't hear anything except a slow steady drip from the sink. I knocked on the door.

"Dr. Rice? Are you in there?" There was no answer. I knocked again. "Dr. Rice?"

My own reflection in the mirror startled me when I opened the bathroom door. The smell of blood and burnt flesh smacked me in the face. Something large and motionless was behind the shower door, obscured by the pattern on the glass.

I took a deep breath and pulled the handle on the door. Juliet, nude, bruised and bloodied, was crammed into the small shower stall. Her face had been beaten into an almost unrecognizable pulp. One of her eyes was swollen shut; the other stared ahead unseeingly, the blue clouding over to white. Her broken nose hung at an unnatural angle; her bottom lip was split. A telephone cord bound her hands behind her back. Cigarette burns covered her arms and legs as if she hadn't been tortured enough. But that's not what caused my knees to buckle. I grabbed the sink for support as I fell back on the toilet.

A small replica of the Eiffel Tower had been jammed to the hilt into the side of Juliet's neck. *My* Eiffel Tower corkscrew. A profusion of dark blood from the wound had run down her neck and between her breasts. A low moan escaped my lips. And suddenly screaming—loud, ragged shrieks—filled the air. I covered my mouth but the screams wouldn't stop.

Because I wasn't the one screaming. It was Meryl Berman. She must have come up looking for me when I took too long. She was standing in the bathroom door looking into the shower. I got up to block her view but she kept screaming. With me shaking so badly, it was a miracle I managed to get the two of us downstairs to the lobby. Meryl sat sobbing on the bottom step while I pounded on the bell for the desk clerk.

"Oui, madame," he said, smiling.

"There's been a murder," I told him.

Within fifteen minutes the hotel was swarming with police.

WE PLAN, GOD LAUGHS. And I'm living proof. Because had anyone asked me yesterday how I *planned* to spend my first night in Paris, I'd have said any number of things. And none of them would have involved sitting in a stark, brightly lit police interrogation room being grilled about the murder of a woman I'd known for all of two hours. I don't know if God was laughing. But I damned sure wasn't.

"Madame Sinclair, if you could just take us through it one more time, we'd be most appreciative," said Police Captain Claude Bellange with a smile.

At least I thought he was smiling. I could barely see his mouth beneath his thick, bushy mustache. But his eyes crinkled. His ruddy skin stretched tightly over his round cheeks, reminding me of baked apples right before the skins split. He was a heavyset man of about sixty and a chain-smoker. Lighting yet another Gauloises cigarette with the still-lit one he'd barely finished, he inhaled and blew a thin stream of smoke out of the corner of his mouth. I was a reformed Benson and Hedges girl, whose nicotine cravings came back during times of stress, and the smell of the smoke was making me twitchy.

Lieutenant Thierry Bernier, Bellange's subordinate, was a gaunt, balding man of about forty with a big gap between his two front teeth. Impatient with restless energy, he stood to stretch his legs before perching on the end of the table. He swung his right leg slowly and glared down at me with his shoulders hunched and rounded like Snoopy doing his vulture routine.

"Look, I've already told you—"

"From the beginning, *s'il vous plaît*," barked the unsmiling Bernier, his voice cracking like a whip. He was the less friendly of the two men, more intense and easily annoyed.

I'd already been over what happened half a dozen times in the two hours I'd been there. At first, I thought my crappy French, combined with both men's heavily accented English, was causing communication problems. However, after I'd been asked to go over my story for what seemed like the millionth time, it dawned on me they were just trying to see if I'd trip myself up and change my story. Not hardly. I'd replayed what happened in my head nonstop since it happened and unlike the air in that interrogation room, it was still very fresh.

By the time I'd finished telling my story yet again it was one o'clock. Bernier had moved from sitting on the table to pacing the room impatiently. Bellange seemed a little antsy as well. He tapped an empty cigarette pack against his hand as if he was hoping sheer will could make a cigarette appear. Bernier cleared his throat and suddenly Bellange snapped to attention. He balled up the empty pack and tossed it in the trashcan in the corner then pulled another pack from his suit pocket.

"Can I have one of those?" I asked impulsively. I hadn't smoked in five years, not since I was in grad school. It seemed like an excellent time to start again.

Bellange was mildly surprised as he slid the pack across the table at me. I pulled out a cigarette and savored the feel of it between my fingers before leaning across the table to let the old French cop light it for me. I inhaled deeply and then began to cough and choke. My chest burned. My eyes watered. Either I'd taken too deep a drag, or my American lungs weren't used to the unfiltered Gauloises. Bernier sighed and rolled his eyes. Bellange fought a smile. I did what most embarrassed people do. I faked righteous indignation.

"Why am I still here? I don't know what more I can tell you that I haven't already."

"Oh, I'm not so sure, *madame*," said Bellange. "What do you think happened to Dr. Rice?"

I was amazed. Surely he knew what had happened. It was clear enough to me.

"Well, it's obvious that whoever stole my bag earlier today and took my hotel key card tried it on every door until they found the right one. Dr. Rice must have still been in the room when he broke in and…and…" My voice trailed off as I relived the horror of Juliet's body in the shower.

I certainly hadn't liked the woman but no one deserved to die the way she had. It was my fault she'd been stuck in a room with me in the first place. And then because my bag had been stolen… Bernier and

Bellange exchanged glances that unnerved the hell out of me.

"Shouldn't you be looking for the person who stole my bag? Maybe one of the hotel staff or one of the guests saw this person."

"If there's one thing we do know, Madame Sinclair, it is Paris pickpockets." Bellange folded his hands over his large belly.

"Meaning what?" The hairs on the back of my neck started to prickle.

"Meaning," said Bernier, pulling up a chair next to me and sitting uncomfortably close, "no self-respecting thief would steal a bag and only take worthless trinkets and leave behind money and valuables. They leave nothing behind, *madame*. They will take everything you have because everything can be sold. Everything."

"You think I'm lying about my bag being stolen?" I was incredulous. "Why would I lie? You can ask them on the cruise I took if you don't believe me. I reported it to one of the crew."

"Ah, but you've already said that you found your bag in the restroom after you reported it stolen. As far as the crew is concerned, you could have just forgotten you left it in there in the first place, no?" concluded Bellange.

"And you are far from a paragon of truthfulness, *madame*. Might I remind you that you've already admitted that your dishonesty regarding your lover's reservation caused the hotel mix-up with Dr. Rice," added Bernier.

Panic began to set in. I wanted out of that room. I wanted to be someplace safe and familiar. I wanted to go home. This trip had been a big mistake. I should have never come alone to Paris. What had I been thinking?

"I didn't have anything to do with Dr. Rice's murder. I was at dinner with a couple from my tour group in a restaurant full of other people. And besides, why would I kill her?"

"No one has accused you of a crime," insisted Bellange. "But you must look at this situation from our point of view. You were the last person with Dr. Rice before her murder, and you were seen arguing with her in the hotel lobby. Witnesses reported Dr. Rice telling you to leave her alone, yet you followed her up to the room you both shared. No one else saw Dr. Rice after that confrontation, but you were seen leaving the hotel in a hurry. Your hotel room was trashed, indicating a robbery, but like the mystery of your stolen bag, nothing was taken. Now, I ask, what would you think?"

Of course, when it was laid out like that the whole thing sounded fishy. But I couldn't help that. They were the police. It was their job to figure out what happened, not mine.

"I wasn't the only one who argued with her. What about the man she was arguing with on the bridge?"

"As you've already said, Dr. Rice denied she was on the bridge when you asked her about it. And as you've also admitted, you had quite a lot of wine to drink with lunch," said Bellange.

"I wasn't drunk. I know what I saw!"

"Why would Dr. Rice lie if you had indeed seen her?" asked a sneering Bernier.

Because she was an arrogant cow who was probably embarrassed that I'd witnessed her argument with that green-eyed hottie, I wanted to say, but didn't.

A knock at the door kept me from having to answer. Bernier got up and opened the door an inch and a manila envelope was handed to him through the crack. He closed the interrogation room door and pulled the contents of the envelope—five photographs—out and examined them one by one. A smirk lifted one corner of his mouth as he handed the photos to Bellange. Bellange took one look at them and then laid them out like playing cards on the table in front of me.

"Tell me what you see." He shoved the pictures roughly toward me. They were photos shot from multiple angles. Each one showed injuries I hadn't seen when I'd found her. Feeling queasy, I pushed back from the table and put my head in my hands.

"Why are you doing this to me? I didn't kill her!" Hot tears flowed down my cheeks. Bernier grabbed my chair from behind and pushed it back up to the table.

"What my partner *meant* to say was, what *don't* you see?" His lips were practically touching my ear.

The asshole enjoyed seeing me so upset. He probably had a hard-on. Not about to give him any more satisfaction, I sat up straight in the chair and reluctantly looked down at the pictures. It was then that I realized what he meant. Everything about Juliet's murder scene was exactly as it was when I'd found her except for one thing, one very big thing. The Eiffel Tower corkscrew—my corkscrew—was no longer in the side of her neck. It was gone.

TROIS

It WAS AFTER two in the morning when they finally cut me loose. I was issued a strong warning to stay in Paris and make myself available for further questioning, at least until they were satisfied I wasn't involved in Juliet Rice's murder—and they were far from satisfied.

I was just relieved not to have been arrested—and to be alive. Whoever killed Juliet must have still been in the room when I came in. After Meryl and I left, he must have taken the corkscrew and disappeared into the night. I shuddered. I could have just as easily been next. What was worse was that Bernier and Bellange thought I lied about my bag being stolen—they thought I tried to make it look like someone else killed Juliet. They just couldn't prove it.

The September night air was cold. I shivered when I stood out on the sidewalk in front of the station. Hugging my bag to my chest, I headed off in the direction of the Hotel de l'Elysee in search of a metro station as a dark green Peugeot with tinted windows pulled alongside me. The passenger-side window began to roll down, but I heard someone call my name. Monsieur Marcel, my tour group guide, stood by a waiting cab parked across the street. His snowy white hair shone like a beacon in the moonlight. I practically flew to him. The Peugeot sped off.

"Madame Sinclair, are you okay? You have not been

harmed, have you?" The Frenchman was genuinely concerned.

He was still dressed in the same immaculate blue suit and red bow tie he'd worn to meet us at the airport. It seemed like a lifetime ago. I assured him I was as well as could be expected and he ushered me into the waiting cab. As it turned out, Brian and Jarrod had called him when the police had whisked me off to the station. He'd been waiting for me the entire time.

"Thank you for the ride, *monsieur*." I could feel the tears coming again. He handed me a crisp white handkerchief with a gold monogram.

"Not a problem, my dear. I'm always happy to help out a beautiful damsel in distress. I've taken the liberty of arranging a new hotel room for you, although, regrettably I was unable to book you into different hotel at this late hour."

"But there were no rooms available until the morning."

"As circumstance would have it, Dr. Rice's murder has made many people upset and fearful for their own safety. Guests checked out en masse. There are now plenty of rooms to be had at the hotel."

"I'm so sorry to put you to so much trouble."

"It is I who should apologize to you. This isn't at all the trip you should be having. It is my sincerest hope that while the police work to clear up that unfortunate professor's death, you can put these bad memories behind you and get to know Paris as you were meant to." He patted my hand and gave me a smile.

I was relieved to be treated like an innocent person, but could I really get to know Paris as if nothing happened?

I SLEPT THROUGH BREAKFAST the next morning. If the maid hadn't knocked on the door I'd have still been sleeping. As long as I was asleep, I didn't have to think about everything that had happened the night before. But a maid running the vacuum would have keep me up, making it hard to escape reality. I asked if she could please come back later to clean my room. She apologized profusely and backed down the narrow hall like she was afraid I might stick something sharp and pointy in her neck. However, one look in the mirror and I understood why I had scared the maid. Wearing slept-in clothes, a puffy, sleep-swollen face and bed-head from hell, I looked like a hot-ass mess. Even a shower wouldn't help matters too much. All of my things, including the new clothes I'd bought for the trip, were now considered part of Juliet's crime scene. I had a feeling I wouldn't be getting them back any time soon.

I started to crawl back into bed when there was yet another knock at my door. Hoping it wasn't the police this time, I opened the door to find Brian and Jarrod loaded down with shopping bags.

"Don't get your undies in a knot, babe." Jarrod pushed past me. "It's just a couple of gays bearing gifts. Are you okay?" He dumped his bags on the rumpled bed and gave me the once-over.

"I'm fine. What's all this?" I ran my fingers through my messy hair, trying in vain to smooth it down.

"We saw the police carting bags full of stuff from your room last night and figured you'd need a few things. I hope this stuff fits. We weren't sure about these European sizes. Things tend to run smaller over here." Brian sat on the bed and started opening the bags.

"Here," said Jarrod, handing me a foam cup of

steaming black coffee and a bag of still-warm crois-
sants and *pain au chocolat* rolls.

Brian pulled out a pair of khaki cargo pants, a pair
of jeans, a black V-neck sweater, a white long-sleeved
shirt, a package of cotton underwear, toothpaste, tooth-
brush, mouthwash, deodorant, soap, lavender-scented
body lotion, half a dozen colorful scarves.

"Oh, you guys are so sweet! Thank you!" I flung my
arms around each one of them and kissed their cheeks.
Brian blushed. Jarrod grinned from ear to ear.

"Where'd you get this stuff?" I took a bracing sip of
coffee before retrieving money from my wallet to re-
imburse them.

"Courtesy of the local Monoprix store around the
corner. We got the scarves and the grub at the street
market under the metro tracks. But that's not important,
babe. What the hell happened last night? We waited
around for you forever, then the next thing we knew the
hotel was crawling with police. Someone said the professor had been murdered," said Jarrod, helping himself
to a croissant.

While I ate, I filled them in on everything. They sat
on my bed, their mouths hanging open.

"Sweet Jesus!" was all Brian could say when he re-
gained speech.

"Are you sure she wasn't a hooker?" asked Jarrod.

"She isn't anything except dead now." I shook my
head. "I'm surprised you two are still here. Monsieur
Marcel said half the guests got scared and checked out
last night."

Brian nodded.

"It was like Exodus. Most of our tour group took
flight. They wouldn't even listen when Marcel tried to

tell them rooms were scarce all over Paris. The city's hosting the World Rugby Cup. Some of them came slinking back this morning and the rest demanded refunds and went home."

"We don't scare that easily. We paid for a Paris vacation and we're not leaving 'til we've had it," said Jarrod matter-of-factly.

"Well, what about that Australian couple from our tour group, the Bermans? Have you seen them? Meryl Berman walked in when I found the body. She saw Dr. Rice in the shower, too. She could tell the police about seeing my corkscrew," I said.

"Sorry, Maya," said Brian, shaking his head. "After the police left last night, her husband packed her and all their crap into a cab and we haven't seen them since."

That was not good. It meant the French police weren't concentrating on anyone but little old *moi*.

"This is just insane! I can't even go home if I wanted to. I've been told I have to stay in Paris until this mess is cleared up. I'm just a librarian from Columbus, Ohio!"

We sat in silence for a few minutes while I polished off the remainder of the bread.

"This is completely ridiculous!" exclaimed Brian, standing up. "Get dressed, Maya. You're coming to Versailles with us. We're not going to let you sit around feeling sorry for yourself and hiding out in this little room like you've got something to feel guilty about."

"Yeah," said Jarrod, laughing. "There's nothing like wandering around the palace of a woman who ended up headless to make you realize your problems aren't all that."

"I can't leave the city, remember?"

"It's not like you're hopping a plane home, babe.

We're only going a half an hour outside the city. Besides, if they thought you were truly guilty they would have just arrested you," Jarrod assured me.

"Take your time. We'll be waiting in the lobby," said Brian, following Jarrod out the door.

They were gone before I had a chance to protest further. I didn't want to go out. Hiding in my hotel room sounded like a pretty good plan to me. But Brian had a point. I wasn't guilty and I had nothing to hide. Why should I act like a criminal? I paid for my trip, or rather Ben had.

It was the thought of Ben that got me out of my chair and into the shower. I owed it to myself to have a great time on his dime. I wasn't about to ruin the rest of my trip. If I had to be stuck somewhere, Paris wasn't too shabby.

I took a long, hot shower and changed into the jeans and black sweater. The jeans were a little loose, so I used one scarf as a belt, another to tie back my hair into a ponytail. I dabbed on a little lip gloss to complete the look. Figuring I looked pretty good for a suspected murderer, I headed downstairs.

AT FIRST I WASN'T SURE he was cop. The guy following us on the RER commuter train to Versailles blended right in. He looked like an aging athlete whose muscle had turned to fat. His polo shirt was rumpled, as though it had been bunched in the bottom of a suitcase too long.

I didn't point him out to Brian and Jarrod because I didn't want to spoil their day when they'd been so nice to me. He seemed just like a tourist amongst all the other tourists headed to Versailles. He sat in front of us and opened a newspaper, but I caught him casting furtive glances in my direction over the paper. And as he flipped through the pages, I noticed an unusual red birthmark on his right forearm.

That's when I realized that like the rest of us tourists he was headed to the Palace of Versailles, one of the most famous sites in France. But unlike us he carried no camera or any other sightseeing paraphernalia. And then I caught a whiff of something familiar—a combination of sweat, stale cigarettes and disinfectant clung to him. He smelled just like the police station. It wasn't a smell I'd soon forget, and he reeked of it.

Brian and Jarrod were oblivious to his presence. They concerned themselves with the day's itinerary and where to eat dinner that evening. As they debated, I made eye contact with the cop and gave him my best dirty look so he would know I was on to him. He returned my glare and smirked at me. What Bellange and Bernier hoped to accomplish by having this guy follow me around was beyond me. If they wanted to waste police time and resources following a dead end, that was their business. But Juliet Rice's killer was roaming free and that made me furious. The cop followed us off the train, hanging back about twenty feet as we made our ten-minute trek from the train station to the palace.

We wove our way around parked cars and tour buses in the dusty, crowded lot located in front of the gilded palace gates. Numerous African vendors in flowing tunics and skull caps hawked everything from handbags and sunglasses to T-shirts and 3-D puzzles of Versailles. The cop from the train was accosted by a particularly persistent vendor who kept shoving a fake Gucci bag in his face. I hurried through the gates and was moving so fast, my heel got stuck in a crack between the cobblestones, pitching me forward. A drop-dead gorgeous guy in dark sunglasses caught me before I ended up flat on my face. Even through the fabric of my sweater, his hands were warm. The gentle way he held me and the subtle tang of his cologne made me forget we were in a crowded courtyard. The stranger made sure I was steady on my feet before letting me go.

"Merci," I mumbled, embarrassed. He flashed me a dazzling smile and my heart beat a little faster, then he disappeared into the crowd. Boy, did I need to get a grip on myself. Men were the last thing on my agenda.

I couldn't help but be impressed by the sheer size of the place, let alone the palace's gold detailing glinting in the bright September sunlight. It was easy to imagine Marie Antoinette and Louis XVI's carriage rumbling across these very cobblestones hundreds of years ago.

Long lines formed at several entrances to the palace. People were taking pictures and babbling in English, French, Chinese, Spanish and other languages I didn't recognize. Dozens and dozens of tour guides held up signs and shouted instructions to groups of people who followed behind them like chicks trailing after a mother hen.

"Crap! The marble court's being renovated. I really wanted to see it." Jarrod gestured toward the very center of the courtyard, which was obscured by scaffolding. I caught a glimpse of black-and-white marble tiles.

"Me, too," I commiserated as we hurried to catch up with Brian, who was headed past the long lines.

For the next two hours we toured the palace and I snapped picture after picture of gaudy fabulousness. Practically everything at Versailles was covered in gold. Even the ceilings were decorated with elaborate frescos framed in twenty-four-karat gold. I took a picture of Brian and Jarrod in the newly renovated Hall of Mirrors. They took one of me in Marie Antoinette's floral-and-gold bedroom by the railing in front of an ornate feather-and-fringe-canopied bed. It was the bed in which she publicly gave birth to all of her children. By the time we emerged from the palace and headed into the ornamental gardens, it was early afternoon. Brian was pale and breathless. Jarrod guided him to a stone bench to rest and catch his breath.

"Is he okay?"

"He's got a heart condition. He couldn't sleep last night with all the excitement at the hotel and now all this walking we've done has wiped him out. I should really get him back to the hotel." Jarrod rubbed Brian's back. Brian didn't protest.

"No…you stay here…Maya," said Brian between breaths when I started to follow them. "We can come back another day."

"Yeah, don't worry about us. You stay and enjoy yourself. Don't forget to see the Petit Trianon. We can meet up later for dinner."

"Okay, here's my cell number." I quickly scribbled my number on a napkin from my bag and thrust it into Jarrod's hand. "Call me and let me know when you want to meet." They left and I felt both concerned and relieved. I wasn't ready to leave. Since ditching the cop, I was finally starting to enjoy my trip.

After the over-the-top grandeur of the palace, the natural beauty of the gardens was a welcome change. I was heading down the garden steps to Versailles' two largest and most famous fountains—the tiered Latona fountain, depicting titaness Latona and her children, Diana and Apollo, and the Apollo fountain, featuring the bronze god Apollo rising from the water, being pulled by horses—when my camera died.

I looked around for a place to put in the extra batteries I had packed. The few stone benches in the garden were taken. I went past the statues lining the walkway to the Apollo fountain and noticed an entrance to the garden hedge maze. Hoping there might be someplace to sit in the maze, I ducked inside. It was cooler and quieter there. Nobody else was in sight. I didn't have to walk far before coming upon an open gate, through which I could see a pond.

In the very center of the pond was a large golden statue of a man struggling to free himself from the pile of black rocks. One golden, muscled arm reached out toward me. He was holding something in his hand that I couldn't make out. A quick peek at the brochure I picked up inside the palace identified it as the Encelade Fountain depicting the fall of the Titans.

Something sailed over my head and landed with a loud splash in the pond. I jumped and bumped into someone.

"I'm so sorry—" I began before I saw it was the cop from the train. My blood started to boil. He dropped the large pebbles he'd been holding.

"Look, you can follow me around all you want but you're wasting your time. I didn't kill Juliet Rice and I don't know what happened to the damned corkscrew. So you can tell Bernier and Bellange to kiss my ass."

"Where's the crucifix, Ms. Sinclair?" he asked, shocking me more by the fact that he was American than the fact that he knew my name.

"You're American? I thought you were with the French police."

"I'm not going to ask you again." There was an edge to his voice that made me uneasy. I hadn't realized just how isolated the spot we were in was until that moment.

I decided to play it cool and just walk away. But he grabbed the strap of my bag and yanked if off my shoulder, knocking me off balance. He shook the bag upside down, emptying the contents on the ground.

"Hey! What the hell is your problem? Give me my bag back!"

He dropped the bag and stood. His brown eyes were cold and hard in the bright sunlight. After shoving up the sleeves of his polo shirt, his hands curled into fists. That's when the small red mark on his arm jumped out at me. It wasn't a birthmark. It was a tattoo of a coiled snake, a cobra. I suddenly realized there could be another reason why he would smell like he'd spent time at the police station, and it wasn't a good one.

"Who are you?" Every hair on my body stood up in alarm.

He didn't answer. Instead, he punched me hard in the stomach. The pain was immediate and intense. I doubled over, clutching my stomach. He grabbed my throat and slammed me up against the side of the lattice walkway. Leaves, vines of ivy and the hard latticework pressed into my back.

"Where's the crucifix?" Tattoo Man hissed at me, bathing my nostrils with his funky breath.

"Wha…what?" was all I could get out. Between the pain in my stomach and the tight grip of his hand around my throat, I could barely breathe, let alone talk.

I struggled to free my hands, which were trapped between our bodies.

"Don't play games with me! I know Juliet gave it to
you. It wasn't in the hotel room! Where is it?" He shook
me by my throat like a rag doll.

"I barely knew her," I gasped. "She never gave me
anything. I swear. Please…don't hurt me anymore!"

I managed to press myself back just enough to free
my right knee and drove it toward his groin. But he an-
ticipated the move and deflected it by turning sideways,
then spun me around pressing my face against the latticework as he tugged my arms up painfully behind me.

"You barely knew her, yet you shared a hotel room!
You barely knew her, yet you showed such concern for
her when you saw her being harassed by that Frenchman on the bridge."

"Please! We didn't know each other! We didn't!"
How did he know about what happened on the boat?

"Don't lie to me!" he screamed in my ear and pulled
my arms up higher. It felt like they were about to break.

"I'm not lying. Please! Please, stop!" Tears streamed
down my face and snot ran from my nose.

"I followed you yesterday. I know you didn't have
the crucifix then. She must have given it to you after
she got back to the hotel."

"I don't know what you're talking about! I swear!"

"What I did to Juliet Rice is nothing compared to
what I'll do to you if you don't give me what I want!
Where is the crucifix?"

The world started to spin. This was the man who
took my bag. This was the man who took my key card
and used my corkscrew to kill Juliet. My legs gave out
and I slid down his body to the ground. He jerked me

back to my feet, turned me around to face him and punched me again, this time in my right side. The explosion of searing pain caused me to fall to the ground and curl into a ball. He grabbed a handful of my hair and jerked my head back.

"Tell me!" he screamed.

My vision began to blur. My attacker let out a grunt. The last thing I heard before passing out was the sound of fists on flesh.

WHEN I CAME TO, I was lying on my back. The most intense pair of green eyes I'd ever seen stared down at me. I'd seen those eyes before.

"Are you okay? Can you stand?" asked the man with the green eyes.

His English was tinged with a French accent. Sunglasses poked out of the front pocket of his faded jean jacket. His white shirt was ripped and his pants were smudged with dirt. This looked like the guy I'd bumped into when I'd arrived earlier. But those eyes made me realize that hadn't been the first time I'd seen him. This was also the man who'd seen Juliet arguing with on the Pont de la Concorde. What was he doing here? I struggled to my feet and felt a wave of nausea wash over me.

"Easy." He reached out to steady me. I pushed his hand away and took long, deep breaths to keep from throwing up.

"We need to get out of here before he comes to." He gestured toward my unconscious attacker lying inside the latticed walkway who had started to groan.

"Come on! Let's go!" he commanded impatiently, grabbing my hand. I pulled away.

"No! We need to call the police! What's the

number?" I fumbled around on the ground for my cell as I tossed as much of my stuff as I could back into my bag.

Tattoo Man groaned again, louder this time.

"Are you crazy? He's coming to! We've got to get out of here!"

"It'll only take a minute!" I tried to turn my cell phone on. But my hands were shaking so badly I could barely push the buttons.

"We don't have time. Come on!" He grabbed my hand again.

He took off running, pulling me behind him. I tried my best to keep up but the pain in my side slowed me down. A bullet whizzed past my head and another hit the fence post near me. Tattoo Man was firing a gun as he staggered behind us.

"He's got a gun!" I screamed at my rescuer.

"No shit! Shut up and keep running!"

We emerged from the maze to see an old, beat-up maintenance truck parked about ten feet away. A workman stood on a scaffold cleaning a nearby statue.

"Get in!" Green Eyes shouted, shoving me into the truck on the driver's side. I scooted over and he jumped behind the wheel. There was no key in the ignition and he slapped the steering wheel in frustration. *"Merde!"*

The man on the scaffold, yelling at us in French, began to climb down. Tattoo Man lumbered out of the maze and ran smack into the scaffold, sending it and the statue cleaner crashing down. While the two cursing men tried to extricate themselves from each other and the wreck of the scaffold, Green Eyes frantically looked for the keys in the glove box and under the floor mat.

"Don't just sit there! Help me!" he yelled, jolting me into action. I checked the ashtray and under the seat, then reached over and pulled down the driver's sun visor. A set of keys fell into his lap. He started the truck just as the back window exploded. I screamed. Tattoo Man was back on his feet and about to fire again.

"Get down!" Green Eyes shouted, pushing my head down as another bullet whizzed through the truck and shattered the front windshield.

He threw the truck into Reverse. *Thud!* I sat up and turned to Tattoo Man on the ground. His gun had been knocked out of his hand. We sped off at top speed and minutes later were on the highway.

"You okay?" he asked, squeezing my shoulder. I wasn't but I nodded yes anyway.

"You were on the bridge with Dr. Rice yesterday, weren't you?"

He looked at me and gave me a disarming half smile, but didn't answer. I had the feeling he used that smile to his advantage quite often. And I bet it worked most of the time.

"Aren't you even going to tell me who you are and what the hell is going on?"

"Aren't you even going to thank me for saving your life?" He smiled at me in an infuriatingly smug way.

"You first." I glared at him. He laughed.

"All in due time, Maya. But first things first." How the hell did he know my name?

"What do you mean? Where are we going?" I demanded while carefully picking shattered glass out of my hair and shaking it out of my clothing.

"Back to Paris. You're not the only one needing answers," he replied cryptically.

QUATRE

AFTER WE DITCHED the truck on the campus of Paris X University in Nanterre, we took the RER train into Paris. Then the metro took us to the Blanche station. As we climbed the stairs out of the station, the sight of a red windmill greeted me. The Moulin Rouge—we were in the red light district. By this time much of the pain in my side had subsided to a dull roar as I trailed along after Mr. Green Eyes. But I was tired and, despite the fact that this stranger had saved my life, apprehensive.

"Stay close to me and watch your bag. There are lots of pickpockets here," he said as he maneuvered around a group of tourists taking pictures of the window display of a sex shop.

"Hold on!" I stopped to catch my breath. He turned and gave me an impatient look.

"I've been following you around for over an hour and I'm not taking one more step until you tell me who you are." I crossed my arms and waited.

He sighed then suddenly reached out and gently ran his fingers through my hair. His warm fingertips grazed my scalp and made my skin tingle. Our eyes met and I blushed.

"Hold still," he commanded softly as I fidgeted. When he pulled his hand away, he was holding a piece of windshield glass that I'd missed.

"I'm…still waiting," I said, suddenly flustered.

"D'accord," he finally said and pulled a worn black leather wallet out of his back pocket, took out a white business card and handed it to me. It read, Simon Girard, Agence France-Presse.

"You're a reporter?"

"I prefer *journaliste.*" He shoved the wallet back into his pocket.

"Is that how you know my name? Were you following me, hoping to get a story on Juliet Rice's murder?"

"Contrary to what most people believe about members of the press, I am not a vulture. However, I do have contacts everywhere, even at the police station, though I admit that like yourself, I'm not one of their favorite people," he said, shrugging.

"That still doesn't explain what you want with me."

"One of my contacts informed me that you were connected to the murder of a woman I've been very much needing to talk to."

"Then it was Dr. Rice you were trying to interview for a story? Is that why you were arguing with her on the bridge yesterday?"

"My business with Dr. Rice was of a much more personal nature than a mere story."

"Were you lovers?"

"Of course not," he said with a look of distaste.

"Friends?"

"I'd never met her before yesterday," he replied flatly.

"Okay, I'm confused. You weren't friends or lovers and you weren't interviewing her. So what was all that about on the bridge yesterday? She slapped the shit out of you."

He ran a hand over his closely cropped hair. It took him a moment before answering.

"I think Juliet Rice was responsible for my brother's murder."

That certainly wasn't what I was expecting. I didn't know what to say. He turned and walked away. I had to sprint to keep up with him. Over my shoulder, the white dome of Sacré Couer loomed in the distance. I followed him down a side street off the rue Blanche called rue de Douai, past restaurants and tiny shops, ending up minutes later in front of a nondescript building with shiny green double doors. There were beautiful ornate floral patterns carved into the center panels.

"This was my brother Luc's place. I've been staying here since I moved back to Paris from Hong Kong six months ago. You should be safe here," he said.

He pushed one side of the door open and I could see a dark foyer with black-and-white tiles on the floor and a winding staircase. He stepped aside for me to enter. I didn't budge. I bit my lower lip while mentally weighing the pros and cons of going inside this building with a complete stranger. He read my expression and laughed.

"You've followed me all the way home and *now* you're having second thoughts?"

"Don't act like I'm a stray a cat when you practically kidnapped me! We should have gone straight to the police. But, no, you had to be all covert and dump the truck in Paris when we could have just left it at the train station in Versailles."

"*Pardonnez-moi, madame,* if I'm not used to having people shooting at me. Forgive me for wanting to get far away and as fast as possible."

"Why won't you go to the police? They need to know what happened."

"Have the police believed a word you've told them

so far? Because I'm guessing if they did, you wouldn't be a murder suspect, right?"

"You're my witness," I insisted. "You can tell them what happened."

"Forget it. I'm not going anywhere near the police until I have the answers I need regarding my brother's death and maybe not even then, considering they've not done a damned thing to help me so far."

I glared at him. Obviously, just because he'd saved me, didn't mean he'd help me. He had his own agenda.

"Maybe I should just go back to my hotel."

"Oh, of course, I understand perfectly why you would want go back to the same hotel where that psycho killed a woman in your room. Smart move. If you go back now, he might even be waiting for you. Why don't I just call you a cab?" he said, with more annoyance than real anger in his voice.

"Shut up," I hissed as I pushed past him.

Once inside, after my eyes adjusted to the dim lighting, I could see there was a tiny elevator underneath the stair. Simon ignored the elevator, probably just to spite me, and sprinted up the steps. We climbed seven winding flights before he stopped on the eighth floor and unlocked an apartment three doors from the black marbled landing.

Just off the small entryway, where Simon tossed his jean jacket over a hook on the wall, was a narrow hallway painted a vivid blue. It was lined with colorful paintings of street and market scenes. Each one was signed "Luc G." The hallway opened up into a surprisingly large and airy living room with a row of tall, narrow casement windows that looked out on the street below.

There was a small kitchenette barely large enough for one person to cook in with a small dorm-sized fridge and an ancient-looking gas stove as well as a compact stacked washer and dryer. The living room was minimally decorated with only a large couch, a black leather chaise. A brand-new computer rested on a glass desk.

"Your brother was an artist?" I sat on the couch and watched as Simon pulled a bottle of bourbon from the kitchen cabinet, grabbed two square-cut glasses from the dish rack and joined me on the couch.

"Oui," he replied. But it sounded like *way.*

"He was talented." I accepted the glass of bourbon. I took a sip and gratefully felt the tingling burn all the way to my stomach.

"He didn't think so," Simon said, after taking a big gulp of his drink. "He painted portraits of tourists on the Place du Tertre. If someone wanted a portrait in the style of Picasso, he could do it. If someone wanted a portrait in the style of Renoir, he could do that, too. But he had no personal style of his own. He called himself a gifted mimic."

"He must have done well being a mimic. That's a new Mac and those flat screens aren't cheap."

Simon sighed, drained his glass, leaned back against the overstuffed cushions on the couch and looked up at the ceiling.

"I'm sorry." I reached out to touch his arm. "Were you really close?"

"Only in the last few years. We didn't grow up together." He pulled a picture from his wallet and handed it to me. It showed a man who bore little resemblance to Simon. His brother had dark red hair, which had started to gray at the temples, a goatee and he wore glasses.

The only thing the two brothers did have in common was their gorgeous green eyes.

"Luc was my father's son from his first marriage," Simon said as if he were reading my mind. "He was eleven years older than me. My father left Luc's mother for mine. She'd been his secretary. How's that for a cliché? Luc's mother took the divorce very hard and never let him come to see us, which tore my father apart. I didn't even meet my half brother until I was sixteen and that was at my father's funeral. He made it clear he wanted nothing to do with me. He was angry and jealous. His mother led him to believe that our father didn't love him anymore, that he only loved me. It's only been in the last five years, since his mother died, that he's shown any interest in getting to know me. When she was alive, I think he thought having a relationship with me would be disrespectful to her."

"How did he die?" I ventured, still nursing my first bourbon while Simon poured himself another.

"Luc disappeared about two weeks ago. No one knew were he was. I called all his friends. Even contacted his ex-wife, Natasha, in Quebec. Nothing. The police were no help. They told me he was an adult and it was his right to disappear if he wanted to. Even suggested that maybe he'd left to get away from me. A week later, they pulled his body out of the Seine. There was a suspicious contusion on the back of his head that could have occurred either before or after death. But the official coroner's report is suicide."

"You don't think he killed himself?"

"My brother was the happiest I'd ever seen him. He and Natasha were getting back together. He was even moving to Quebec to be with her. The last time we talked he was making plans and had already bought a one-way ticket to Canada. There's no way he'd kill himself. No way!"

"I don't understand. How does Juliet Rice come into all of this?"

"My brother didn't earn enough money painting portraits to earn a living. He used his artistic skills to supplement his income in ways that weren't legal, mostly through forgeries of art and antiquities. Luc could duplicate anything you put in front of him—paintings, sculptures, pottery, you name it. He could even take a bed sheet, some tea and a paintbrush and make a replica of the Shroud of Turin that could fool the experts. He was that good and he'd never been caught. You can probably imagine how in demand his skills were. And he was going to give it all up for Natasha. It was the only way she'd take him back. He told me he had one last job to do for some American woman before he left and she was paying him a lot."

"And you think it was Juliet Rice?"

"I know it was her. I found her card in his things after he disappeared as well as a check from her for twenty thousand euros. I tracked her to the Ritz-Carlton to ask if she'd seen him but she'd already checked out. I finally tracked her to the Bienvenue yesterday and saw her hop in a cab, so I followed her."

"What did she say when you confronted her?"

"Told me I had the wrong person and she didn't know my brother. I could tell she was lying because every time I tried to show her his picture to jog her memory, she refused to look at it. There was definitely something off about that woman."

"In what way?" I didn't disagree but wanted to hear what he thought.

"I did some checking on Dr. Rice. She'd recently quit her professorship at Stanford after teaching there for twenty years and had just been granted tenure. She sold her house and came here three weeks ago but kept moving around. I managed to track her to three different hotels in the last week—each time she'd be gone before I got there. She'd stay at each place for a couple of days and then leave. She was running from someone, probably that wacko who attacked you."

"Wait a minute!" I exclaimed, suddenly remembering. "He said Juliet had something that belonged to him. He kept asking me about a crucifix. He thought she gave it to me."

Simon got up abruptly and walked over to the cabinets under the bookshelves and pulled out a large sketchpad.

"That would explain this," he said excitedly, sitting down next to me and flipping the pad open. I couldn't help but notice the warmth of his thigh pressed against mine and kept my head down so he wouldn't see my flushed face.

There were a dozen sketches in all. Each one a more detailed variation of the same image of a crucifix. It showed two figure eights, with the smaller one positioned crosswise, and the larger one placed lengthwise. An inlaid scene on the handle depicted a nun kneeling in front of a serene winged angel. With one hand, the angel presented the nun with a book whose cover contained a horizontal figure eight. The letter *S* was written in one of eight's sections, the letter *M* in the other. With the other hand, the angel held up a sword. The nun's head bowed reverently; the folds of her habit obscured her face. She clasped her hands as if in prayer.

Both characters were bathed in rays from a brightly shining sun in the upper right-hand corner of the picture. Dimensions, four inches wide by six inches long, were listed in the margins. I'd seen that letter and figure eight combination before. And it had been recently. I just couldn't remember where.

"And you think your brother was killed because of this?"

"*Oui.* Luc must have been hired to make a replica of this crucifix for Juliet Rice. I think the minute Luc turned it over either she or someone connected to her killed him because he knew too much. Juliet must have stolen the real crucifix and left the fake in its place. The guy she stole it from killed her and now he thinks you have it. This has to be what this is all about."

"But I don't get it! What makes this thing worth two people's lives?"

"I don't know. But since Luc died I've been doing research on that symbol on the book the angel is holding." He got up and grabbed a file folder lying next to the laptop and opened it. "That figure eight on its side is the symbol for infinity. I didn't know what the *S* and the *M* meant until I found this."

He handed me a sheet of paper that looked like it had been printed from an online book. The title, *Secret Societies of France,* was in the upper left corner. The page number at the bottom was 315. The page was a list of strange symbols and Greek letters, as well as the names of the societies they represented. Simon had highlighted in yellow the infinity symbol with the *S* and *M* about halfway down the page. Underneath, it read, "Society of Moret."

"Society of Moret? What is it, some kind of secret society like the Freemasons or something?"

"Unfortunately, that's the only page of this book available online. It was published by a small university press in 1992 and is out of print now. I haven't had any luck finding a copy anywhere let alone finding another mention of the Society of Moret anyplace else. However, as luck would have it, the author lives right here in Paris. Her name is Dr. Evalyn Hewitt. She recently retired from teaching medieval studies at the American University. After I put you in a cab to the airport tomorrow morning, I plan to go see her."

"Oh, really?" I fixed him with a hard look. "I don't remember saying anything about leaving Paris."

"You need to go home where you'll be safe."

"I need to stay here and clear my name. Do you know how it'll make me look if I leave the country? They might even arrest me for trying. At least now I have a chance to prove I didn't kill Juliet."

"They didn't arrest you. Did they take your passport?"

"No. But—"

"Then you can go home. If they were truly trying to keep you here, they'd have confiscated your passport. They were just trying to scare you."

"Well it worked! I'm not going home and you can't make me."

Simon let out an exasperated sigh.

"Your life is in danger. Two people have already died. You need to get out of here before—"

"Forget it, Simon." I stood, letting the sketchbook

slide onto the floor. "I'm not going home to spend everyday looking over my shoulder waiting for either the French police or that crazy fucker who killed Juliet to come after me. I need to lay low and find out what the hell is going on."

"When I find out exactly what happened to Luc, I'm afraid of what I might do," Simon said quietly. "Do you want be a part of that with the trouble you're already in?"

We stared at each other. I had to break my gaze because he was dead serious. He also had a point. Did I really need to add Simon's troubles to my own? His eyes held a deep sadness that made my heart ache for him. And the last thing I needed was to get into more trouble over some stranger, even one with beautiful, green, sad puppy dog eyes.

"Why don't we wait until tomorrow to see what Dr. Hewitt has to say? If she doesn't know anything useful, then we can go our separate ways and you can do whatever you want. Now, if you really want to do something for me," I said, sitting back down, "you can feed me. I'm starving."

I WOKE WITH THE BIRDS the next morning in Simon's brother's bed. Simon slept on the couch. We'd spent the rest of the previous evening in awkward companionship, making occasional small talk punctuated by long lapses of silence. I sensed Simon was much more personable and charming under normal circumstances, and so was I. But we were both so tired and these were hardly normal circumstances. The only edible things to eat in the tiny fridge, that didn't resemble a science project, had been some eggs, a wedge of Gruyere cheese and a pint of strawberries. Simon made a large omelet and we'd shared it along with the strawberries before he gave me one of his old T-shirts to sleep in and went to bed. He was still asleep, lying on his stomach with his left arm hanging over the side of the couch, when I walked into the living room and pulled up the blinds, flooding the living room with bright sunlight.

"Rise and shine, Sleeping Beauty. We need to get a move on."

Simon jerked awake with a groan and fell off the couch. When he scrambled to his feet, he was completely naked, and the only part of him that was awake and alert was below his waist. Wow! No wonder he could run up all those flights of stairs. He had the trim, well-muscled body of an athlete. He was in excellent shape. In short, his body was bangin'.

"*Mon Dieu!* What are you trying to do, kill me?" He hastily grabbed two pillows from the floor to cover his front and back and sidestepped me.

"Well, I am suspected of murder after all," I joked, hoping he hadn't noticed me admiring his anatomy.

"What time is it?" he asked.

"Ten 'til seven."

"Why did you wake me so early?" he asked grouchily as he dropped the pillow covering his ass and rubbed his scruffy face.

"You said you had an appointment with that professor this morning."

"At eleven. A civilized hour," he snapped, grabbing his pants from where they were draped across the chaise.

"Sorry," I said, slinking off to the kitchen. "I didn't realize you weren't a morning person."

"There is only one reason a woman should wake me first thing in the morning. And it's not for an appointment." He eyed my bare legs. I tugged at the T-shirt.

He came into the kitchen and walked toward me. Due to the limited space, I couldn't get out of his way fast enough and ended up backed into a corner. At first, I was afraid he was going to try and kiss me, and I could tell by his smile that he knew it. Instead, he reached over my head to the cabinet above and pulled out a bag of coffee beans and a grinder. I noticed for the first time he had a small diamond stud in his left ear.

"Do you think she'll still talk to you if you bring me along?" I asked to mask my embarrassment.

Simon looked down at me, started to speak and stopped abruptly. A horrified look spread over his face. He leaned down to look at my neck. Rattled, I headed off to the bathroom to see what the problem was. Simon followed. What I saw made me gasp. Livid purple bruises from where I'd been choked the day before encircled my neck.

"Does it hurt?" He probed the bruises with tender fingers. I could feel his warm breath on my neck and jumped away from him like I'd been burned.

"A little," I said, though in truth it didn't hurt at all.

"Are you hurt anywhere else?" He promptly pulled up the T-shirt to reveal my white cotton bikini panties as well as another large bruise the size of a baseball on my right side. This bruise was tender and I flinched when he touched it.

"I should have killed that bastard when I had the chance!" exclaimed Simon through gritted teeth.

"I'm fine!" I quickly yanked the T-shirt down again. "Now get out of here so I can take a shower."

Simon paused in the doorway of the bathroom before leaving. "Luc's ex, Natasha, left some clothes behind that might fit you. They're in the bedroom armoire."

"Thanks." I waited for him to go but he just stood there smiling at me. Was he expecting an invitation to wash my back? Like that would happen. I finally closed the door.

NATASHA GIRARD HAD a much frillier and more feminine taste in clothing than I did. She was also a lot taller than me. The only things of hers I was willing to step out of the apartment in were a gray turtleneck sweater that covered the bruises on my neck and a pair of black slacks that fit just fine once the waistband was rolled up a couple of times.

While I was putting Natasha's clothes back into their box at the bottom of the armoire, I found a snapshot. Two tanned, smiling couples stood on the beach. Simon's brother, Luc, wearing an unflattering yellow Speedo and a red polo shirt, had his arm around a tall, willowy blonde in a pink string bikini. This had to be Natasha.

The other couple was made up of Simon and a curvy redhead in a black one-piece. Her gorgeous curly hair hung gracefully around her shoulders. The redhead wasn't traditionally pretty, but she had a beautiful smile and was quite striking. Simon smiled at her like a love-struck teenager. I flipped the picture over, but all it said was *St. Tropez 2004.* I wondered who the red-head was. Simon was clearly crazy about her. Of course a man like Simon had someone special in his life, probably several someone specials. How cute. I tossed the snapshot back in the box and slammed the armoire shut with a force I hadn't intended.

DR. EVALYN HEWITT LIVED on the Ile St. Louis, the smaller of two islands in the center of Paris. Once Simon and I crossed the Pont Louis-Philippe, the bridge that connected the island to the Right Bank, it was as though I'd stepped into a small village.

I walked with Simon down narrow, cobbled one-way streets past shops, galleries, restaurants and elegant seventeenth-century townhouses. We strolled past an ice cream parlor that had a line of customers so long it was winding down the sidewalk. Simon told me it was Berthillon's, an ice cream parlor that had the best ice cream in the world.

Once we were away from the busy rue St-Louis-en-l'Ile, a short street running the length of the island, the side streets were much quieter and tranquil, and it was possible to catch glimpses of the Seine between the buildings lining the quay. Residents of the island went about their daily business, pulling grocery and laundry carts down the street and relaxing at cafés.

Dr. Hewitt lived on the rue Poulletier in a building built in 1637, according to the plaque mounted on the outside of the honey-colored building. The building was a walk-up and I could see Simon resisting the urge to laugh at my pained expression as I started up after him. Thankfully we were only going to the third floor.

Simon was just about to knock on Dr. Hewitt's door when it was suddenly flung open by a slender woman in her late sixties with short white hair pinned down on either side of her head by black barrettes. She wore a gray twinset and skirt.

"Dr. Hewitt?" asked Simon.

"Oh, yes. Do come in. I've been so looking forward to your visit, Monsieur Girard," the woman said excitedly. She had an English accent but rolled the *R*'s in Simon's last name like a French native.

She stepped aside and we walked into a large spacious apartment. Our shoes clicked on the polished hardwood floors. The first floor of the apartment was decorated in what I would bet my next paycheck was authentic Queen Anne furniture. I spotted a staircase in the corner of the dining room. This place had to have cost a fortune.

"I hope you don't mind that I've brought my assistant, Madame Sinclair, with me, Dr. Hewitt?"

"Oh, not a problem. Not a problem. You know I was just telling Agnes the other day. It's not every day we have a filmmaker come to visit us. It's all so exciting."

Filmmaker? I shot Simon a look and he ignored me.

"The pleasure is all mine, Dr. Hewitt. I'm just happy an important woman such as yourself was able to squeeze me into your busy schedule." He took her hand and brushed the top of it with his lips. Dr. Hewitt giggled like a little girl. I rolled my eyes.

"Agnes thinks it would be an excellent idea if we take our coffee up in the library. I have it all laid out. Follow me."

We followed Dr. Hewitt upstairs. White-washed brick walls and exposed wood beams in the ceiling gave the room a homey, rustic feel. Walls were lined with bookshelves holding row after row of leather-bound books.

An overstuffed plaid couch and a worn leather recliner were arranged by a fireplace. A tray with a

Bodum coffee brewer, cups and a dome-covered platter of cheese, fruit and French pastries were laid out on the low table in front of the couch. Curled up on a leather footstool was a fluffy Bichon Frise.

"Here we are, Agnes," Dr. Hewitt announced as she sat. The dog looked up briefly then jumped off the stool and onto Dr. Hewitt's lap. It was clear the two adored each other.

Once we were settled, Simon got down to business.

"Dr. Hewitt do you mind if I ask you few questions about your book, *Secret Societies of France?*"

"Ask away, *monsieur.* It's not everyday one's book gets made into a documentary. Isn't that right, Agnes?" The dog yawned.

I cringed but didn't dare look at Simon. I couldn't believe he'd lied to this sweet old lady.

"I'm aware of many of the societies mentioned in your book. But this one," he said, pulling out the computer printout he'd shown me and handing it to her, "is one I'm completely unfamiliar with." He gestured toward the symbol for the Society of Moret. Dr. Hewitt put on her glasses and peered at the printout.

"Ah, yes, the Society of Moret." She reached into the drawer of the small, round table next to her chair and pulled out a hardbound book. It was a copy of *Secret Societies of France.* "You know I seriously thought about not including this one in the book. It's actually more of a myth than anything else."

"It that so?" said Simon. He was sitting on the edge of the couch, leaning forward in anticipation.

"Except for a handful of stories handed down over the years, there's no real proof it ever existed," said Dr. Hewitt, clearly happy to have a captive audience.

"And what are those stories?" Simon asked after taking a swig of coffee.

Dr. Hewitt started to speak and then looked pointedly at me, and then back at Simon. My mouth was full of luscious pear tart and by the odd look she'd just given me, I was afraid I might be drooling.

"Isn't your assistant going to take notes?"

"Ah, you must forgive her, Dr. Hewitt. She's new." He turned to wink at me on the sly then pulled a note-pad and a pen out of his backpack and plopped it on my lap. I quickly wrote the words *Society of Moret* at the top of the page.

"As I was about to say," continued Dr. Hewitt. "According to legend, the Society of Moret was founded in Moret-sur-Loing France by an obscure seventeenth-century nun named Sister Louise-Marie Therese. She was known to the locals of the time as the Black Nun of Moret."

"Why'd they call her the black nun?" I asked, still writing.

"Well, because she was a woman of color like yourself, my dear. She was born Louise-Marie Therese, the illegitimate daughter of Queen Maria-Theresa of Spain, wife of King Louis XIV of France, and her African lover, a servant named Nabo," she said matter-of-factly.

Dr. Hewitt flipped through the book until she found the page she wanted. She turned the book to show us a painting of a black woman wearing a habit. Her skin was the color of cinnamon and her large brown eyes overwhelmed her long narrow face. She seemed sad and forlorn. My pen froze over the page. This story sounded familiar. Then it came back to me. When I'd toured Versailles with Brian and Jarrod, I'd overheard a tour guide telling her group about a French queen who'd given birth to a black baby at Versailles. I'd just thought it was some exaggerated gossip to shock and titillate the tourists and it had annoyed me at the time. But this had to be the same child.

"You're telling me a French queen had a baby by a black servant and managed to keep her head?" I asked.

"Luckily for the queen, the workings of human reproduction weren't well-known back then. We're talking about a time when people thought a man merely looking at a woman could influence her pregnancy. And that's what Louis XIV was lead to believe, that Nabo startled Queen Maria-Theresa while she was pregnant, causing the child to be born black."

Simon let out a low whistle.

"What happened to the baby?" I asked.

"Everyone was told the baby died at birth, but she was sent off to be raised by a wet nurse on a farm. She was raised along with the farmer's other children for several years and then sent to a convent in Moret-sur-Loing. She spent the rest of her life there and took her vows at the age of thirty-one. A representative of the king made sure she was always well taken care of and wanted for nothing."

"Except a family you mean?" I was shocked by the bitterness in my voice.

Simon looked at me quizzically. I went back to writing, feeling puzzled by the kinship I was suddenly feeling toward this unwanted, unloved, illegitimate child born so long ago.

"Please go on, Dr. Hewitt," urged Simon.

"The legend goes that around the late 1600s Sister Louise-Marie was walking in the woods near her convent when she was visited by an angel who entrusted her with a book and told her to protect it and keep it hidden at all costs."

Simon and I shot each other a look. What she'd just described was identical to the scene on the crucifix handle.

"What kind of book?" asked Simon.

"Are you familiar with the *Mutus Liber?*" asked Dr. Hewitt, stroking Agnes affectionately and causing the little dog to go limp with pleasure.

"Isn't *liber* Latin for book?" I asked. I struggled unsuccessfully to remember more of my high school Latin.

"You are correct," replied Dr. Hewitt. "*Mutus Liber* is Latin for mute book. It was an illustrated book of alchemy published in France sometime in the 1670s by a Huguenot named Isaac Baulot. It contained only illustrations—fifteen to be exact—and no words. So it is known as the mute, or silent book, as some refer to it."

"And this mute book is what the angel supposedly gave to Sister Louise-Marie?" Simon asked.

"No. Actually, the *Mutus Liber* is a well-known book in alchemy circles. Its illustrated panels reportedly show how to make the philosopher's stone, which can turn metal into gold as well as prolong life. However, no one has ever been able to decipher what the panels mean."

I started to laugh and Simon shot me a warning look. I couldn't help it. It sounded like something straight out of a kid's book.

"I know what you're thinking, my dear." Dr. Hewitt was not offended by my outburst. "But the philosopher's stone is very real and goes back centuries before Harry Potter was ever dreamt up."

"Sorry. I just don't believe in that kind of thing," I said.

"No need to apologize. I certainly don't begrudge anyone his beliefs, or disbeliefs," Dr. Hewitt said with undisguised amusement.

"But you think the philosopher's stone is real?" I asked.

"I believe within every great legend lies a grain of truth. But that's beside the point. History itself proves the philosopher's stone could indeed be real."

"You've got to be kidding," exclaimed Simon, looking over at me.

"Not in the least. How would you explain figures such as Methuselah, who by some accounts lived to be 969, or Ramses the Great, who lived to be nearly 100 years old at a time when the average life span was thirty? The Abkhazia people in the mountains of southern Russia who live well into their hundreds? Something certainly contributed to their longevity. Who's to say it wasn't the philosopher's stone?"

"Aren't those just more myths and legends? It's impossible to know if any of them truly lived that long," I countered.

"My dear, just because something seems implausible doesn't make it impossible. Think about how long people believed the world was flat."

I was incredulous. I couldn't believe an educated woman believed in an elixir that could prolong life. Then again, she did let her dog decide where we would have coffee.

"If it's real, why doesn't everyone know about it and use it?" I asked.

She considered my question for a long moment, her

eyes never leaving mine, before answering. "Tell me," she said, looking down at the dog on her lap. "Would you believe me if I told you my Agnes is almost forty years old?" Agnes's ears perked up at the sound of her name.

"No. It's impossible for a dog to live that long," I replied. I'd had a roommate in college whose beagle lived to be twenty-two—but almost forty? Nonsense.

"Well then there you have it. Knowledge and belief are two different things. I've given you a bit of knowledge that based on conventional wisdom you've decided isn't true. Most people, like you, are skeptics when it comes to the unconventional. They aren't going to pursue something they don't believe in even if they know about it, even if the knowledge of it goes back centuries."

"But—"

"We'd love to debate this further, Dr. Hewitt," Simon said impatiently, cutting me off, "but could you finish telling us about the *Mutus Liber?*"

"Ah, yes, we did get a bit sidetracked, didn't we?" she said with a laugh. "The *Mutus Liber* wasn't considered a dangerous book because no one could decipher the illustrations. In fact, a copy of it was kept in the library at the Louvre back when it was still the primary residence of the French royal family. However, an updated version of the book, complete with about five hundred pages of text describing what the illustrations meant, was supposedly published some ten years later by a student of Baulot."

"Why would this book be considered dangerous?" Simon asked.

"Surely you can answer that question yourself, Monsieur Girard," said Dr. Hewitt. She put Agnes down, and the dog sat looking longingly at the half-eaten plate of cheese and fruit on Simon's lap.

"The book was considered dangerous because it threatened the church," I said. Dr. Hewitt nodded enthusiastically.

"That's right," said Dr. Hewitt, warming to her subject. "Why would people need the church if they had a book with a recipe for immortality *and* turning base metals into gold? You could live forever and be rich. No need to go to church to confess, or repent, or pray for your soul's salvation if you never had to worry about dying and going to hell in the first place."

"But they couldn't possibly believe what was in this book was real?" I persisted.

"Why not? They believed a black man could startle a pregnant white woman and turn her baby black," Simon pointed out.

Dr. Hewitt nodded in agreement. "It was more about what the book represented than what was actually in it that worried the Catholic Church. Any ideas that didn't align with their own were considered heresy. Remember Baulot was a Huguenot, a member of the Protestant church, and they there were persecuted in France. By the time the second book was published, Louis XIV had revoked the Edict of Nantes and declared Protestantism illegal."

"So then this *second* book is what was given to Sister Louise-Marie to protect?" I was starting to get impatient.

"Yes," Dr. Hewitt replied, nodding vigorously.

"Why her?" Simon and I asked in unison.

"I'm getting to that." Dr. Hewitt got up and walked over to the bookshelf behind us.

We turned and watched her peruse the shelf until she came upon a thick, red leather-bound book. She pulled it out and sat back down, flipping through it until she finally found what she was looking for. She turned the book to show us an illustration of the same image depicted in the handle of the crucifix in Luc's sketchpad.

CINQ

WELL, IT WAS ALMOST the same scene. Once I got a closer look, the differences were apparent. This was a tapestry, not a drawing or painting. The kneeling nun was no longer faceless. It was clear she was a black woman. The angel's wings and robes were longer and more elaborate than in Luc's sketch. The book with the infinity symbol was there, but its cover was jewel-encrusted. And while the infinity symbol was still present, the letters *S* and *M* were missing. The sun in this image was smaller and less imposing than it was in Luc's drawing. The scene included a detailed background of large trees filled with songbirds, lush greenery and a huge castle-like building. Simon stared at it, speechless. I finally broke the silence.

"What is this?"

"This, my dear, is the Moret Tapestry. It was found at the turn of the century in the cellar of a private home in the village of Fontainebleau not far from Moret-sur-Loing. It dates back to the late 1600s, but nobody has been able to identify the artist. The French art historian Bernard Fouquet theorized that since the book was never found, a society must have been formed to protect it. He could never prove it conclusively, though.

"Fouquet believed that this tapestry is the blueprint on which a crucifix was created. The so-called Moret Crucifix supposedly provides the clues for finding the actual book the society protects, but no one has ever found it. Unfortunately, there is no evidence it even exists beyond Fouquet's wild theories."

Simon shot me a glance. His eyes shined with excitement. "Do you know this Fouquet? I'd love to talk with him about his theories for the documentary."

"Unfortunately, I never got a chance to meet the man. We didn't exactly move in the same circles. Sadly, he died in obscurity about ten years ago. The academic community deemed him a crackpot. I found my information from his early writings."

"That still doesn't answer why Sister Louise-Marie was chosen to protect the book," I prodded. Dr. Hewitt was silent for a moment.

"All I have is a personal theory of my own to explain that."

"Yes?" I said anxiously.

"Despite the ridiculous excuse Louis XIV bought into, he had to know she wasn't his child. Poor Louise-Marie was never acknowledged or recognized by the royal family. She was an embarrassment to the king. She was never supposed to know about her background or where she came from. But someone told her who her mother was and as a result, she became a big problem."

"What do you mean?" I asked.

"According to the few known accounts of her life, Louise-Marie kept running away from the convent to try and gain an audience with her mother, the queen. She wanted her rightful place at court. She was always found, usually somewhere on the grounds of nearby Fontainebleau Castle. She was always persuaded to go back to the convent, that is, until she fell in love."

"How'd she manage that, living in a convent?" I

asked incredulously. I could barely find dates living in a big city.

"People of color weren't exactly in abundance back in seventeenth-century France. So she was quite a curiosity to the members of the royal court. Many of them visited her at the convent when they were staying at Fontainebleau Castle. One of them, Philippe d'Orleans, the Duke of Chartres, was the king's nephew, they fell madly in love and he snuck her out of the convent with every intention of marrying her."

"And did they get married?" I asked.

"No. Louis was never going to grant his nephew permission to marry the woman he'd hidden away since birth. That would have defeated the purpose of hiding her. Instead, he arranged a hasty marriage between the duke and Mademoiselle de Blois, the daughter he fathered by his mistress Madame de Montespan."

"What did Louise-Marie do?" I asked.

"What could she do? She was powerless. In those days women had few options. They could either become wives, mistresses, whores or nuns. And some women, depending on their circumstances, experienced each option at various points in their lives. In the end, Louise-Marie had no choice but to return to the convent."

"I doubt the duke ever really intended to marry her. I bet he just used her and dumped her," I said, channeling my recent relationship failure.

A curious half smile lifted one corner of Dr. Hewitt's mouth. From inside her shirt she pulled a thin silver chain from which hung a silver band ring. She unfastened the chain to retrieve the ring and handed it to me.

The ring was slightly domed and etched with a chain of interlocking figure eights circling its circumference.

"What is this?" I asked.

"It's a posy ring. They were quite popular with couples from about 1400 through the seventeenth century. The silver ones were used as engagement rings and were replaced with a gold one upon marriage. Posy comes from the term *poesy*. It refers to the secret messages of love that were engraved inside each one."

I held the ring up and turned it so I could read the message. It read: *de mon amour soyez sure.*

"Of my love be sure," translated Dr. Hewitt. "What you're holding is the ring that I believe Philippe d'Orleans, the Duke of Chartres, gave to Louise-Marie as a token of his love and his intention to marry her."

"You believe? So you don't know for sure?" I asked, eyeing the ring in my hand.

"I found that ring in an antique shop in Moret-sur-Loing when I was doing research for the book. The shop's owner told me it had been found at the bottom of an old well on the site where Louise-Marie's convent once stood. It's long gone now."

"But what makes you think it belonged to her?" I asked.

"Take a closer look inside. What else do you see besides the message?"

I took another look and opposite the message was a small mark. At first it looked like a *G* with an underline. But upon closer inspection it was actually a *G* engraved over an *L*. "What's GL stand for?"

"It's the jeweler's mark for Gilles Lagere. He was a court jeweler and engraver during the time of Louis XIV."

"Still seems like a bit of a stretch," said Simon.

"Oh, I don't know. Maybe I'm just a hopeless old romantic, Monsieur Girard, but the duke and Louise-Marie were in love. So a ring dating back to the late 1600s, found on the site of the convent where she once lived and commissioned by a member of the French royal court makes it highly likely as far as I'm concerned that this was her engagement ring."

"I'd call you neither hopeless nor old and I insist you call me Simon," he replied smoothly.

While Simon and Dr. Hewitt continued to chat, the shiny silver ring seemed to glow in my palm. I don't know what compelled me to slide the band on my ring finger but I did. And once it was past my knuckle, everything went eerily silent like someone pushed a mute button. The acrid stench of burning sugar filled my nostrils. Dizziness hit me hard, making the room spin. I gripped the cushion of the couch to keep from sliding off as the ringing of a church bell filled my ears, far off at first, then clanging so loudly the walls were vibrating. Then, just as soon as it started, it was over. What the hell had happened?

"Maya? Are you okay?" asked Simon.

"Didn't you...?" I began and then thought better of it. From their concerned expressions, neither Simon nor Dr. Hewitt had experienced what I had. "Never mind... I'm fine," I said with a nervous laugh and shook my head to clear it. "I was just thinking how devastated Louise-Marie must have been when they couldn't get married and she had to go back to that convent."

"As any woman in love would have been," said Dr. Hewitt. "And to make matters worse, the king gave his priest the task of making sure she never left the convent again. This was also around the time that the church came into possession of the second version of the *Mutus Liber.* The priest killed two birds with one stone by—"

"Giving Louise-Marie something to occupy her?" I ventured. Dr. Hewitt nodded.

"The theory is that the priest gave her the book, telling her that her marriage wasn't approved because she'd been chosen by the king for a higher purpose. She was to keep a dangerous book out of the wrong hands. She probably thought her family loved and needed her after all and she embraced her new role. She eventually took her final vows and remained in the convent for the rest of her life, no doubt forming the Society of Moret to watch over the book after she was gone."

"She spent the rest of her life guarding a worthless book?" said Simon, looking disgusted.

"Oh, I wouldn't say that, Monsieur Girard. You saw the tapestry. The book is bound in solid gold and covered with precious gems. In fact, the name of this second book is allegedly the *Aurum Liber,* the Gold Book. Forget about what's inside, the cover alone would be priceless, that is, if it even exists." She winked at Simon.

"How is the crucifix the key to finding it?" asked Simon.

Dr. Hewitt fixed Simon and me with an odd look and my heartbeat quickened. So far she'd been very forthcoming. Was she starting to smell a rat?

"Will this be in the documentary? I think it should be, you know. I watched the one the BBC did on Dan Brown's book and feel quite strongly that a story of missing treasure would really pull in the ratings, don't you?"

Neither of us spoke.

"My publisher will be forced to reissue *Secret Societies of France,* or better yet, I will be able to get a new publisher." She rubbed her hands together and stared off into space, no doubt imagining fame, glory and fat royalty checks.

Simon looked like a deer caught in headlights. I wanted to go…now. I checked my watch and abruptly stood

"Monsieur Girard, have you forgotten your 1:00 p.m. appointment with your lawyer? If we don't get going, we'll miss it and his next opening isn't until next week and you can't go then because you'll be in America." I pulled Simon roughly to his feet.

"Oh, dear," said Dr. Hewitt, looking disappointed. "Don't let me keep you, Monsieur Girard. Can we finish up another day, perhaps when you return from America?"

"It would be my pleasure, dear lady, and I thought I told you to call me Simon." Simon kissed her hand again.

I pulled him down the steps to the front door. Before we could leave, Dr. Hewitt called out.

"Oh, Simon! Don't you want to know the answer to your question?"

"Pardon?"

"Your question about how the crucifix is the key to finding the book?"

"Ah, *oui,* how could I have forgotten? Do tell, *s'il vous plaît.*"

"According to Bernard Fouquet's theory, it's all to do with the sun."

"The sun? You mean the sun on the tapestry?" I asked.

"I'm not sure. One interpretation of the sun depicted on the tapestry is that it represents Louis XIV. He was the sun king, you know. The sun shining down on the nun and the angel is thought to represent Louis's blessing of Louise-Marie being given the book. Personally, I'm not so sure. I think the sun is the key to finding the book. I just don't know how," she concluded sheepishly.

"*Merci,* Dr. Hewitt. I will be in touch." Simon bowed and blew her a kiss, which made her blush.

ONCE OUTSIDE AND SAFELY down the street, Simon shed his gentlemanly demeanor and rounded on me.

"What the hell is your problem? Why did you drag me out of there when she was telling us everything we needed to know?"

"Did you have to lie to her? How's she going to feel when she finds out you're a fraud? You may not have a problem lying. Most men don't. But I—"

"It was the only way I could get her to talk to me!" he snapped. "I'm trying to figure out what happened to my brother and I don't need some silly American woman with man problems fucking everything up. I didn't ask you to come with me!"

"Man problems?" My face was flaming.

"It's written all over you. You're mistrustful and uptight and angry. You're here in Paris, the most beautiful city in the world, yet you wouldn't know *joie de vivre* if it bit you in the ass. You may as well have 'I've been dumped' tattooed on your forehead. You're so miserable and sorry for yourself it's pathetic!"

He was more right than wrong. But that didn't mean

I had to like it, or take it. I closed my eyes, took a deep calming breath and let it out slowly while counting silently to ten. It usually helps when I'm trying to avoid making a scene. But when I opened my mouth to give the arrogant bastard a piece of my mind, I found I was so pissed off I couldn't talk.

"What's wrong?" he asked. "Has the cat caught your tongue?"

"It's *got* not *caught*," I snapped. "And screw you, dickhead! You don't know a damned thing about me. Forget the fact that I'm a murder suspect and the real murderer attacked me yesterday. Nooo! If I'm angry and mistrustful, it *has* to be because some man dumped me. Well, you know what? You can kiss my *joie de vivre*." I shoved the notepad at him. "And thanks a lot for saving my life. I'm outta here." I walked away.

"Where are you going?" He grabbed my arm. I shook him off.

"The agreement was that we'd see Dr. Hewitt together and then go our separate ways, remember? Good luck finding out what happened to your brother. I've got problems of my own. *Au revoir!*"

I took off running down the cobbled street back toward the crowded rue St-Louis-en-l'Ile.

"Maya! Come back here! That psycho is still out there! Maya!"

I ducked into a nearby gallery just in time to see Simon run past me. He looked around frantically for several minutes and then headed back toward the Pont Louis-Philippe.

Simon was right. I couldn't go back to the hotel. I knew I should check in with Bellange and Bernier to them and tell them about what happened at Versailles.

But Simon was right. They hadn't believed me so far. The thought of going back to the station and being grilled for hours in that room kept me from calling. And I knew after the incident at Versailles, they'd waste no time issuing a warrant for my arrest.

I ended up sitting at a sidewalk café, racking my brain trying to figure out what to do next. I suddenly remembered the U.S. Embassy. Wasn't the U.S. Embassy considered U.S. soil in Paris? They wouldn't be able to arrest me there. Surely the embassy could help me. I dug around in my bag for my Paris guidebook and discovered another big problem. I still had on Dr. Hewitt's posy ring! I tugged on the ring with every intention of going back to return it. But it wouldn't budge. Shit! I tried again with no luck, which was odd since it wasn't too tight. In fact, it was a perfect fit.

"Calm down, Maya," I whispered. I didn't have time to panic. I'd have to return the ring when this mess was over. I just hoped Dr. Hewitt hadn't called the police and reported it stolen.

I located my guidebook and flipped through it until I found the address for the U.S. Embassy.

On my way back off the island, I passed by Berthillon's again. A familiar-looking woman with short brown hair and glasses stood in line for ice cream. Meryl Berman! I couldn't believe my luck.

"Meryl!" I shouted. "Meryl, hey! How are you? You left the hotel before I got back from the police station. Are you okay?"

"Maya," she said, slowly looking around. "Where'd you come from?"

To say she didn't seem pleased to see me was an

understatement. A vacant look in her eyes made me wonder if she was on medication.

"You okay?"

"Of course. Why wouldn't I be?"

I was skeptical but didn't push it. "Look, Meryl, I really need your help. Did you tell the police about everything you saw the other night? It's really important."

Meryl's hands flew to her mouth. "Oh, that poor woman." She shook her head. "That poor, poor woman."

"I know. It was horrible. But I need to know if you got a good look at her in the shower. Do you remember seeing something in her neck?"

"Remember? I don't want to remember! I've been doing everything I can to forget."

"Did they ask you about seeing something in her neck?"

She shook her head no.

"But you did see it, right?" I was getting frantic.

"I saw something. But I can't say what it was or wasn't."

"That's okay, Meryl," I said hopefully. "The police don't believe me about the corkscrew because it's missing. They think I had something to do with her death and I need you to tell them you saw something in her neck, too. I need you to back up my story so they'll know I'm not the one who removed it. Please? This is really important."

Meryl shook her head and tears filled her eyes. "Please leave me alone. I just want to finish me vacation in peace. Ted went to look for a loo. If he comes back and sees you here he won't be happy."

"I don't give a damn about Ted. I need your help! Please, Meryl." I don't know if it was the desperation in my voice or that she just wanted to get rid of me, but Meryl slowly nodded her head yes.

"Thank you. I wouldn't ask if it wasn't really important." I pulled out the card Captain Bellange gave me.

"What's all this then?" exclaimed Ted Berman. Berman snatched the card from me and tore it up. He grabbed his wife's arm.

"The police need to talk to Meryl again about what she saw in my room the other night. It's important, Mr. Berman."

"Stop harassing my missus! Look at her! Can't you see she's traumatized? She already told them cops all they need to know. She ain't got nothing else to say. Now fuck off!"

He pulled her out of the line and down the street. "Wait! Meryl!" I shouted in vain.

Meryl looked back and mouthed, "I'm sorry," and then they were gone, swallowed up by the crowd.

People in line began to whisper. Tears burned in my eyes. Not wanting to make more of a scene, I figured I should get out of there fast. I ran all the way across the Pont de la Tournelle. As I came off the bridge, the hem of the too long pants I was wearing got caught on my heel and I went down face-first on the pavement. My bag flew into the middle of the street. And as if I hadn't suffered quite enough, I watched in horror as a cab rolled over it.

I'd also skinned my knee and it was on fire. I limped over to the curb. The traffic showed no signs of slowing down. Car after car ran over the bag, flattening it to a canvas pancake. Just as I was about to give up on getting my bag back again, a man on a black Vespa took pity on me and scooped it up. I gave him a teary *"Merci."*

Realizing I seriously needed to chill out—I hobbled over to a café and ordered a bottle of red wine. I downed a glass before I had the courage to examine the damage.

Miraculously, my cell phone was okay as it had been at the very bottom of my bag. My sunglasses were bent in half. They snapped in two when I tried to bend them back. No big loss. They were cheap knock-offs. But my expensive digital camera was completely crushed and the insides were rattling around inside. The cover over the battery compartment was cracked and stuck, but I wanted to try to get the batteries out before they leaked. I pounded the remains of the camera on the table in frustration, and the battery cover bounced off, but there were no batteries. Something small, rectangular and silver was nestled in the compartment. I pulled it out and recognized it as Juliet Rice's pendant. She must have hidden it in my camera. But I couldn't figure when, let alone why she could have done it. We'd only been in the room together twice and the first time she was definitely wearing the necklace. It had to have been when she came back to the room, after Simon confronted her on the bridge, and while I was in the bathroom.

I ran my fingers over the engraved J on the front and then turned it over. There was a small raised mark on the back. I couldn't make out what it was. I held my empty wineglass in front to magnify it and discovered a tiny infinity symbol with an S and an M. The Society of Moret's symbol. Why on earth would it be on Juliet's pendant? I must have inadvertently pressed it because a retractable USB prong popped out of the bottom. It wasn't a pendant at all. It was a flash drive. Now all I needed was a computer.

ACCORDING TO MY GUIDEBOOK, the nearest Internet café was on Boulevard Saint-Michel, near the Luxembourg Gardens. Since my knee was sore and aching, I opted for the metro. The Micro Café consisted of two long, narrow rooms with computers lining the walls. I paid two euros for thirty minutes of computer time and settled in at one of the available Macs.

After I punched in the access code given to me by the clerk, I plugged Juliet's flash drive into the computer's USB port, and an icon with the initials *JR* popped up on the desktop. I clicked on it, only to be disappointed when a login screen popped up. The flash drive was password protected. I tried to guess the password, but it was slow going. The European keyboards weren't arranged the same way as the keyboards back home and I had to hunt and peck. I tried *Stanford, art, art history* and *professor.* When those didn't work, I threw in *Moret, Society, nun, Mutus Liber, book* and a dozen or so other words without success. In the meantime, the café had filled. Several people patiently waited for their turns near the front counter.

A timer popped up in the bottom right of the computer screen, indicating that I had about five minutes left on my allotted time. I knew I'd have to give up my computer and get back into the queue if I wanted to use it again. I gave it one more try and typed in *Dior.* I was immediately greeted with menu of dates that went back as far as 1978. I clicked on a random entry and the screen filled with lists of numbers and symbols. The file was encrypted. I clicked on two more entries and found those files were encrypted as well before my computer screen reverted back to the "Welcome" menu. My time was up.

SIX

THE NEXT STOP was the U.S. Embassy. Hopefully, someone there could advise me on my current situation. I was hoping the key to Juliet's murder was on her encrypted flash drive and I planned on handing it over to someone at the embassy.

One of the things mentioned over and over in all the books I read before coming to Paris warned tourists who wanted to remain unnoticed by muggers and pickpockets not to stare at people on the metro. The message was reinforced strenuously by Monsieur Marcel on the bus ride from the airport to our hotel. So, following instructions, I avoided making any eye contact with anyone. I sat next to the window and stared out.

It wasn't very long before I sensed someone was staring at me. An elegantly dressed older woman reading *Le Monde,* a Parisian newspaper. She kept looking from me to her paper. She certainly didn't look like a pickpocket, but who knew? If I were at home in Columbus riding the COTA, I'd have looked her in the eye and said hello. But I wasn't at home. I ignored her and turned back to the window. Her cigarette-roughened voice startled me.

"Est-ce vous?" She gestured toward the newspaper in her hands.

"Je ne parle pas français," I said, ignoring the paper and hoping she'd get the hint that I didn't speak her lan-

guage and wanted to be left alone. The woman was un-deterred and quickly switched to English.

"She could be your twin, no?" She gestured again to the front page of *Le Monde*.

Frustrated, I finally turned to look at what she was pointing at. The shock made me sit upright. Splashed across the front page of the newspaper were two com-posite sketches of a man and a woman. Simon and me. And though the sketches were pretty generic and lack-ing small details such as the diamond stud in Simon's left ear and the small beauty mark above my right eye-brow, there was clearly enough detail for anyone obser-vant enough to recognize the resemblance. The headline read, *Couple cherché dans la mort de tir à Versailles.* The woman was watching me closely and I knew I had to keep my cool if for no other reason than so she could translate what the article said. I smiled at her and willed my voice not to shake.

"Maybe a little around the eyes. But my mouth is fuller don't you think?" I said with a nonchalant laugh.

"Perhaps." The woman looked skeptical.

I sure hoped no one was listening to our conver-sation. But the only person close to us was a filthy bearded man with grime-encrusted fingernails who was sleeping in the seat across the aisle.

"Who are they? Can you read it for me?" I leaned forward. She seemed more than happy to oblige. It took everything in me to remain calm as she relayed the grim details. The headline read, Couple Sought in Shooting Death at Versailles. According to the article, a maintenance worker at the Chateau de Versailles, iden-tified as Bruno Allard, was shot and killed during a car jacking on the palace grounds. The only witness to the crime, who asked to remain anonymous, saw the couple attack and shoot Monsieur Allard when he tried to stop them from stealing his maintenance truck. The witness tried to stop the couple from leaving but was knocked down by the truck as it fled the scene. The composite sketches were based on the witness's descriptions. The article went on to say authorities were still looking for the truck and that the couple was armed and highly dangerous. The witness was treated for minor injuries at a local hospital and released.

"Mon Dieu," exclaimed the woman when she finished reading me the article. "What is the world coming to? So many crazies roaming the streets."

She could say that again. I'd stepped out of the frying pan into a bonfire. And by helping me, Simon was getting burned, too. Not wanting to leave a witness behind, the asshole who killed Juliet and attacked me, must have killed that poor statue cleaner after we drove off in his truck. Juliet Rice and Bruno Allard's killer was a material witness while Simon and I were Bonnie and Clyde.

"That's horrible. I hope they catch them." I shook my head. We arrived at the next stop, which wasn't the one I needed but I had to get off so I could think. I stood to go. *"Merci, madame."* She nodded but was still looking at me strangely and I had to work hard to keep from running out the door.

I paced up and down the metro platform trying to figure out what to do next. If the newspapers had just hit the newsstand as I suspected, then it was possible Simon hadn't seen it yet. He could be walking around looking for me, unaware that he was a wanted man. I couldn't decide whether I should go to Luc's apartment to warn him since, after all, he had saved my life, or go to the U.S. Embassy as planned and leave him to his own devices. After all, he was the one who refused to go to the police in the first place. Not that it would have mattered since it was the "witness's" word against ours.

Then there was the matter of the truck. Neither of us had bothered wiping our prints from it before we dumped it. It was only a matter of time before they found the truck and ran our prints. I suddenly remembered I'd been fingerprinted the night of Juliet's murder, which meant I was screwed. As bad as I felt for Simon, I needed to get to the embassy and tell my side of the story before I was arrested. Then I suddenly remembered I still had Simon's business card. I could call and warn him.

I was just about to hunt for the card in my bag when I noticed the filthy bearded man from the train I'd just exited. He stood about twenty feet away from me showing a baby-faced, uniformed police officer the newspaper cover and pointing at me. He must have overheard the entire conversation between the woman and me. The officer and I made eye contact and I froze. He squinted at me then back at the newspaper. The lighting on the platform wasn't exactly the greatest. Quickly, I walked away, heading for the stairs to the street above.

"Madame!" He called out. I kept walking.

"Excusez-moi, madame!" His voice was louder this time, more commanding. I still didn't stop. *"Arrêt, s'il vous plaît! Arrêt maintenant!"*

Blood was pounding in my ears as I rounded the corner. I pushed through the turnstile and felt the strap of my bag get caught, pulling me back. *Crap!* I tugged frantically at it. The officer rounded the corner just as I managed to get the strap free. Pushing past people,

I ran like hell and took the steps to street level two at a time. My skinned knee made each step painful. The officer behind me yelled.

"Arrêt, police!"

I was almost at the top of the stairs. A cab was idling at the curb several feet away—just a few more steps and I'd be able to jump into that cab and escape. A hand grasped my ankle. The officer had dived face-first onto the staircase to reach me. He was lying in the middle of the stairway on his stomach. He was reaching for his gun with his free hand. Instinctively, I kicked out. The officer struggled to hold on to my ankle but in doing so bumped against a young woman walking up the stairs backward, pulling a baby stroller. She lost her grip.

"Mon bébé!" the young woman screamed.

The stroller bumped down the steps. He looked back at me, and for just a split second, I could tell he was torn. But he let go of my ankle and flew down the steps to catch the stroller before it could hit bottom and overturn. It was the break I needed. I ran up the remaining steps and practically flew into the cab.

THE U.S. EMBASSY in France was located just off the Place de la Concorde. Because several tour buses were blocking the street near the embassy's entrance, I got out in front of the Hôtel de Crillon, which was next door and across a narrow side street, I quickly maneuvered around the well-dressed, wealthy people coming and going from the hotel, and the abundance of picture snapping. The security around the embassy was understandably heavy with a multitude of white concrete pylons and metal gates in front of the main entrance. There had been similar reinforcements around all the government buildings on my recent trip to D.C. It should have made me feel secure. Instead, I was afraid that at any moment one of the guards would throw me facedown on the ground and point a gun to my head.

I went inside the embassy, and after wandering aimlessly, I finally got up the nerve to ask where I could find help with a serious legal issue. I found out from an embassy employee that I needed to go to the consulate office. But by the time I finally located the consulate it was closed. The hours posted indicated that it was only open from 9:00 a.m. to noon. I was more than two hours too late. I sagged against the door. I'd just have to come back tomorrow. In the meantime, I had to warn Simon. That is, if he hadn't already been arrested, or was even speaking to me after running away from him. There was only one way to find out. I needed to call him. Unfortunately, I soon discovered I'd lost the business card he gave me. This just wasn't my day. Seeing as he'd saved my life, I owed it to him to warn him in person.

I left the embassy and headed back to the hotel, thinking it would be the best place to catch a cab. While I waited for a cab to stop, I happened to notice a group of photographers snapping pictures of two men, one in an expensive suit, and the other dressed more casually. They stood posing next to a stretch limo. I didn't pay them much mind until the voice of the more casually dressed of the two men caught my attention. My blood ran cold. Tattoo Man, my attacker, was standing right there, laughing and talking to the man in the gray suit.

Thankfully, he was oblivious to me, so I took advantage of the opportunity to get a good look at him. I didn't see the snake tattoo since his long sleeves covered it, but what was easy to see was the cut across the bridge of his nose and the nasty purple bruise on his right cheek, courtesy of Simon. Hoping I was safe with so many people around, I crept a little closer and stood on the other side of a large luggage rack parked near the curb to try and hear what they were saying. But as soon as I moved, the men got into the limo. Who was that guy? I headed over to one of the hotel's uniformed doormen.

"Excusez-moi, monsieur. Parlez-vous Anglais?" His eyebrows shot up as he took in my slightly disheveled appearance, but to his credit he smiled politely, if somewhat insincerely.

"Oui, madame. How may I assist you?"

"The man in the white shirt that just left in that limo. I think I may have gone to college with him. Do you know if his name is John James?"

The doorman let out a sharp, harsh laugh. *"Non, madame.* The man you are referring to is Monsieur Vincent Garland, Ambassador Garland's son."

"The American ambassador?" I was unable to keep the shrill disbelief from my voice. He had to be kidding.

"Oui, madame, Ernest Garland, the American ambassador. His son, Vincent, is an attorney."

"You're sure?" The doorman sighed heavily. His allotment of good humor spent on someone who wasn't a guest at the hotel was limited, and I was about to tap it out.

"Absolument. He luncheons here quite often, *madame."*

I stared at him but he didn't blink an eye. He wasn't kidding. I was faint.

"Are you okay, *madame?"*

Hell no, I wasn't okay because when it came right down to it, who were the French police going to believe, me—a murder suspect—or an ambassador's son who was also an attorney and had diplomatic immunity? Even if I had proof he killed Juliet, he was untouchable unless the U.S. revoked his immunity, and I wasn't holding my breath. I couldn't believe it. I was officially fucked.

"I'm fine. *Merci, monsieur.*" I pressed a five-euro note into his palm, which brought a real smile to his face. He thanked me by putting me into a cab. I gave the driver Luc's address.

IF I WONDERED HOW THINGS could get any worse, I was answered by the sight of the police barricade outside Simon's brother's apartment on rue de Douai. I had the cab drop me off around the corner and then walked back to join the crowd of people gathered at the barricade, careful to keep my head down and not make eye contact with anyone. Two police cars were parked out front and I strained to see if Simon was in either of them. He wasn't as far as I could tell. My heart was beating so loudly I was surprised no one could hear it. They must have found the truck. Officers were leaving the building carrying items I recognized from Luc's apartment—including his laptop—but still no Simon. Where was he? Had they already taken him away?

Lieutenant Bernier emerged from the building followed by Captain Bellange, who had a Gauloises dangling from the corner of his mouth. I took off walking in the opposite direction and didn't stop until I came to a place identified by a green sign as Square Berlioz.

I had no idea who Hector Berlioz was but I hoped

he didn't mind me hiding out in his square. I sat on an empty bench. I was completely exhausted and the enormity of my situation hit me like a Mack truck. Tears streamed down my cheeks and I did nothing to stop them.

"Maybe I should just turn myself in," I said to the pigeon pecking the ground around the bench.

"Like hell you will."

"Simon!" He was standing behind my bench looking just as he had that morning. Not so much as a hair out of place or a worry line marring his handsome face.

"Shh! Not so loud." He looked around with a sly smile. "I'm a wanted man." I punched him in the arm.

"That's not funny. We're in so much trouble. That poor man whose truck we stole is…is dead!"

I really didn't want him to see me cry but couldn't stop the flow of tears. He put his arms around me. I buried my face in his chest and sobbed. He stroked my hair and held me tight and it was a good thing, too, or I might have slid into a heap on the ground.

"It's going to be okay, Maya."

"How?" I pushed away from him. "How can this possibly be okay? This is as far from okay as it gets! Do you even have any idea who the man who tried to kill us is?"

"Vincent Garland, Ambassador Earnest Garland's son." He reached out and put a finger under my chin, gently closing my mouth after it fell open. "Look, I told you I have contacts everywhere, including the DCJP headquarters. When those sketches of us hit the paper, I called my contact to find out who this so-called witness was. And that's not all I found out."

Just then a couple with their two kids and dog entered the square.

"Come on. This isn't the place to talk about this." He took my hand. "I know somewhere we should be safe for tonight."

SIMON TOOK ME TO a tiny apartment over a café in Montmartre belonging to his best friend, Max, a performer on a cruise ship who was out of town. Simon insisted we walk to Montmartre separately, in order to blend in with the tourists, which was fine for him since he was in such great shape. I, on the other hand, was sweaty and out of breath by the time we climbed the steep and sloping cobblestone streets to Montmartre. The turtleneck clung to the sweat on my back. I had to hurry to keep him in my sights so I wouldn't lose him. Each step took us closer to the white domed cathedral of Sacré Couer. I wondered if I should stop in there to say a prayer for us, but, realizing it meant climbing more than one hundred steps, quickly put it out of my mind. Once he had safely deposited me in the cramped studio apartment, Simon told me to make myself at home, donned a baseball cap and sunglasses and went to get us some food.

When he'd gone, I moved a pile of clothing from a black lacquered futon with a yellow-and-red flowered mattress and sat. I gingerly rolled up my pant leg to examine my skinned knee. The fabric of the pants had stuck to the dried blood. I held my breath and tugged it free, causing it to bleed a little. I fished out the first aid kit in my bag and squeezed on some antiseptic gel before covering it with a large square bandage. Afterward, I started to nose around. The pile of clothes I'd moved was all women's clothes. I'd assumed Max was a man but the high-heeled shoes and lacy underwear strewn all over the floor proved I had been mistaken. Was Max the redhead in the picture I'd found?

I got up and went into the tiny bathroom and stripped off my clothes. I took a long hot shower, lathering my body with the lemon-scented body wash I found in the bathroom cabinet.

By the time I emerged from the bathroom wrapped in Max's red silk robe, Simon had returned and was laying out food on the table in front of the futon. When he spotted my still-damp body wrapped in the clinging robe, he smiled. I avoided his eyes and sat, careful to keep myself covered. He told me what he'd found out about Vincent Garland over hot *croque-monsieur* sandwiches, cucumber salad, chocolate éclairs and wine. Who says fugitives can't eat well? But unlike the food, what he told me was not good. Not by a long shot.

According to Simon's source at the DCPJ, Vincent Garland had only been in Paris for several months. And had recently been caught up in a scandal involving his girlfriend, an ex-beauty queen and aspiring actress named Shannon Davies, who went missing during a visit to Paris just a week ago. Garland says they argued and she packed and left. Yet there'd been no activity on her passport or credit cards. She had yet to contact her friends and family and they were all pointing the finger at Garland, insisting he'd been abusive and must have done something to her. No charges against him had been filed. And as if that weren't bad enough, what Simon told me next practically made me choke on my food.

"You mean he was waiting for me at the police station that night?" I exclaimed.

Apparently, according to Simon's source, the night of Juliet's murder, while Bernier and Bellange were questioning me, Vincent Garland showed up to explain my rights to me under French law. He claimed the American Embassy sent him. He'd waited around for two hours but since technically I hadn't been arrested, they wouldn't let him into the interrogation room. He had left in a huff. No wonder the man had smelled like the police station when he was at Versailles.

"He was going to kill me that night, wasn't he? Whether I'd had the crucifix or not, he'd have killed me. That's why he followed me to Versailles the next day. I bet he was outside my hotel all night waiting for me to leave."

Simon slowly nodded while I digested the fact that I had dodged a very big bullet not once, but twice. Garland must have been the person in the mysterious green Peugeot that night. If Monsieur Marcel hadn't shown up, I probably would have gotten into Garland's car if he'd claimed to be from the American Embassy. He could have killed me and dumped my body someplace, and no one would have known a thing. But that wasn't all. Vincent Garland had a serious gambling problem and had racked up a lot of debt to some very scary people in Paris.

"That explains why he was trying to get his hands on the Moret Crucifix. If he used it to find the *Aurum Liber* he'd be set for life." I took another sip of wine.

"But he'd have had to be damned certain it even existed."

"I think he was certain. And I think he found out

from Juliet Rice." I retrieved Juliet's flash drive from my purse and tossed it across the table at Simon. He caught it with one hand.

"I found this hidden inside my digital camera's battery compartment. It's Juliet's. She must have hidden it to keep it from Garland. Check out the back."

Simon examined the pendant and when he saw the tiny Society of Moret symbol his head jerked back in surprise.

"It's a flash drive, see?" I reached over and pressed the symbol and watched the USB prong pop out.

Simon's eyes glinted devilishly and he quickly pulled a black laptop from his backpack.

"Don't bother. It's encrypted. I already checked."

"Merde!" he exclaimed, then his face lit up. "Not to worry. I know someone who can help us out." He fired up his laptop and logged onto a wireless connection.

He plugged in the flash drive and emailed the data to applederry.francoise@worldnet.fr.

"You're sure this Francoise can break the encryption?"

"Absolument. It should be a slice of cake, you'll see."

"You mean a piece of cake, right?" I laughed.

"Slice—piece—makes no difference. Francoise will take care of it. So stop worrying, *d'accord?"* He grinned and shoved an entire éclair into his mouth.

We were finishing up our food when Simon suddenly became serious. "Can I ask you something?"

"Sure."

"When we were at Dr. Hewitt's and she was talking about that nun, Sister Louise-Marie, and how she'd been sent away by her family after her birth, why were you so upset? I could tell it bothered you a lot."

I had been holding my breath as he spoke and now I let it out slowly. "Because I understand what she must have gone through. We both had mothers who didn't want us. She grew up in a convent. I grew up in foster care. I never knew my parents, either. I guess you could say I felt a kind of…I don't know…kinship, or whatever you want to call it, to poor Louise-Marie." Hearing about Louise-Marie's love affair gone wrong made that connection feel even stronger. The silver ring on my finger was suddenly warm. Simon poured us each another glass of wine.

"Have you ever thought about looking for your birth mother?"

"Why? If she didn't want me when I was born, why would she want to see me now?" I used to fantasize about meeting my mother when I was a little girl. But I wasn't a little girl anymore and I couldn't go through another rejection from her. Tracking her down was not an option.

"You'd rather go through the rest of your life not knowing why she gave you up? I don't understand."

"If I ask *you* something, will you tell me the truth?" I asked quickly to change the subject. Only it wasn't just a move to distract him. There really was something that had been bothering me, ever since the police were outside Luc's apartment.

"Depends on what it is." He licked chocolate from his fingers. He was smiling until he saw the look on my face. "What is it?"

"The police had my prints on file because I'm a suspect in Juliet's murder. Why do they have yours?"

I could tell I'd caught him off guard. He stared off into space for a long time, his brow creased in concentration. Then he stood and began picking up our dinner containers. A grim expression marred his handsome face and I was afraid to hear what he might tell me.

"Simon?" I grabbed his hand and gently pulled him down beside me. "It can't be that bad, can it?"

He shrugged. "I assaulted a cop, broke his nose."

"Oh." I took another big sip of wine. "I take it that's why you're not popular with the police, then?"

"I was at a student protest trying to conduct an interview with the head of the student union when things turned violent. This cop body slammed a girl to the ground. She was pregnant. I just snapped, went berserk, grabbed him by the throat and started pounding him. The next thing I know, I've got his blood all over my hands. I got tasered and woke up in jail. A week later I was reassigned to our bureau in Hong Kong where I've spent the last two years."

"Hong Kong? You weren't convicted?"

"Other witnesses backed-up my story, and the cop had a history of using excessive force. And," he said quietly, "I think they cut me some slack because they knew…" His voice trailed off and he looked away.

"About what?"

He pulled a picture from his wallet and tossed it on the table. It was a picture of him with the same striking redhead from the picture I'd found at Luc's place. Simon was sitting in a chair. The woman was behind him. Her arms wrapped around his shoulders. Her long, curly hair fell onto Simon's cheeks. Simon beamed into the camera. She was laughing. They looked so happy.

"Who is she?" I asked, still looking at the picture.

"My wife…Justine." His voice was low and slightly hoarse, like it took everything in him to speak her name. "My late wife," he added, like he'd just remembered she was gone.

"Oh. I'm sorry. What happened?"

"She was a freelance photographer and had gone to London for a job shooting some actress for a magazine article. While she was there her rental car broke down and she got on the tube to get back to her hotel. That was on July 7, 2005, the day of the terrorist bombings in the London Underground. She was twenty-eight years old and…five months pregnant with our first child."

"Oh my God," I said softly. "Simon, I'm so sorry."

He went over to the trash can. I got up, too, and when he turned around. I put my arms around him. It was *supposed* to be a supportive hug from one wounded person to another. But his eyes held so much raw pain in them that I kissed his cheek, then his other cheek, then his chin, and his forehead. Simon's hands pressed me against him. I could feel their warmth through the thin robe. He buried his face against my neck and his lips blazed a moist trail along my collarbone, his stubble was rough against my skin. I should have pulled away. Hadn't I promised myself not to go down this road again? But who the hell was I kidding? I'd wanted him since the day I'd spotted him on the bridge and gotten caught in the high beam stare of those green eyes of his.

The red silk robe fell open. Simon pulled it roughly off my shoulders and it fell to the floor. Our mouths met, tongues intertwined. He tasted like chocolate, smelled like soap. He only took his hands off me long enough to take off his shirt. I tugged on his belt, unbuckled it and unfastened his pants. I slid my hand down inside his black boxers and grasped his rock-hard erection. Simon gasped as my thumb encircled the engorged tip. I stroked his smooth head and his breathing became louder. I let my hand slide down the thick shaft of his penis to the base. I tightened my grip and slid up again.

His head fell back and he let my fingers work him for another minute or so before he pushed my hand away. He reached into his back pocket and hastily pulled a condom from his wallet. Impatient, I took it from him. As I gently rolled the condom onto his erection, he sighed and let my fingers caress him.

He tugged his pants down around his hips and lifted me up so my legs could wrap around his waist then entered me so abruptly I gasped. The pain was exquisite and intense, laced with pleasure. My nails dug into his shoulders. Each thrust pushed me closer and closer to the edge.

This wasn't about love, or tenderness, or even friendship. This was a pure, raw need for release. I started to whimper and moan and he quickened his pace until I was practically coming apart at the seams. I cried out and buried my face against his neck. He groaned once and his body jerked then relaxed. He turned and gently lowered me onto the bed and lay on top of me, breathing heavily while I stroked his back.

"Don't move," he whispered as he hastily removed his pants all the way and retrieved another condom.

He smiled and kissed me deeply as he entered me again. Pinning my arms above my head, he started moving his hips, thrusting very slowly and gently while whispering French words in my ear. He could have been calling me everything but a child of God but it sounded damned good and felt even better. Sweat beaded our bodies as he continued his maddeningly slow rhythm. I couldn't take it anymore.

"Please, Simon," I moaned, grinding against him.

He quickened his pace and the sound of our heavy breathing filled the room. I could feel the intensity building as each thrust sent him deeper and deeper inside me until finally my hands clutched the sweat dampened sheets and my back arched as a near scream escaped from my lips. Simon looked down at me, watching—waiting—before groaning loudly. When his breathing returned to normal, he rolled to his side, propped himself up on one elbow and smiled at me. I kissed him and traced the outline of his lips with my fingertip and he bit it playfully.

"So, tell me about this idiot who sent you running off to Paris all alone."

Before I could answer, he bent down and stuck his tongue in my belly button. I laughed. It felt so good. And for the first time in two months, I forgot why I'd been so unhappy.

I STOOD IN THE CORNER of a small, darkened room that resembled a cell. A figure slept in a narrow bed in the corner. I couldn't make out who it was. Then a thin shaft of weak sunlight streamed in from a small arched window set high up in the stone wall. The figure sat up and swung its legs over the side of the bed. It was a woman. But I still couldn't make out her face. She held her hand out to me. I didn't want to take it but did. And suddenly, I was no longer in the corner. I was the woman in the bed.

A sense of purpose drove me to the chair next to the bed where a pair of thick black woolen stockings was draped. I put them on then retrieved a long black habit hanging from a hook on the back of the wooden door. I pulled it over the white cotton chemise I'd slept in. Next came the white hoodlike coif, which I adjusted until it covered the top, sides and back of my head as well as my shoulders, leaving only my face free. Lastly, I draped the long white veil over the coif. Black veils were for the professed sisters.

There was no mirror in the room for me to see my reflection. But I knew what I would see if there were—a long, narrow face with large brown eyes, a broad nose and full lips, the face of Louise-Marie, the Black Nun of Moret. As I slipped into the one pair of shoes I owned, happiness filled my heart and lightened my mood. I would be leaving this place soon.

Dawn was giving way to morning and the hall outside my cell was filled with sunlight as I hurried past the empty cells of the other sisters. I avoided the back stairwell that led directly into the chapel where mass had been going on since 4:00 a.m. I didn't have much time. Soon mass would be over and it would be time for the morning meal. I'd run away before and they would be suspicious if I was late. And even though it had been years ago, they still watched me constantly. Instead, I headed the opposite direction down the main stairwell and nearly collided with Sister Jeanette. Why wasn't she in mass? Was she lying in wait for me? Did she know what I was up to? Thankfully, the long sleeves of my habit hid the ring on my finger.

"Excusez moi, Soeur." *Excuse me, Sister.*

I stepped aside so the portly woman could pass. The burnt-sugar smell clinging to her habit assaulted my senses but failed to completely mask her strong personal scent. Sister Jeanette didn't respond or even look my way. She hated me. She found my brown skin odd and offensive. And if that wasn't bad enough, she coveted my job in the convent library looking after the books and illuminated manuscripts. Sister Jeanette used to weave tapestries. But the palsy that caused her hands and limbs to shake had grown worse over the past year, making weaving impossible.

She'd been sent to the kitchen to train as a confectioner with the sisters who made the candy. She'd argued bitterly with Mother Elizabeth that I should be the one sent to the kitchen so she could have my job. But Sister Jeanette didn't have a wealthy patron paying for her keep as I did. She had to work to earn her stay as did all the other sisters. Most of the nuns were widows without family to care for them or daughters who by misfortune of birth order had to become nuns because their families could only afford a dowry for the eldest daughter to wed. I was an odd case. I lived in a sort of limbo. Not a nun, and with no family who would claim me, I'd been sent to the convent when I was eight. Not bound to the same rules as the professed sisters, I didn't have to work. I wanted to. But I wasn't free to live my own life, at least not yet.

The convent's candy was what brought in the most money. Sister Jeanette was the culprit behind the three batches of burnt sugar this week alone, not to mention the ruined pots and the acrid stench that hung in the halls for days. She was doing it on purpose, hoping to get moved to another job. So far it had not worked. I dug deep into the pocket of my habit and pulled out a bright yellow piece of the sugar candy. I had pilfered it the day before and popped it in my mouth. As it melted, it released its mellow caramel flavor to bathe my tongue.

The library was empty when I arrived. I closed the heavy wooden door behind me and hurried across the polished wooden floor, past the long wooden tables. I inhaled the sweet scent of beeswax from the previous night's melted candles. Numerous books and large manuscripts lined the shelves that occupied three levels. Colorful light shone down through eight large stained-glass windows, four on either side of the room. They depicted saints and angels, the stained glass making them appear as if they were trapped inside a colorful kaleidoscope.

The library was my refuge. The only place in the convent I belonged. Books didn't judge me...or abandon me. I would miss this room dearly. With little time to spare, I headed to a small table at the very back of the room that served as my desk. I was in charge of book donations from the clergy, scholars and the nobility and my desk was usually piled high with parcels. But there was only one I was interested in. I located it almost immediately. It was thin and square and wrapped in the purple paper and gold twine of the French royal court. I unwrapped it, careful not to tear the precious paper. It was a novella, Le Voyage de Fontainebleau *by Jean de Prechac.* The Voyage to Fontainebleau.

The book itself was of no consequence. It was the message I'd been waiting for. Impulsively, I began spinning the silver ring around on my finger, the ring that would soon be replaced with a gold band once we were wed. Tonight my love, Philippe, the Duke of Chartres, would come and whisk me away to nearby Fontainebleau Castle. And by his side, I would finally live the life I'd been born to live, a life that had thus far been denied me. The bell calling us to the morning meal began to ring and I quickly left.

SEPT

THE SOUND OF church bells jolted me out of sleep. It took me a minute to realize it was close to noon and I was with Simon in Max's apartment. But that dream had felt so real… It must have been all the stress I was under.

I could smell coffee brewing and by the time I wrapped myself in the red robe and dragged myself from the bed, Simon was sitting on the couch, nursing a cup of coffee with only his laptop covering his nakedness.

"We're in luck," he said excitedly. "Francoise has broken the encryption and saved the files to another flash drive. We'll have to go pick it up."

"We can't do that. Our names and faces are probably all over the news by now. Everyone in Paris is looking for us. And how do you know this isn't a trap to lure us out into the open?"

Simon chuckled. It annoyed me that he was taking this so lightly. "The charge on my laptop is almost dead. The police have Luc's laptop. We need a way to look at the files on Juliet's flash drive, so Francoise is loaning me a laptop. And you worry too much. When you meet Francoise, you'll understand why we have nothing to fear."

"Whatever," I replied, rolling my eyes and wondering how a man who fucked with such intensity could be so nonchalant about everything else.

"Hey, I don't want to go to jail, either."

"You sure don't act like it," I said, sitting next to him and feeling grumpy.

"Ah, mon petit pessimiste." He leaned over to kiss my forehead. "What do I have to do to wipe that frown from your pretty face?" His green eyes were soft and seductive and he leaned in and kissed my neck, sending a delicious shiver down my spine. The scruff on his face was a day away from being a full-grown beard and I had the beard burn all over my body to prove it.

"That's an easy one." I pushed him away. "Feed me."

After a meal of coffee and leftover éclairs, I got into the shower. Minutes later Simon joined me, insisting it would save time to shower together. As we slowly kissed and lathered each other, our wet, soap-slicked bodies practically welded together. I stood still under the spray of hot water as Simon's soapy hands roamed all over my body, lingering on my breasts and belly. I soaped his chest and rinsed him off with the handheld showerhead, mesmerized by the water running down in rivulets on his rock-hard pecs, then slowly retraced the water's path with lingering kisses. Simon moaned then turned me to face the shower wall and ran his tongue down my spine. I arched like a cat and leaned against the wet wall as he entered me from behind. He gripped my hips, rocking me to a climax so intense my knees buckled and I would have fallen if Simon hadn't caught me.

WE STEPPED OUT OF THE SHOWER and Simon busied himself by toweling my body with the softest towel I had ever felt. He had just turned his attention to my hair and was blotting it dry when we heard a door slam in the other room. We froze. Someone was in the apartment. Simon pressed a finger to his lips, signaling me to be quiet.

He grabbed a broom from behind the door, and wearing nothing but a towel, he crept out of the bathroom. Was this it? Had the police, or worse yet, Garland found us? I was searching the bathroom for a weapon of my own when there were loud shouts followed by laughter. What the hell? I flew out of the bathroom, nearly tripping over a large steamer trunk, to see Simon hugging a six-foot-tall black figure wearing pink pumps, a pageboy haircut, a vintage pink-and-black suit and pillbox hat à la Jackie Kennedy.

"Maya, this is Max," said Simon, grinning with his arm around the stranger.

"That's the Amazing Max, *mon cher,*" said Max in an American accent and held out a gloved hand for me to shake.

Though Max's makeup was flawless, it wasn't good enough to hide an Adam's apple. I'd been right in my first assumption. Max *was* a man, or a transvestite to be exact. When I'd noticed the woman's shoes and undies all over the place I'd obviously neglected to notice the sizes.

"Nice meeting you." I held out one hand while holding the towel together with the other one.

There'd been an E. coli outbreak on the cruise ship Max worked on as a headliner in their *La Cage* show where he—or was it she?—portrayed Diana Ross. They'd been forced to turn around and come home early. Max talked nonstop about knowing there'd been something wrong with the *boeuf bourguignon,* but no one would listen even though he was one of the few people who hadn't gotten sick.

"I've got a sixth sense about such things," he said as he unpacked the steamer, not at all fazed by the fact that he'd come home to find two half-naked people in his apartment.

"That bad, huh?" asked an amused Simon.

"I'm telling you it was enough to turn this stone cold carnivore into a vegetarian on the spot, but enough about me. What kinda trouble have you gotten yourself and this poor girl into?"

"So you've heard then?"

"Have I heard? You mean about the gun-toting French maniac and his murderous American girlfriend going around shooting folks fulla holes and stealing trucks? You mean have I heard about that?"

"I'm not a murderer!" I said indignantly. "Or his girlfriend," I mumbled under my breath.

Max took off his hat, kicked off his size-twelve pumps, sat on the couch and crossed his shapely legs. "Alright let's hear it. I know this ought to be good. Should I make some popcorn first?"

We took turns filling him in on everything that had happened, and when we were done, Max just sat there with one perfectly shaped eyebrow raised.

"You two are in some deep shit, alright. And just how are you planning to get yourselves outta this? You know I'll do whatever I can to help you out but I can't harbor fugitives. Max wouldn't do well in prison. Stripes make me look fat. And Marlena would shit a brick. You know ever since that nasty little run-in she had with immigration she's allergic to cops."

"Marlena?" I asked, looking from one to the other.

"Max's girlfriend," replied Simon. A smile tugged at his lips when he saw my shocked expression.

Max took off his wig and scratched his shiny bald head. "It ain't that kinda party, sweetheart. Just 'cause I dress my inner girl don't make me gay," he said matter-of-factly, putting me in my place.

Once his wig was off, Max's voice had deepened to its original baritone as if his female persona solely resided in the wig and clothes.

I quickly changed the subject. "We just have to make the connection between Vincent Garland and Juliet Rice. Garland's a lawyer and an ambassador's son. We can't turn ourselves in until we have all the proof we need."

Simon added. "We'll be out of here as soon as we can get dressed. Don't worry. No one will ever know we were here."

"You going out looking like that? 'Cause you'll get arrested before you even hit the corner."

"What choice do we have?" I said.

"Oh, you always have a choice," he said, looking us over. "Simon, all you need is some different clothes, and maybe a hat. And don't shave. That beard you got going will do the rest. But you," he said, shaking his head, "need a lot of help. Come on over here and let Max hook you up." He took my hand and led me over to his closet.

While Simon dressed in the bathroom, Max pulled out an array of wigs, clothing and makeup and got busy transforming me.

"How long have you known Simon?" I asked as Max made up my face.

"'Bout ten years. We met one night outside a club

in Nice when I got jumped by punks who didn't appreciate seeing a big black dude in a sequined minidress. Simon jumped in. Between the two of us, we wiped up the sidewalk with those fools and I was wearing four-inch heels! Been friends ever since. I'm the one who introduced him to his wife, Justine, after she photographed me for the cruise line's promotional brochures. We really hit it off and I knew they'd be perfect together. I sang at their wedding. Sang at her funeral, too," he said shaking his head.

"What was she like?"

"A ball of energy. I got tired just being around her. Nothing ever got that girl down. She was always smiling. She saw the bright side of everything but she was no pushover. She also had a temper. Really lived up to that red hair. She kept Simon on his toes, too."

We were silent for a moment before Max asked, "So, are you two…?" He let the question hang in the air and it took me a few seconds to realize what he was getting at.

"No," I said quickly. "We're not a couple. Just two people in trouble trying to help each other out."

"Oh, really." He looked pointedly at the rumpled bed. "'Cause from the noises I heard coming outta that bathroom when I walked in here, it sounded like the only thing you were helping each other do was get off." He tossed his head back and laughed. My face burned.

"Oh, don't get all embarrassed. No one can blame you. You're in Paris and when you add big trouble and an okay-looking dude like Simon to the mix, things are bound to get hot. And I'll tell you something else."

"What's that?"

"Even with all the trouble he's in, I haven't seen him

this alive since before Justine died. And that's saying a lot. He was a mess after she died. You're good for him."

"It's not like that," I insisted.

"Whatever you say, girlfriend," Max said, chuckling. "Whatever you say."

HALF AN HOUR LATER, Simon and I were on our way. Simon was dressed in a charcoal-gray Brooks Brothers suit. It was a Christmas gift to Max from his ever-hopeful Mama back home in Baltimore. According to Max, his mother was still hoping he'd become a suit-wearing success instead of the son she could share clothes with. Simon also sported a black beret and sunglasses to cover his distinctive green eyes. Max had dressed me in a short, curly gray wig and big, red horn-rimmed glasses. He also gave me a large fake mole on my chin and another on the side of my nose. Except for a navy blue poncho, Max's clothes didn't fit me. I was stuck wearing what I'd had on the day before. We cinched the poncho with a black leather belt looped double around my waist.

Simon and I sat apart from each other on the metro and did our best to act like we didn't know each other. Thankfully, no one paid us the least little bit of attention because they were all too busy reading about us in the paper. We'd made the front page again, only this time our names had been given, along with my passport photo, which already looked like a mug shot, and Simon's Agence France-Presse photo showing him smiling and clean shaven. Simon was sitting a few rows ahead of me. He was discreetly reading the paper over the shoulder of the woman sitting in front of him. He slumped down into his seat. Whatever he'd just read wasn't good and I had a feeling it had something to do with us. When we reached the Tuileries metro stop, Simon stood and signaled me to follow him. Once we emerged from the station and rounded the tall hedges separating the Tuileries Gardens from busy rue de Rivoli, I got my first close-up view of the Louvre Museum. That's where we were meeting Simon's hacker friend, Francoise. The large glass pyramid sat in the center of the museum's massive courtyard. Visitors sat along the edges of triangle-shaped fountains surrounding it. The sheer size of the museum was breathtaking; it was far larger than I had imagined. I found myself gaping in amazement, and then shock. The museum's guards carried large assault rifles and were dressed in fatigues. I was so fixated on the big guns, I wasn't watching where I was going and ran right smack into Simon's back, causing him to stumble.

"Observez-le, vieille dame!" he growled at me, purely for show in case anyone was watching. I didn't know what he'd said but could tell from his tone it wasn't nice.

"Baisez vous!" I replied, pushing past him. I may not know much French but I could say "fuck you" in four languages.

It was Francoise who'd insisted that we meet inside the Louvre. Simon had to buy a ticket. In order to avoid the long line at the pyramid entrance, he headed toward the entrance down the stairs in the Jardins du Carrousel next to the arch, while I headed toward the Passage Richelieu. I could use my museum pass there. I flashed my pass and smiled at the guard manning the entrance. He gave it a cursory glance and ushered me through the metal detector. I rode the escalator down to the main lobby of the museum. The three separate wings of the museum, Denon, Sully and Richelieu, were accessible from this large, crowded hall. After waiting ten minutes for Simon to show, I began to worry that he'd been arrested, but just as soon as I started to tell myself I needed another plan, someone brushed up against me.

"Pardon, madame," Simon said and winked. I followed him to the escalator leading to the Denon Wing of the museum.

Once we made it into the museum proper, and figuring no one was paying us much mind, I caught up with Simon.

"Where are we supposed to meet your friend?"

"In one of the galleries up on the second floor. It's not much farther. Just stay close and don't get lost. It's easy to do in here."

I had to walk fast in order to keep up with Simon's long strides. All of the paintings, sculptures and antiquities I passed became a blur as I wove in and out of people and found myself inadvertently walking into a couple of photos being taken just as the camera flashed.

"Pardon," I mumbled without stopping. This was no way to see the Louvre for the first time.

We entered a long, wide corridor with vaulted ceilings. Ancient Greek statues lined both sides of the hallway. At the end of the corridor one of the Louvre's most famous statues, *Winged Victory,* sat at the top of a staircase. I had to admit it was an impressive sight and clearly I was only one of the statue's many admirers. Dozens of people surrounded it, snapping picture after picture. Simon walked past without so much as a glance and turned right to head up yet another flight of stairs.

I stopped for just a few seconds to get a good look then realized Simon was more than ten feet away.

"Pardonay mwaa, *madame*. Could you take my picture, see view play?" asked an older woman with big hair and a Texas twang. She thrust a digital camera into my hands without even waiting for my response and struck a pose in front of the statue with her hands firmly placed on her wide hips. I snapped a quick picture and shoved the camera back into her hands.

"Mercy!" she called out after me as I rushed off to catch up with Simon. But it was too late. He was gone. I frantically looked around for him but I'd lost him in the crush of museum-goers.

Panic started to build and I willed myself to stay calm. I couldn't decide if I should stay put. Surely Simon would notice I wasn't behind him and come back to look for me. Or maybe I should just go look for him. I was sweltering in the turtleneck and poncho. Sweat ran down my back, so I yanked off the poncho. I went to sit in one of the window wells, my poncho folded in my lap. Five minutes passed and still no sign of Simon. I rooted around in my bag for the museum map and spotted a small white card sticking out of my Paris guidebook. That's where Simon's business card went! Should I call him? Would the police be tracking our cells? Surely one quick phone call couldn't hurt, could it? I headed into the nearest women's restroom and went into the first empty stall I could find. I flipped open my phone. It was the first time I'd turned it on in two days. I had six missed calls and four voice mail messages.

The first message was from my best friend, Kelly, asking how the trip was going. I laughed out loud. The second one was from a tearful Jarrod informing me that his partner, Brian, had had a massive heart attack on the way back from Versailles and was in the American Hospital of Paris. With everything that had happened the past couple of days, I'd completely forgotten about Brian and Jarrod. The second message was also from Jarrod and had just come in that morning.

"Maya, please pick up. What's going on? Are you okay? You're all over the news. I know what they're saying about you can't be true! Listen, there's a man from the American Embassy who says he can help you. He's a lawyer. I gave him your number. He's supposed to be calling you. Jesus! I hope you get this message. Please, call me if you can."

I went numb with fright. Garland had seen me with Brian and Jarrod on the RER on the way to Versailles. He'd probably even seen me leave the hotel with them. He must have tracked them down at the hospital. He had access to them and they had no idea how dangerous he was. The phone rang in my hand, causing me to jump. I quickly answered it.

"Jarrod?"

"Ms. Sinclair, you're a hard woman to get a hold of. You and I must speak," said Vincent Garland.

"We have nothing to discuss. Leave me alone, you psycho." I tried my best to keep my voice down so no one would hear me on the phone. The last thing I needed was to be reported to the museum's guards.

"Oh, but I beg to differ. You have something I want and I have something you need."

"I told you I don't have that fucking crucifix. Juliet didn't give it to me. And you couldn't possibly have anything I need."

"How about an Eiffel Tower corkscrew with your fingerprints *and* Juliet Rice's blood on it?"

I was speechless.

"Yes. I thought that'd get your attention. I propose an even exchange, the crucifix for the corkscrew. Once you hand it over, I'll gladly give you the corkscrew and tell the police I was mistaken in what I witnessed at Versailles."

"I can't give you something I don't have," I insisted.

"Well you best be finding it then, hadn't you? Meet me tomorrow night at 7:00 p.m. at the Medici Fountain in the Luxembourg Gardens. You can even bring your French boyfriend. The more the merrier. But don't even think about showing up without my crucifix or bringing the police, Ms. Sinclair. I'd hate for your two gay friends to suffer any ill effects from being associated with you."

"Don't you dare hurt them," I said. But I was talking to the dial tone. He'd hung up.

I left the restroom in a daze and ran, literally, right into Simon. He saw the phone in my hand and snatched it from me.

"Are you crazy? They're probably tracking us through our cells," he whispered.

"My friends Jarrod and Brian from my tour group are in trouble I need to—"

"You need to come with me," he said, cutting me off. "Francoise isn't here yet. Come on. Let's go before we're late."

He grabbed me by my hand and pulled me along after him through the various galleries. We flew by painting after painting by French masters. Simon finally stopped when we arrived at a gallery with red walls and shiny parquet floors. There were four long, narrow black benches down the center of the room. Two were occupied. Simon sat on an empty bench in front of the largest painting in the room. The massive painting depicted a group of men—some dying, others merely terrified—clinging to a raft for dear life as it tossed on a dark, churning, tumultuous sea.

"The Raft of Medusa, an excellent choice," came an American voice from behind us.

We turned to see a pretty, young girl dressed in a school uniform. Her wavy brown hair hung to her shoulders. A backpack was strapped to her back.

"Merci, mademoiselle," Simon said, standing up and smiling.

"Do you know who painted it?" asked the girl. She was looking at Simon as though he were the only person in the room.

"Why I believe it was Edward Wong Hau Pepelu Tivrusky IV," concluded Simon in all seriousness. The girl nodded.

"No it wasn't. The plaque says Theodore Gericault," I protested.

The girl sighed and rolled her eyes. Simon leaned over and whispered in my ear.

"It's our code, Maya."

"Code for what?" I was confused.

"Who's the old lady?" the girl stage whispered, giving me the once-over. I took offense at the word *old,* forgetting I was dressed like a giant Mrs. Beasley doll.

"This is my friend Maya," Simon said to the girl then turned to me. "Maya, this is my goddaughter, Francoise."

"*This* is Francoise, Francoise the hacker? Are you crazy, Simon? She's just a child," I growled at him, careful to keep my voice down. If I'd been offended by the word *old,* Francoise clearly wasn't feeling the word *child.* She bristled.

"I am a Leo. I'm also a member of Mensa and a vegan. But what I am *not* is a child. A child is defined as someone under the age of twelve. I'm thirteen, a *teenager.* Do I need to define what the word *teen* means, too?" she asked with her arms crossed and her head held high.

"Child, teen, it's all the same to me, sweetie, meaning you're too young for grown folks' business," I replied, refusing to let this girl get to me.

"Marie Antoinette was engaged to be married when she was twelve," she said matter-of-factly.

"Honey, this isn't the eighteenth century and you're no Marie Antoinette. And shouldn't you be in school with all the other *kids?*"

Francoise's face turned bright red and Simon grabbed me by the elbow and pulled me to the side.

"Do you want to know what's on that flash drive or not?"

"Of course I do, but she's just kid. We can't involve her. She could get in trouble for helping us."

"Do you have a better idea? 'Cause if you do, I'd love to hear it."

"No, but—"

"But, nothing. We're in a bind. We have no choice. Besides, I've known her since she was little. We can trust her."

He left me standing there and joined Francoise on the bench. I sat next to Simon just as Francoise pulled a small silver-and-black flash drive and a black laptop from her backpack. She handed both items to him. And he in turn handed them to me to put in my day bag.

"It was a fairly standard encryption program," she said with a nonchalance she probably thought made her look grown-up. "Anyone with the right software could have unlocked it. Not at all up to my skill level. I could have decoded it blindfolded with my arms tied behind my back."

"You're a lifesaver, Francoise. I owe you one."

"Yes, you do. And I collect on all my debts," she said with complete seriousness, slinging the backpack over her shoulders and standing up. "And don't worry." She looked around to make sure no one was listening. "If anyone asks, I haven't seen you…or the old lady." She tossed out that last bit as an afterthought.

We watched her walk away and discreetly rejoin a group of similarly uniformed schoolgirls gathered near the gallery's entrance, which answered my question as to why we'd had to come all the way to the Louvre to pick up the laptop and flash drive. She was on a fieldtrip. Simon chuckled.

"Thirteen going on thirty-five. And don't let the attitude fool you. She's a great kid. Smart like her old man. Real name is Phoebe. Francoise is just her hacker name, after some Japanese anime character—"

"Garland called me," I whispered. Simon's eyes grew wide.

"If I don't find the crucifix Juliet hid and bring it to him in the Luxembourg Gardens tomorrow night, he's going to kill my friends Jarrod and Brian. And he has my corkscrew. The corkscrew he used to kill Juliet. He must have worn gloves when he did it. But my prints are still on it."

"Merde." Simon groaned and buried his head in his hands.

"Give me my phone. I need to warn Jarrod and Brian."

"You can't use this phone anymore. It's too risky."

"It's my fault they're in danger. I can't just sit back and do nothing. I have to warn them. Give me my phone."

"We still have until tomorrow night. They'll be safe enough until then. We need to see what's on this flash drive first."

"Fine. But I don't trust Garland. After we check out the flash drive, I'm calling them."

We left the Louvre and found a shady, secluded spot in the Tuileries gardens to view what was on Juliet's flash drive. I laid the poncho on the grass for us to sit on and started to take off the scratchy wig.

"Leave it on unless you want to get dragged kicking and screaming to the police station," Simon said as he inserted the drive into the USB port on the side of the laptop.

"This thing is driving me crazy." I stuck a finger under the wig to scratch my itchy scalp.

"There's a fifty-thousand-euro reward for our capture or information leading to our arrest. It was in the paper this morning. I read it on the metro when we were on our way here."

I left the wig on.

The files on Juliet's flash drive turned out to be journal entries. The earliest entries looked to have been scanned pages from a paper journal. The entries started in September of 1978 when she was a doctoral candidate at the Sorbonne. Her advisor had been a Dr. Bernard Fouquet.

"Fouquet?" I said. "That name sounds familiar."

"Isn't he the art historian Dr. Hewitt said studied the Moret Tapestry?" asked Simon.

"Yes, he's the one whose theories the Society of Moret legend are based on."

"Apparently they were more than just theories. Listen to this," he said and read me an entry dated November 13, 1978.

I've worked hard to prove myself since Dr. Fouquet approached me last year. He thinks I'm finally ready to take the next step. I've been invited to his home in Moret-sur-Loing for the weekend. As to what will happen, I can only guess. Fouquet insists he can only do so much, and it's up to the committee to approve my admittance to the society. I'm worried about Oliver. He's hated me since I ended it. Saturday is Sister Louise-Marie's birthday. I think it's a good sign. I'm extremely hopeful.

The next entry was dated November 17.

I kissed the crucifix. I made my promise. I'm in!

"So the Society of Moret not only exists, but both Juliet Rice and Bernard Fouquet were members and they found the Moret Crucifix," I said.

"*Oui.* And that also means Juliet stole the crucifix from a society she'd been a member of for thirty years. What would make her do that? Money?"

The last time I'd talked to Juliet, she'd said, "I broke my promise." She hadn't been talking about a man. She'd been referring to her promise to the Society of Moret. She'd said she'd given up everything and it had all been for nothing. I could only think of one reason why a woman would act so foolishly.

"Love," I said. Simon shot me a skeptical look. "I'm serious, Simon. She quit her job, sold her house and came to Paris. She and Garland must have planned on using the crucifix to find the book and run away together, only she had second thoughts and hid the crucifix from Garland and he killed her when she wouldn't tell him where it was."

"If that's true, I wonder what changed her mind."

I shrugged. "Maybe she found out what happened to Garland's last girlfriend, the one who's missing."

Simon shook his head. "I'm not so sure about that. I have a hard time seeing Vincent Garland and Juliet Rice as a couple. She was a snobby art history professor a good decade older than him and he's a thug and a bully with a gambling problem."

"Yeah, but he's also an attorney and an ambassador's son, which would have appealed to someone like Juliet Rice."

"I don't know. Still seems like a stretch to me."

"Only one way to find out." I tugged on the wig. "Let's keep reading. And if I'm right, I promise I won't say I told you so if you let me wear your beret."

HUIT

FOR THE NEXT hour, Simon and I took turns reading Juliet's journal. It was slow going. She wrote down everything. Grocery lists, recipes, what she'd had for dinner, books she'd read. She'd even meticulously documented her weight each morning. Despite the minutia, a picture of the woman she'd been slowly emerged from the journal entries. She'd never married and had been devoted to her job at Stanford. She rarely dated, traveled extensively, though mainly to lecture on her specialty of medieval art, and loved expensive designer clothes. She also appeared to have had very few friends. I was disappointed that with the exception of the two earlier journal entries, there appeared to be no other references to the Society of Moret, though starting on April 5, 1980, and every year after that on the same date, the only entry was a hand-drawn star. What did it mean?

After reading entry after entry my eyes were starting to cross. But I sat up when I reached the one dated April 5, 2007. Instead of a star, there was an entry.

Lecture at the Sorbonne went well. Richelieu Auditorium was almost full. Spent an hour at Jean Taris's yesterday morning then went shopping. Bought a new red Dior. Wore it last night to the embassy reception. Can't believe I was thinking of not going. So glad I did. After all this time I met the one I've been waiting for.

There wasn't another entry until two months later on June 10.

Never knew I could feel this way, so alive, and so happy. Had no idea what I was missing. Nothing else matters except for this. We've held nothing back. There are no secrets between us. It's all hush-hush for now. Soon we'll be together forever.

The next entry was dated August 17.

Turned in my resignation. Wasn't as hard as I thought it would be. Everything is in motion and falling into place. I feel so full of purpose and no longer have any doubts. This is all for the best. I have every faith that the committee will see that this is for the greater good. I truly believe Sister Louise-Marie would approve.

Juliet's final entry was dated September 5, less than a week before her death.

I'm beginning to question our course of action. I must keep any doubts to myself so as not to cause more anger. I'm seeing a side I didn't know existed and it scares me. I pray that when this is over things will be back to the way they were five months ago. Don't know if I can go back to being alone.

"I knew it." I stabbed a finger at the computer screen. "She met Garland at an embassy reception and fell in love with him. He must have rocked her little uptight world and she spilled her guts to him about the society. Garland needed money and somehow talked her into stealing the crucifix in order to find the book and somewhere along the way, before she could hand it over to him, she found out what he really planned to do with it."

"And somewhere along the way, one of them murdered my brother to cover their tracks. My money's on Garland," said Simon grimly.

I rubbed his arm and thought about Garland's brutal torture and murder of Juliet, and his violent attack on me. He enjoyed inflicting physical pain. I'd never forget the look in his eyes as he was hurting me. Hitting someone over the head and chucking them into the Seine hardly seemed like his style. I kept it to myself, though, sensing it wouldn't be something Simon would want to hear.

"So you agree with me that Garland was the one Juliet was in love with, the one she stole from the society for?"

"You're probably right," conceded Simon, rubbing his neck. "But from reading this I get the impression that Juliet thought she was doing something noble."

"I bet Garland talked her into donating the book to a museum or something and she found out he planned to sell it to cover his gambling debts. That's probably why she hid the crucifix, to keep him from getting his hands on it. She drank the Kool-Aid and when she realized what was really going on it was too late to spit it out."

"Kool-Aid?" said Simon, looking confused.

"It's an American saying. It's when you accept what someone tells you without question," I explained. "Poor woman. What a waste." I closed out the last journal entry.

"And poor us. She never mentions Garland by name so we still can't make a connection between them and I was hoping there'd be a mention of where she could have hidden the damned crucifix." Simon ripped the beret off his head in frustration.

"Wait. There's another file here." Underneath the last journal entry was a document labeled *dissertation.doc*.

"It's just a copy of her dissertation," Simon said dismissively and stood to stretch his legs.

I clicked on the file to open it. Simon was right. It was a copy of her dissertation entitled "Deciphering Signs and Symbols in Medieval Tapestry." I quickly scrolled though it and saw that there was a whole section devoted to the Moret Tapestry. On the last page were the names of Juliet's dissertation defense committee and the date she successfully defended her dissertation, September 8, 1979, almost a year after she joined the society. I read the names.

"Look at this." I grabbed Simon's hand and pulled him back down beside me. The names of Juliet's dissertation committee were: Dr. Bernard Fouquet, Dr. Anna Schroder, Dr. Oliver Renard and Dr. Evalyn Hewitt.

"Dr. Hewitt?" Simon said in disbelief.

"She lied to us, Simon. She knew Fouquet. And look at that third name, Oliver Renard. I bet that's the same Oliver Juliet mentions in the journal that she ended it with. I bet they had an affair and she was worried he'd keep her from joining the society."

Simon's brow was creased in concentration.

"What is it?"

"What if these people weren't just her dissertation committee? What if they could also be the same committee she refers to in her journal, members of the Society of Moret?"

"It would make sense. She said in the journal that Fouquet approached her a year before she joined the society. He was her advisor. Maybe her dissertation was her ticket into the society."

"Come on," he said excitedly. "We've got to go back and see Dr. Hewitt."

I wanted to know why Dr. Hewitt had purposely misled us about Fouquet, but I was also hoping she'd be able to help me get this damned posy ring off my finger. It was still stuck. I was putting the poncho back on when I suddenly remembered Garland's threat.

"Wait! I need to warn Jarrod and Brian first." Simon ran his fingers through his hair in frustration, making it stand on end.

"Fine, warn them, but make it quick." He handed me my phone. "And after this, no more using this phone, understand? You've got to get rid of it. Promise me, Maya."

"I promise!" I checked my incoming calls log until I found Jarrod's number and pressed redial. He answered on the second ring.

"Maya? Where the hell are you?" I could hear the panic in his voice.

"I can't tell you that. Are you and Brian okay?"

"No, I'm not okay! Brian's in surgery and I'm freaking the hell out."

"Jarrod, I don't have much time. I need you to stay away from Vincent Garland, the man from the U.S. Embassy. He's not trying to help me. He's very dangerous."

"Hello? Maya? You're breaking up. What did you say? Are you still there?"

"Can you hear me?" I yelled into the receiver.

"Maya? Maya?"

He was cutting in and out. I was loosing the connection. I shook the phone in frustration and the display went black. It was dead, which shouldn't have been a big surprise. I hadn't charged it since I'd gotten to Paris. And my charger was back at the hotel.

"Shit!" I threw the phone on the ground.

I was on the verge of asking Simon for his phone when the sound of police sirens filled the air. I peeked over the bushes we were sitting behind to see a caval-cade of police cars converge on the Louvre's courtyard. Bernier and Bellange emerged from one of the cars and they, along with a group of uniformed officers, rushed inside the museum while another group of officers fanned out into the Tuileries garden. Simon had been right. They'd been tracking our cell phones. He was in such a rush to meet Francoise that he hadn't turned my cell off when he'd taken it from me in the museum. It had been on the entire time, enabling them to track us down. My first reaction was to run but Simon grabbed my wrist and pulled me back down behind the bushes.

"If we run, it will attract attention. We have to stay calm," he whispered and put the beret back on, pulling it down over his ears.

"Oh, yeah, that'll be easy."

"I'm going to walk through the Tuileries to La Grande Roue. I'll meet you there."

"Where are you going?"

"The big white Ferris wheel," he said, pointing off into the distance, toward the Place de la Concorde where a large Ferris wheel turned slowly.

"You're not leaving me here, Simon Girard. I'm coming with you."

"*Non!* We don't want to raise suspicions. I'll go first. Then in a few minutes you follow me, *d'accord?*"

I barely had time to nod before Simon took off walk-ing like he hadn't a care in the world while pretending to talk and laugh on his cell phone. A chill crawled down my spine as a police officer eyed him before turning his attention to a young interracial couple sitting on a blanket about twenty-five feet away. The woman had my coloring and build but short hair. The man had blond hair and looked nothing like Simon. The officer was barking orders at them in French and they fumbled in their bags for ID.

I glanced around the garden and saw other officers checking people lounging in chairs around a nearby fountain and waiting in line at the stands selling food and beverages. None of the officers were looking my way. I put the poncho back on and emerged from behind the bushes and took off in the direction Simon had gone. I still wore the wig, glasses and fake moles, but I couldn't help but feel as though my name was tattooed across my forehead in neon ink. I walked slowly, focusing on putting one foot in front of the other, when someone touched my arm.

"Excusez-moi, madame."

A tall police officer was holding out a black-and-white photo of Simon and me, the same pictures that had been in the newspaper that morning. A thin trickle of sweat ran down the side of my nose, threatening to dislodge my fake mole. I forced myself to smile.

"Oui," I replied, pronouncing it *way* like Simon did.

"Avez-vous vu ces personnes?" he asked. I didn't understand what he'd asked but assumed he was asking if I'd seen the people in the photos. I shook my head vigorously.

"Non." I started to walk away but he blocked my path.

He shoved the picture in my face again but a loud

cry from the direction I'd just come from caused him to look away. I looked, too. Another police officer was waving something in the air. It was my cell phone. He must have just found it on the ground where I'd thrown it.

"Merci, madame," said the officer dismissively as he rushed off to join his colleague.

I kept walking as other officers rushed past me to see what had been found. I didn't look back and the farther I walked, the less I could hear of what was going on behind me. I went down the dirt path past a couple of restaurants set amongst the trees, past school kids playing on a playground, tourists resting on benches, an ice cream stand and around a large round fountain where a man was playing a guitar. Finally, I reached La Grand Roue. The bright sun forced me to shade my eyes as I searched in the crowds for Simon. He wasn't there.

"Hey!" came a familiar voice from above.

Simon was on the Ferris wheel. He was at the top, waving his arms wildly. I laughed. Another bullet dodged.

WE COULD HEAR AGNES, Evalyn Hewitt's Bichon Frise, barking like crazy when we knocked on her door. Faint strains of chamber music came from inside the apartment. When we knocked again, Agnes frantically scratched at the door. She whined and yipped. Simon and I both came to the same conclusion at the same time. Something was wrong.

"Dr. Hewitt!" I pounded on the door. "Dr. Hewitt, are you okay?"

Simon turned the doorknob. The door was unlocked. "You wait out here," he said as he pushed the door open.

I was in no big hurry to see what was on the other side of that door. And once it was open, my fears were validated. Agnes, who was spinning in circles and barking, had tracked bloody paw prints to the door. Simon was apprehensive. He sidestepped the blood and went inside. Seconds later, the music stopped. I paced in the hall for what seemed like forever. Laughter drifted up from the staircase in building's hallway. Someone was coming up.

I ducked inside the apartment, closing the door behind me, and followed the bloody paw prints. I didn't have very far to go before coming upon Evalyn Hewitt's body lying on her kitchen floor in a dark pool of congealed blood. Her skin was so pale it looked translucent. Her lips were white and bloodless. Her throat had been cut from ear to ear. Agnes had followed me in and now was lying across her master's chest. I had to clamp my hands over my mouth to keep from screaming.

"Maya, up here." Simon leaned down over the second-floor railing.

I hurried past poor Dr. Hewitt's body and flew up the steps to find Simon standing by the largest bookshelf in the room, where a handful of books had been pulled off and lay on the floor.

"Someone was looking for something?" I said.

"It must have been Garland looking for the crucifix. He must have found out we came here, Maya, and thought we gave the crucifix to Dr. Hewitt. We probably got her killed," said Simon. He looked angry.

"No." I shook my head. "If that were the case then why pull four books from just this one shelf and not the others? Did you check the other rooms? Were any of them disturbed?"

Simon shook his head. "*Non.* Not as far as I could tell. Just this room."

"Then whoever did this was most likely looking for a specific book."

"You don't think Garland thought the book the society was protecting was here, do you?" he asked.

"I hardly think they'd go to so much trouble to hide the damned book for it to end up in plain sight on a retired professor's bookshelf." I walked over to the bookshelf.

Each book lay on the floor underneath the spot on the shelf from where it had been pulled. As I read the titles, images from the weird dream I'd had came back to me. There was something so familiar tugging at my memory. What was it? Was it the smell of beeswax or the brightly colored purple paper? The book. What was the title? Something about a voyage? *Le Voyage de Fontainebleau?* It had been a message. Yes! The book was a message.

"Maybe he wasn't really looking for anything," said Simon. "What if Garland did this to make it look like a robbery or something?"

"Or maybe he didn't do this at all," I said slowly. "Maybe Dr. Hewitt did this herself. Do you notice anything about these books?"

He looked down at the floor and then at me. "What are you talking about? It just looks like a bunch of books on the floor."

"Yes. But check out the titles." I knelt next to a leather-bound copy of *Les Liaisons Dangereuses, Dangerous Liaisons,* the famous French novel about a devious marquise and vicomte who play games using sex to manipulate and wreak havoc on those around them.

The other books were Shakespeare's *King Lear,* Robert Louise Stevenson's *The Strange Case of Dr. Jekyll and Mr. Hyde* and Dashiell Hammett's *The Maltese Falcon.*

"They're all books I was forced to read when I was in school?" said Simon.

"Not that," I said impatiently. "They're books about sex, greed, ambition, violence, betrayal, murder and insanity. Now, who do all of those words describe?"

"Vincent Garland and Juliet Rice," he said, nodding his head like he finally understood.

"Exactly. I bet she knew she was about to die and pulled these books off the shelf as a message, or a more like warning." I pulled a pen and a scrap of paper out of my bag and scribbled down the titles.

"But a warning to who?"

"The other society members." I stood "I just want to know why Garland came here if he wasn't looking for the crucifix or the book."

"I don't know but we really need to get out of here. Come on." Simon grabbed my hand and led me back down to the first floor where Agnes still held vigil by her master's body.

"I hate to just leave her like this. Can't we at least cover her up?"

"*Non.* We need to leave everything just like we found it." He wiped his prints off the CD player and the doorknob with his sleeve before we left.

Once we were back outside he looked at me and said, "I think we should make sure they get it."

"Get what?"

"Dr. Hewitt's warning," he replied. "I think we need to track down the other society members. If we tell them about Dr. Hewitt's murder maybe one of them will be rattled enough to tell us where Juliet could have hidden the crucifix."

"Sounds like a plan."

SIMON AND I HEADED ACROSS the Pont St. Louis to the Ile de la Cité and a beautiful little park near Notre Dame called Square Jean XXIII where Simon said he could get wireless access. We sat on a bench underneath a large tree and Simon fired up Francoise's laptop and looked up information on Juliet Rice's dissertation committee, starting with Bernard Fouquet. Apparently, Dr. Hewitt hadn't lied about Fouquet being dead. Simon found his obit online showing that he'd died on March 20, 1997, of a heart attack. Next we tried Dr. Anna Schroder and found out she'd died recently of a stroke in Cambridge, England.

"Talking to her is out of the question. What about Dr. Oliver Renard?"

Simon plugged Renard's name into a search engine. There were several Oliver Renards but only one who was a professor of history at the Sorbonne. There was also a picture of him that showed him to be a stern-looking man in his sixties with a comb-over, a thin mustache and thick glasses.

"Wonder why he didn't like Juliet?"

"Look at him. He doesn't look like he likes anybody. I bet a good fuck would do him a world of good," said Simon.

"He must have had something going for him if Juliet had an affair with him. Maybe he's hung like a horse."

"Or he's rich. For a woman like Juliet Rice, he could

be hung like a mosquito as long as he has money," he said, making me laugh. He squeezed my hand.

"It's good to see you laugh, Maya. We're going to get through this." He brought my hand to his lips and kissed my fingers. I smiled and gently pulled away. We needed to focus on finding Dr. Renard and Simon's kisses were too distracting.

"So now what? Do we go the university to see him?"

"Too risky. We need to find out where he lives."

"How're we going to do that? I work at a university and believe me, they're very strict about giving out personal information on faculty and staff."

"Ah, but you are forgetting we have a first-class hacker at our disposal. Francoise could hack into the university's personnel files and find Renard's address in no time flat," he said, clapping his hands.

"Are you serious? Decrypting a flash drive is one thing. Hacking into a university's personnel files is something else entirely. It's against the law. Don't you care whether your goddaughter gets into trouble?"

"What I care about is saving a man's life, Maya. Garland could be targeting the committee, wiping them out one by one to make sure Juliet didn't tell them about him. If she had a change of heart about handing over the crucifix to Garland, then maybe she also confessed to them about what she'd done. Either way, they're in danger. And Francoise is good. She never gets caught. She's the one who hacked into the computers at the coroner's office and got me a copy of my brother's report before it was officially released."

I stood and looked down at him.

"What?" He threw his hands up in exasperation. "If

she gets caught I'll take the blame. I'd never let her get into trouble."

"It bothers me that you'll use anyone to get what you want regardless of the consequences."

"And it bothers me that you're so damned uptight," he snarled at me. "In case you haven't noticed we're wanted for murder. I'll do what I have to and use whatever connections are available to me to save a life and to clear my name. And if you don't like it, maybe you should just turn yourself in and let me go warn Renard on my own. I certainly wouldn't want to offend your impeccable sense of justice," he concluded stiffly.

He turned his attention back to the computer on his lap. I reluctantly sat back down next to him. I didn't want to admit he was right. Between Francoise getting caught and Renard getting butchered by Garland, I knew what the lesser of the two evils was.

"Fine. You do what you have to. I just didn't want to see another innocent person mixed up in our mess." He leaned over and kissed me on the cheek then got busy emailing Francoise with the details of her new job.

Less than an hour later we had an address. As it turned out, it was a good thing Simon had contacted Francoise for help. Oliver Renard was not currently teaching at the university. He was on sabbatical. Francoise even emailed us the details of Renard's leave of absence. He was currently taking a year off from teaching to write a biography of Louis XIV's second wife, Madame de Maintenon.

"What's this info going to cost you?" I asked while we waited for the metro.

"I have to take her to her favorite veggie restaurant and to see some teenaged boy who sings like a dying frog in concert next month." He looked anything but excited.

"Isn't vegan French food an oxymoron?"

"The only moron is me for agreeing to eat bean sprouts and tofu and having my eardrums punctured by loud music and a bunch of screaming girls. I think I'd rather be shot out of a cannon into a brick wall."

I laughed. "Now who's being uptight?"

OLIVER RENARD LIVED IN NEUILLY, a wealthy suburb of Paris, in a private four-story mansion on rue de la Renaissance. His wrought-iron front gate was unlocked when we arrived and we walked down a stone path and through a garden to get to the front door.

"Wow," I said, looking at a bronze sculpture of what looked like a Greek god holding court among the flowers and greenery. "The history professors where I work sure don't live like this."

"See, I told you he was probably rich. I bet it's old family money."

The front door was black and heavily carved. It was open just a crack. We heard moaning and rushed in to see a figure lying on the floor at the bottom of a staircase. But it wasn't Oliver Renard. A young woman lay bleeding from a cut above her right eye. A ribbon of blood ran down the side of her face into her thick black hair. Her stocking was torn and her knee was bloody. A red pump lay in the middle of the staircase. The other was still on the woman's foot. Simon knelt beside her and pressed two fingers to her neck to check for a pulse.

"Is she alive?" Her eyes fluttered open. They were large, blue and terrified.

She pushed away Simon's hands. With a grimace, she

forced herself to a sitting position, scooting backward like a fleeing crab until she hit the wall. She pressed herself hard against the wall as though she was trying to disappear into the woodwork.

"It's okay." I crept closer. "Don't be afraid. We're not going to hurt you."

"What's your name?" asked Simon gently. "Do you know Dr. Renard? Is he home?"

At the mention of Renard's name, the young woman wailed, "Papa!" and buried her face in her hands. That wasn't a good sign. I looked at Simon and shook my head.

"You stay here." He sprinted up the stairs.

"Is anything broken? Can you move everything?" The woman just stared up the steps after Simon and didn't answer.

"Parlez-vous Anglais?" I asked.

She finally nodded her head slowly. *"Oui...* I mean yes."

"Is Dr. Renard your father?" I pulled a handkerchief out of my bag and gently dabbed at the blood on her forehead.

She simply nodded and her eyes filled with tears. "I'm Sylvie Renard."

"Do you live here, Sylvie?"

"Yes. I've been away in Barcelona visiting my fiancé since last Friday. I just got home." She gestured toward a large yellow suitcase sitting in the entryway next to the front door. "My father was supposed to pick me up from the airport but he never came. I knew he was probably tied up working on his book and I took a cab. When I got here I went up to let him know I was home and..." She started sobbing again and couldn't continue.

"It's okay." I sat next to her.

"After I found my father I heard a noise in the hall-way. I went out to the landing and someone pushed me down the stairs and ran out the front door."

"Did you see who it was?"

She shook her head no.

Simon came downstairs and waved me over. The look on his face said it all.

"How bad is it?" I whispered, looking over my shoulder at Sylvie who looked like she was in another world.

"He's up in his study with his throat slit just like Dr. Hewitt's. You find out who she is?"

"She's Renard's daughter, Sylvie. She just got home from Spain and found him dead. Garland must have still been in the house when she got home. She said someone pushed her down the stairs and ran out."

"That hardly makes sense," said Simon, looking confused. "From the way it smells up there, Renard's been dead for days. Why come back here?"

"I don't know. But she looks pretty banged up. She needs to go the hospital. She could have a concussion or internal bleeding or something."

"Who are you two? How do you know my father?" Sylvie suddenly asked, looking more alert.

She rose unsteadily to her feet and lurched forward. Simon rushed over and caught her before she hit the ground. She looked up at him with her big blue eyes and I could have sworn Simon blushed. He'd obviously noticed the same thing I had the minute I'd laid eyes on her. Sylvie Renard was a very beautiful woman. I could see nothing of her father in her.

"I'm fine," Sylvie said as Simon helped her to sit on

the bottom step of the staircase. I came and sat on the step directly behind her.

"We should get her to the hospital, Simon," I repeated.

"I'm not going anywhere until you tell me who you are," Sylvie insisted. She turned to look at me.

"We're friends of Dr. Juliet Rice. We came to speak to your father about her. Do you know Dr. Rice?" I asked. I figured since Sylvie had been out of the country in Spain she hadn't heard about Juliet's murder.

"She's an acquaintance of my father's. They both belong to the same club."

"Club?" said Simon looking at me.

"*Oui,* it's a book club."

"Is it called the Society of Moret?" I asked. Technically speaking, the Society of Moret *was* a book club, just a book club that was only interested in one book.

NEUF

Sylvie nodded and winced. "It was started by my father's late colleague Dr. Fouquet. They're just a bunch of old academics that meet every year in Moret-sur-Loing to discuss some boring old history books. They've been doing it for years."

"When was the last time you saw Dr. Rice?" Simon asked.

"She came to visit my father last Friday but they argued and she didn't stay long."

"About what?" Simon and I asked in unison.

"I don't know. Why?"

"Can you please try to remember, Madame Renard? It's very important." Simon knelt in front of her and took her hands in his. Simon was a master at working that charm of his.

"I believe it was about something she took," Sylvie said. "My father was very, very angry. He told her if she didn't return whatever it was, there would be big trouble. Dr. Rice told my father she was the only one strong enough to do what needed to be done. My father called her a traitor. It sounded like he spat at her and she ran out crying. Then my cab came for the airport and I left."

"Have you ever heard of a man named Vincent Garland?" I asked.

"The American ambassador's son?"

"Oui," replied Simon.

"What about him?" Sylvie looked confused.

"Do you know if he knew Dr. Rice?" I asked and then held my breath.

"Of course," she said.

"And you know this for a fact?" I could barely contain my excitement. We'd finally be able to connect Juliet to Garland.

"I work at the U.S. Embassy as a translator. I introduced them at an embassy reception months ago when she was in Paris lecturing. Now, please, no more questions. My head is spinning." She clutched her head in both hands.

"I'm going to call the emergency squad. Where's your phone?" Simon got up and looked around.

"My car is in the garage. It will be quicker to drive." I helped Sylvie up. "What about my father?" Tears filled her eyes again.

"We'll call the police as soon as we get you to the hospital," I assured her.

SIMON DROVE US TO the nearby American Hospital of Paris in Sylvie's black Mini Cooper. As soon as we entered the emergency room, Sophie filled out a form and was whisked away by a nurse. Simon located a pay phone and made an anonymous call to the police to report Renard's murder and the attack on Sylvie Renard.

"She's in good hands and the police are on their way. Let's get out of here," he said.

We were out of the hospital, halfway down the street, when it suddenly dawned on me that the American Hospital of Paris was the same hospital that Brian and

Jarrod were in. I could warn them about Garland in person.

"You don't even know what room he's in," protested Simon. "Are you going to just wander around the hospital looking in every room?"

"Why not? According to Francoise, I look like some old lady. I'll just pretend I got lost."

"That's your plan?" he said, looking at me like I was crazy. "The police will be here soon, Maya. You'll have to be more careful than that."

"Don't worry. I'll think of something. You stay out here if you want. I won't be long," I told him, then rushed off before he could protest further.

Once I got through the hospital's main revolving doors, it was as if I stepped into the lobby of an upscale hotel. A long, highly polished wood information desk to my left was manned by a receptionist giving directions to an older couple. Fresh flowers were everywhere. I kept right on walking past the information desk and headed down the hall as if I knew where I was going. Luckily, once past the entry, a male nurse came my way, pushing a wheelchair down the hall.

"Could you please tell me what floor the cardiac care unit is on?"

"B Wing. Level O," he told me. "You can take the elevator. It's one floor down."

When I stepped off the elevator, signs on the walls in both French and English pointed the way to the cardiac unit. But I was stopped by a nurse at the nurse's station when I tried to go down the hall toward the rooms.

"Peux-je vous aider?" she asked, then switched to English when I gave her a blank look. "May I help you?"

"I'm here to visit a friend of mine who had heart surgery this morning."

"Name please?" she asked with a friendly, I'm-here-to-help smile.

I racked my brain to try and remember Brian's last name as the nurse took in my odd appearance and her expression changed from friendly to suspicious. I didn't exactly look like I had friends who could afford such a ritzy hospital.

"What is the patient's name, please?" she asked again.

I was thinking back on the day I met Brian and Jarrod. The nurse kept looking at my poncho as if I might have a bomb under it. Her fingers were inching toward the phone when a name suddenly popped into my head.

"Mitchner," I said, letting out a breath. "His name is Brian Mitchner."

Satisfied, the nurse consulted the computer on her desk. "Monsieur Mitchner has been moved to recovery and is resting. I'm afraid he cannot have visitors."

"Oh…well…what about his partner, Jarrod…ah… Perlman? Do you know if Mr. Perlman is here in the hospital?"

"I just came on duty, *madame.* But if you can wait, I'll check for you." She picked up the phone and pressed a button. After a short exchange in French, she hung up and gave me a tight smile that made me nervous. "The nurse attending to Monsieur Mitchner is not sure where Monsieur Perlman is, but suggests you check the snack bar."

She gave me directions to the snack bar and I got back onto the elevator and looked back to see the nurse still staring at me oddly. The elevator stopped on the first floor and two uniformed police officers got on. I could have fainted, but I kept my head down, and tried to slow my breathing. Neither of them paid me the slightest bit of attention as they conversed in French. Thankfully, they got off on the next floor.

I got off the elevator on the next floor and ran right smack into Jarrod.

"Excuse me." He pushed past me, looking like he had the weight of the world on his shoulders, even his gel-spiked blond hair looked limp.

"Jarrod," I whispered. His head snapped around and he looked at me like I was crazy before recognition finally flashed across his face.

"Maya?" he said uncertainly.

"Not so loud." I put my finger to my lips and looked around. There was a closed door behind me and I jiggled the knob. It was unlocked. I grabbed Jarrod's arm and pulled him through the door of what turned out to be an empty office.

"Boy, am I glad to see you." He pulled me into a tight embrace.

"I'm glad to see you, too. How's Brian?"

"Groggy. But I'm assured that he'll be sitting up and taking nourishment as soon as tomorrow."

"That's great. But I came to warn you. Has that man from the U.S. Embassy, Vincent Garland, contacted you again?"

"No. He was supposed to be calling *you,* why?"

"Don't trust him. Do you understand me? He's a very dangerous man. Just as soon as Brian is well enough, you need to go home, or at the very least, switch hospitals."

Jarrod laughed nervously. "You're not making sense, Maya."

"Please trust me on this. He's killed four people and you and Brian could be next."

"A killer? That's insane. He was nothing but nice to us. Did you know his father is the American Ambassador to Paris?"

"And he's also a stone cold killer who set up me and Simon."

"You actually saw Garland kill someone?"

"He tried to kill *me!*" I blurted out in frustration. Jarrod was stunned. I couldn't tell if he believed me. I started to explain how Garland attacked me and tried to shoot us when a shrill chirp interrupted me. Jarrod pulled a cell phone from his pocket and flipped it open.

"Yes, I have that information now," he said into the phone as he shot me a nervous look. "That's right. Okay. I'll be here. Send them over right away." He ended the call and put the phone back in his pocket. But his hand was trembling.

"Everything okay?"

"Just my insurance company. They're faxing some forms here for me to sign." His voice sounded normal but he wouldn't look me in the eye. Beads of sweat had popped up on his brow. He was lying.

"I should go." I headed for the door but he blocked my path. Guilt and anguish distorted his features.

"Can't let you do that."

"Who was that on the phone, Bellange or Bernier?"

"They know about my criminal record, Maya. They've been harassing me since you went on the run, accusing me of aiding and abetting. Threatening me with criminal charges if I don't help them catch you!

They're the ones who made me keep calling you, hoping to lure you here. I can't take much more of this on top of what's going on with Brian. This is your mess, not mine!" His voice cracked with emotion.

"Oh my God. I'm so sorry for getting you involved in this, Jarrod. But Simon and I are innocent, too."

"Then you have nothing to worry about. Captain Bellange and his partner are on their way here now. You can tell them all about it."

"No! Get out of my way!" I tried to get past him but he grabbed me by the shoulders and shook me hard.

"Don't you realize how guilty all this running makes you look?" He opened his mouth to say more, then stopped. He looked at me closely then gave a mirthless chuckle. "Now I get it. It's written all over you. Bright eyes, glowing skin. You slept with that French guy, didn't you?"

My face flushed hotly and I jerked out of his grasp. Could he really tell?

"Trust me, babe. I've been right where you are back when I was boosting cars with Jake, my ex, and I know you wouldn't do any better in prison than I did. But it's not too late. I can help you get a good lawyer."

Was he insane? A lawyer got me into this mess. "It's not like that, Jarrod! You have no idea what's going on!"

If I couldn't get past him then I'd just have to run over him because I was getting out of that office. I rushed at Jarrod and tried to tackle him but he shoved me again and the momentum sent me sprawling on my ass. Jarrod knelt in front of me.

"Can't you see I'm just trying to help you? No man is worth spending the rest of your life in prison over."

"I'm not dick whipped!" I shoved him hard and

jumped up, making a break for the door, but Jarrod was on his feet in an instant.

He got a handful of my poncho and jerked me backward away from the door. I was struggling to get free when Jarrod suddenly let me go. He was wide-eyed and his mouth hung open in shock. All the color had drained from his face. And then I heard it, too. It was an announcement on the hospital's PA system. *"Code Blue...level O...room 0518. Code Blue...level O...room 0518."*

"Oh my God! That's Brian's room!" Jarrod paled and his knees buckled. I put an arm around his waist to steady him.

"Go to him! Now!" I shouted, opening the office door and shoving him out. He took off running down the hall and disappeared into the elevator. Talk about a close call. I sagged against the door jam, willing myself to stop shaking and praying Brian would be okay.

Once I got back down to the lobby, the two officers that had been on the elevator were talking to a nurse. They looked annoyed. I didn't know what they were saying but could have sworn they said the name Sylvie Renard. I couldn't hang around to listen. I had to get out of there. I knew Simon had to be wondering why I was taking so long. I started toward the lobby entrance when someone called out to me. To my right a nurse was rushing toward me.

"Madame! Excusez-moi, madame!" It was the nurse who checked Sylvie in at the emergency room.

Just then Bernier and Bellange pushed through the hospital's revolving doors. They were deep in conversation, probably about me. How had they gotten here so fast? I turned toward the emergency room nurse and away from the lobby.

"Yes?"

"The young woman you brought in, Madame Renard, do you know where she is?"

"No, why?"

"I'm embarrassed to say that Madame Renard has gone missing. We put her into an exam room to be treated and when the doctor arrived—*poof*—she was gone. No one has seen her."

So that's why the uniformed cops were in the lobby. They'd had an anonymous tip about Sylvie Renard being attacked and came to take her statement, and now she was gone.

"You mean you lost her?" I tried my best to sound indignant.

"I'm so sorry for the mix-up, *madame.* I don't know what could have happened."

"You'd better find her fast. She's in need of treatment." Bernier and Bellange were getting closer. I could hear them laughing about something.

"There are some officers here. I'm sure they'd appreciate any information you could give them about Madame Renard."

"Of course, but I need to go to the restroom first. Is there one nearby?"

She pointed down the hallway from where she'd just come. An exit sign glowed just beyond the restroom. I was steps away when a police officer called to me. The nurse I'd just spoken to was following him.

Stopping, I held up a hand. *"Un moment, s'il vous plaît,"* I said and headed into the restroom.

Now what was I going to do? I had no intention of

talking to him but didn't want him chasing me if I ran. Unlike the cop in the metro, there would be nothing to keep him from catching me. And Jarrod was right. Running would just make me look guilty. There was one large window in the restroom. But it was too high up for me to reach and I didn't want to take the chance of sounding an alarm if I tried to open it.

The door to the restroom swung open and I expected to see the nurse coming to see what was taking me so long. Instead, it was woman wearing a long white lab coat. I made a show of washing my hands as she took off her lab coat and hung it on a hook on the wall. As I was reaching for the towel dispenser, my bag slipped off my shoulder and fell onto the floor.

"I'll get that for you, *madame*." The woman quickly bent down to pick up my bag. "Here you go," she said in that tone people used on babies and the elderly. Instead of handing it to me, she looped the strap over my shoulder and patted me gently on the back before entering a stall. And then it dawned on me that she thought I was an old woman—and so did the nurse and the cop!

I peeled off the poncho, that awful wig and the fake moles. After fluffing out my hair with my fingers, I grabbed the lab coat from the hook and put it on. I stuffed my disguise into the trashcan by the door and threw my glasses in my bag. I walked out just as the nurse, who'd come looking for me, was coming in. She didn't give me a second look. I walked past the waiting cop without incident.

Once through the exit, I took off running. I ran and ran. I kept running for at least two blocks. When I finally stopped to catch my breath I headed down an alley next to a bistro. I was taking off the lab coat when a firm hand gripped my shoulder. I yelped. But it was only Simon.

"What the hell happened?"

I filled him in, explaining that Bellange and Bernier tried to use Jarrod to catch us. When I told Simon about Sylvie being gone from the hospital, his face fell.

"We don't know that Garland has her," I said, reading his mind. "She has a head injury. She could be wandering around the hospital in a daze or she could have just gotten scared and left." I pulled the same handkerchief I'd used on the cut on Sylvie's forehead from my pocket to wipe my sweaty palms.

"Don't you see? If something has happened to Sylvie, she won't be able to tell the police about Garland's connection to Juliet Rice. *Merde!* I just wish we could catch a break!" He angrily kicked the side of the Dumpster, making me flinch.

A small flash of gold on the handkerchief in my hand glinted in the sunlight, catching my eye. I stared at it, noticing for the first time that this was the same handkerchief Monsieur Marcel had given to me to wipe my eyes when he'd picked me up at the DCPJ headquarters after my interrogation. Now that I had time to really look at the monogram in the bottom right corner, I could see that it was actually a gold infinity symbol with the letter *S* in one section and *M* in the other. I remember thinking when he'd given it to me that the initials stood for Sebastian Marcel. It didn't. *This* was why the Society of Moret's symbol had looked so familiar to me. I'd seen it before, on Monsieur Marcel's handkerchief.

"What's wrong now?" snapped Simon.

I held up the handkerchief and grinned. "I think our luck just changed."

BEING A TOUR GUIDE for TransEuro Tours made Sebastian Marcel an easy man to find. All I had to do was look at my tour group's itinerary—still crumpled at the bottom of my bag—to see that today Monsieur Marcel was scheduled to take anyone from our group who was interested on a tour of the Palais Garnier, which included stops at the nearby Fragonard Perfumery and the Galeries Lafayette department store.

It was the middle of the afternoon by the time Simon and I reached the Palais Garnier, also known as the Paris Opera House. Along the way, Simon bought me a black baseball cap from a street vendor and I tucked my hair underneath it and put the horn-rimmed glasses back on. The sun was bright as we approached the opera house, making the two gilded statues of L'Harmonie and La Poesie, which sat majestically atop the building, gleam like highly polished gold coins. The area was thick with people. Traffic was heavy and several tour buses lined the nearby side streets.

I had no idea which bus belonged to Monsieur Marcel's group. The back of the opera house faced rue Scribe, the street that the perfumery was on. According to Simon, the Galeries Lafayette was a mere block away. Now all we had to do was wait.

"I hope we haven't missed him." I scanned the street for the dapper, white-haired Frenchman.

"If so, I can always enlist Francoise," he said teasingly.

"You've done enough corrupting of a minor for one day."

"Have you always been this uptight?" asked Simon as he leaned against the doorway of the entrance to the Fragonard Perfumery's museum.

"I'm not uptight. I'm just cautious." He was definitely starting to annoy me.

"I bet you've never had so much as a parking ticket in your life, have you?" He somehow made it sound like something to be ashamed of.

"No, I haven't. But I'd say the mess I'm in now more than makes up for it, wouldn't you?

"That's him." I nudged Simon in the ribs. A man with snowy white hair stood about a half a block away with a group of people, half of whom I recognized from my tour group.

I headed toward him, but Simon grabbed my arm.

"Easy, Madame Cautious. You can't just run up to him waving a bloody handkerchief in his face. Let's follow him and see if we can catch him alone."

We waited and watched from the doorway as Marcel addressed the small group. A minute later, the tourists had left, heading in various directions, a few of them looking at their watches. Monsieur Marcel headed off past the opera house and Simon and I rushed to keep him in sight. Half a block later, he disappeared inside the Galeries Lafayette.

"Hurry up! If we lose him we'll never be able to find him in there," I said.

The store was packed with shoppers loaded down with bags bearing designer names I would never be able to afford. And Marcel was nowhere in sight.

"I told you we'd lose him in here!"

"Is that him?" Simon pointed toward a spot in the crowd about twenty feet away where a bright white head of hair bobbed in a sea of blonds, redheads and brunettes.

We followed him and found ourselves at a wine bar in the women's clothing department. He perched on a stool and ordered wine.

"Un verre de Cabernet sauvignon pour moi et mes deux amis, s'il vous plaît."

The bartender looked taken aback and looked at the empty stools on either side of Marcel.

"What did he say?" I whispered to Simon.

"He just ordered wine for himself and two friends. Is he nuts?"

"Au contraire, Monsieur Girard, le vin est pour vous et Madame Sinclair," Marcel said, swiveling around to face us and giving me a toothy smile.

So startled that he'd addressed Simon by his name, I actually jumped. The bartender sat three glasses of red wine in front of Monsieur Marcel.

"I've been expecting the two of you. Please, come sit and have a glass of wine with an old man."

I wasn't expecting such an invitation. I'd thought we'd have to corner the man and plead for his help. He not only expected us, he welcomed us with wine. Was this a trap? Only after seeing the warmth and genuine concern in his eyes, I made the decision to join Monsieur Marcel at the bar.

"Maya," Simon whispered and tried to pull me back. I slipped out of his grasp.

"You and your friend have nothing to fear from me, my dear," Monsieur Marcel whispered as I sat next to him.

"It's okay," I said. Simon hesitated a few seconds before sitting on the stool on the opposite side of Monsieur Marcel. He wasted no time taking a large gulp of the wine.

"You've been expecting us?" I asked in a low voice, keeping my eye on the bartender to make sure he wasn't listening. He was busy tending to other patrons.

"I had high hopes that you and your friend would seek me out, Madame Sinclair."

"You gave me that handkerchief on purpose? You wanted me to see the Society of Moret symbol?"

"Not exactly on purpose," he said simply. "It was more as a precaution."

"Some precaution. Why didn't you just tell Maya you knew Juliet Rice? Why didn't you warn her?" Simon slapped his wineglass down a little too hard on the bar.

A faint blush colored Monsieur Marcel's cheeks and he regarded Simon calmly. "It was my greatest wish that the police would clear Madame Sinclair of all suspicion in poor Juliet's murder. By the time I realized the situation was so serious," he said, glancing over at the bartender and lowering his voice farther before turning to me, "you were on the run. And I was too afraid to contact you for fear they would be tracing your cell phone. They can do that kind of thing" he concluded matter-of-factly.

"But how could you be so sure I'd figure it out?"

"I could not be sure. I could only hope you'd put it all together. And might I add that I overheard you telling Madame Berman when you arrived that you are a librarian. I have great respect for librarians and have yet to meet one who didn't possess extraordinary problem-solving powers."

Not exactly the answer I was looking for but somehow just being in Monsieur Marcel's calm, reassuring presence was making me feel hopeful that Simon and I were going to come out of this nightmare okay. I squeezed his hand.

"We need answers, Marcel. What the hell is going on?" asked Simon.

"Yes, of course, Monsieur Girard. I will answer all of your questions to the best of my ability, but not here. We need privacy."

DIX

HE TOOK US to the empty tour bus parked in front of the Fragonard Perfumery's museum. The bus driver was too busy smoking and talking to the driver of the tour bus parked across the street to pay much attention to us as we climbed onto the bus.

"Alright," said Simon, leaning across the aisle once we were seated. "What do you know about this Moret Crucifix? Do you have any idea where Juliet could have hidden it?"

"Juliet's killer wants us to bring it to him tomorrow night in exchange for the murder weapon he used to kill Juliet. It has my prints on it," I explained.

"Mon Dieu," said Marcel, letting out a breath. "I'm so sorry. I have no idea what Juliet could have done with it. I didn't even realize it was missing until Oliver called me last Friday. It was his turn to have the crucifix and he called me in quite a state, saying it had been stolen and a fake left in its place."

"How did he know it was a fake?" asked Simon.

"Sixteen ninety-four, the year the Black Nun of Moret took her final vows as a nun, and the year we believe the crucifix was given to her, was engraved on the back of the crucifix. It wasn't there anymore."

"What do you mean it was Dr. Renard's turn to have the crucifix?" I asked. Simon appeared equally confused.

"Oh dear, I'll have to start at the beginning I'm afraid."

"Please do," prompted Simon. I nodded for him to continue, as well.

"Well, it all started back when we were students at the Sorbonne back in 1957. Bernard Fouquet, Evalyn Hewitt, Anna Schroder, Oliver Renard and I were all great lovers of history, you see. We were in many of the same classes and studied together. It wasn't long before we were inseparable. But it was Bernard who was the glue that held us all together. He was the one with all the grand ideas and theories. He was brilliant."

"He was the one who studied the Moret Tapestry," I said, then added, "Dr. Hewitt told us."

"You've spoken to Evalyn?" He looked surprised.

"She's dead, *monsieur*," said Simon bluntly, causing the old man's eyes to instantly fill with tears. I could have kicked him.

"I was supposed to have lunch with her today. She called and told me not to come. It was most odd. She didn't sound like herself at all. I should have known…"

"She may have saved your life," said Simon a little more gently this time.

"I'm afraid Dr. Renard is dead, too." I took his hand. "I'm so sorry about your friends. We found both of them today. That's why we really need your help. We have to stop the man who's doing this."

"I'm the only one left?" he said in a hollow voice.

"And you could be next," Simon added.

Monsieur Marcel nodded and rubbed his eyes then cleared his throat before continuing. "In answer to your question, yes, Bernard was the one who studied the tapestry. His research proved that the original design of the Moret Tapestry had been altered during an attempt to restore it in 1920. He discovered that the restoration destroyed one of the major clues to finding the book entrusted to Sister Louise-Marie."

"What clue?" we asked simultaneously.

"When the tapestry was found in Fontainebleau, it was in a state of disrepair. There were many places that were faded and threadbare. One of those worn places was the area on the front of the kneeling nun's chest. The restorers filled in the spot with solid black, the color of her habit. But in closely examining the few surviving photographs taken of the tapestry before it was restored, Bernard was certain that the nun had originally been wearing a crucifix."

"The Moret Crucifix!" I said as a warm feeling of excitement flowed through me. But it was more than that. I somehow *knew* Bernard Fouquet's theory was right.

"*Exactement!* It was all just speculation of course. Bernard believed the crucifix was commissioned by the Duke of Chartres who was in love with Louise-Marie and gave it to her as a gift and a reminder."

"To stay in the convent," I said and Marcel nodded.

"And of her higher purpose of protecting the book. Sadly, no one in the academic community paid Bernard's theories much attention. Then the Moret Tapestry was stolen in 1959 and Bernard was unable to substantiate his theories. Even the four of us had our doubts. Eventually, we all drifted in different directions, taking up faculty positions at various universities after graduation and moving on with our lives. We lost touch with each other. But then something amazing happened. In 1970 we all got an invitation from Bernard to visit him at his home in Moret-sur-Loing. He told us he'd found something and it would be very much worth our while to show up."

"He found the crucifix?" Simon asked.

"*Oui.* You see, he'd always theorized that the crucifix must have been hidden someplace where Sister Louise-Marie spent a great deal of time."

"The convent," I added again with certainty. He nodded.

"Bernard believed Louise-Marie was a member of a Benedictine convent in Moret built in 1638 called the convent of Notre-Dame-des-Anges.

"Notre Dame of the Angels," said Simon to no one in particular.

"The convent disappeared during the French Revolution. But fortunately for Bernard, the Benedictine nuns of Moret were famous for their barley-sugar candy making. Their candy—"

"Candy!" I blurted out. It wasn't possible, was it? How could I have dreamt about being a nun in a convent where they made candy? Had Dr. Hewitt mentioned it? Had I read about it someplace and just forgotten? That must have been it. I'd read about it. There was no other explanation unless… I fingered the silver ring and shoved my left hand under my thigh so the elderly Frenchman wouldn't see it and recognize it as belonging to Dr. Hewitt.

"But what has candy got to do with the Moret Crucifix?" Simon asked, ignoring my odd outburst.

"Let the man talk, Simon."

"I'm sorry," said Monsieur Marcel, blushing. "I do get carried away."

"It's okay, *monsieur.* Go on," I said.

"After the revolution, the nuns once again began their

candy making in Moret and set up shop in a little house next to Notre Dame Church. In 1970 they turned over the recipe to a local family in Moret who owned a candy shop. Much of what had been in the nuns' house was given to Notre Dame Church. One of the priests knew that Bernard was a historian and asked him to take a look at the items from the house to appraise their historical value. Most of it was directly related to candy making but some of it was items belonging to the nuns that dated as far back as the early 1700s. Among the items, Bernard found a prayer journal from 1732 belonging to a young novice nun named Sister Cecile. One of the entries gives an account of the night she sat up praying with an elderly, dying black nun named Sister Louise-Marie. Before Louise-Marie died, she gave Cecile something and made her kiss a gold crucifix as a promise to keep it safe."

"She gave her the *Aurum Liber?*" asked Simon.

"Well, the item was not mentioned but, yes, Bernard assumed it was the *Aurum Liber.* He assumed Sister Louise-Marie may have also given Cecile the crucifix. Cecile fell ill and died in 1734 before taking her final vows as a nun. Through old church parish records, Bernard was able to discover Sister Cecile's family name was Lambert. She'd belonged to a wealthy family in Fontainebleau. He thought that stories about the book or the crucifix had been handed down through the family. Bernard traced her family tree and found a direct descendent of Cecile's family, a woman named Albertine Dumaire.

"But by the time he found an address for her, she'd already died. Bernard just happened to show up at Madame Dumaire's tiny apartment the very day her possessions were being auctioned off. He was wandering through her home when he spotted a grimy, dusty blackened crucifix hanging on the wall above her bed. He had a hunch and bought it for a franc. Once he cleaned it up, he discovered his hunch was right. It was the Moret Crucifix and it had been hanging on the wall in that poor woman's derelict little apartment for who knows how many years."

"But what about the book?" asked Simon.

"He never found it. It wasn't in Madame Dumaire's apartment. Somewhere between the time of Sister Cecile's death in 1734 and Albertine Dumaire's death in 1970, someone in the family must have hidden the book. That's why Bernard invited us to Moret-sur-Loing. He formed the Society of Moret and recruited all of us to study the crucifix for clues as to the book's whereabouts. Each year one member of the society was given the crucifix to study for an entire year, after which we would meet at Bernard's house to share our findings with the society."

"You mean Sister Louise-Marie didn't create the Society of Moret to protect the book after her death?" I asked.

Monsieur Marcel chuckled humorlessly. "I see you've been reading Evalyn's book, Madame Sinclair. Evalyn wrote *Secret Societies of France* as a textbook for one of her classes. Only fifty copies were printed. And do you know what one of the questions was on the final exam for that class?"

I shrugged and shook my head.

"What secret society listed in your textbook is not a real centuries-old society?"

"The Society of Moret?"

"If you'd gotten to know her better, you'd have discovered Evalyn had a wonderful sense of humor," he said as he looked off in the distance.

I had to admit, she got us good. Dr. Hewitt must have known Simon wasn't really a filmmaker. She'd had a bit of fun at our expense, which is exactly what we deserved for lying to her. I wondered what else she'd lied to us about. By the set of his jaw, I could tell Simon wasn't ready to appreciate the humor just yet.

"But that nun's family could have just sold the book. It's worth a fortune, right? How can you be so sure it was hidden?" Simon asked, looking highly skeptical.

"We've discovered that the inlaid stained-glass scene in the crucifix's handle isn't as old as the rest of the crucifix. It was added a good hundred years or more after Sister Louise-Marie's death. Bernard believed—as did the rest of the society—that the scene had been added by whoever hid the book in order to serve as a map to the book's location."

"Dr. Hewitt told us Dr. Fouquet believed the sun was the key to finding the book. Was that a lie?" I asked.

"We all believe the sun is the key. The sun is not the largest object in the Moret Tapestry but for some reason it dominates the scene in the crucifix's handle. It has to be a clue. And I'm afraid poor Juliet must have figured it out at last, only instead of sharing what she'd found, she betrayed us."

"Why would Juliet even bother stealing the crucifix if she had the opportunity to have it for an entire year?" I asked.

"It was Anna's turn last year. Oliver's turn this year. It was my turn next year and Evalyn's turn after that.

It's been two years since Juliet had her turn and she was going to have to wait another three years."

"She stole it from Dr. Renard," said Simon. "Remember Sylvie said they'd argued about something she took?"

"Sylvie? You've spoken to Sylvie?" Marcel appeared shocked.

"She found her father's body shortly before we arrived, why?" I asked. He opened his mouth to speak but Simon cut him off.

"She's disappeared, Marcel. So we need to know everything you know."

He nodded and sighed. "Juliet came to see Oliver a few weeks ago out of the blue. He told me he was surprised to see her. They've never gotten on. Oliver could be a bit of a snob when it came to Americans. He felt Juliet was too flashy to be taken seriously as an academic."

"He took her seriously enough to have an affair with her, right?" I asked.

Monsieur Marcel blushed. "It was long ago. And they both paid dearly for it."

"Finish what you were telling us," said Simon impatiently.

"Ah, yes, Oliver was eating lunch in his garden when she arrived. It was no secret that he kept the crucifix in his study. He thinks she switched it when she went inside to use his restroom. He'd been so busy working on his new book that he didn't notice something wasn't right about the crucifix until last Friday."

A tap on the bus's door made me jump. A half dozen people from Monsieur Marcel's group were waiting to get back on the bus. Monsieur Marcel pressed a set of keys into my hand.

"There is still much to discuss. Please wait for me at my apartment."

Simon and I exchanged looks.

"You'll be safe there. Of that you have my promise," he insisted.

"What about you? You need to be very careful."

"Don't worry. I should be home within the hour."

He gave us the address of his apartment in the Marais district and ushered us off the bus, oblivious to the stares from our tour group. A sudden thought came to mind and I grabbed his hand.

"I think Dr. Hewitt left you a message, *monsieur,*" I whispered.

He gave me a startled look and I quickly explained about the books we'd found on the floor of Dr. Hewitt's apartment and handed him the list of titles. He read them and all the color drained from his face. More members of the group arrived. I pulled the tour guide into a nearby doorway.

"Maya, let's go…now," Simon ordered. I ignored him. He cursed under his breath.

"These titles mean something to you, don't they?"

"Oui," he whispered. "They mean that all is not as it seems, Madame Sinclair. I'll explain later. Now, please go before you're recognized."

He'd barely gotten the last word out before Simon grabbed my hand and dragged me away.

Sebastian Marcel's apartment on rue de Poitou was above an antique shop. Compared to Oliver Renard's mansion and Evalyn Hewitt's fancy Ile St. Louis digs, it was a closet. But what it lacked in space, it more than made up for in charm. Much like those of his late friend Dr. Hewitt, the walls of his apartment were covered in floor-to-ceiling bookshelves. Well-worn leather furniture, antique lamps and oriental rugs made the apartment feel cozy. A Siamese cat sat, swishing its elegant tail atop a counter that separated the kitchen from the living room. Simon didn't hesitate to make himself at home. He uncorked a bottle of Pinot Noir from Monsieur Marcel's wine rack and poured us each a glass.

"I wonder if these are the other society members." I asked, looking at a black-and-white framed photo on the wall. It looked like it was taken in the late '50s or early '60s. I leaned closer for a better look.

Five carefree twentysomethings sat around a table at a café. I recognized Monsieur Marcel who looked much the way he did now, only his thick, wavy hair was jet-black. He gazed adoringly at a young and very pretty Evalyn Hewitt, who in turn only had eyes for the handsome, serious-looking black man sitting next to her. He was the only one staring directly into the camera. Sitting on the opposite side of him was a grinning Oliver Renard who had a headful of blond hair. A busty dark-haired girl with glasses sat on his lap. She must have been Anna Schroder.

I took the picture out of its frame and flipped it over. There was a note on the back: *Le grand jour á Bernard.* Bernard's big day. I flipped the photo over and looked again at the handsome black man. So *this* was the infamous Bernard Fouquet? The info we'd found on him on the web didn't include any pictures. I don't know why I was so surprised he was black…or hot. With his slim build, sensual lips and brooding gaze he could have been a model.

I put the picture back and turned my attention to the bookshelves. Much like those in Dr. Hewitt's library, many of Monsieur Marcel's books were in French and English, leather-bound, and looked well-worn. But his tastes leaned heavily toward nonfiction with one whole shelf devoted to books on alchemy and in particular, the philosopher's stone.

I took one off the shelf and flipped through it. It was in English but may as well have been a foreign language. I couldn't make heads or tales of what I was reading. I started to close it but something was stuck to one of the pages. It was a faded snapshot of Dr. Hewitt. But she looked older than in the black-and-white group photo on the wall, maybe early to mid-thirties. She was sitting on a blanket in a grassy area. The Eiffel Tower was in the background. And sitting in her lap was a Bichon Frise puppy.

"Agnes?" I whispered and then laughed at myself. Of course it couldn't be Agnes. Lots of people remain loyal to a breed of dog. I flipped the snapshot over and saw the year, 1970, written on the back.

"Looks like Dr. Hewitt may not have been the only who believed in the philosopher's stone," commented Simon, who had come up behind me. I quickly shoved the snapshot back in the book.

"I own a copy of Grimm's Fairytales but that doesn't mean I believe in them," I said.

Simon chuckled. "Why is it so hard for you to believe that something like the philosopher's stone could exist?"

"Don't tell me you believe what Dr. Hewitt told us? You don't strike me as the type to believe in hocus-pocus and magic elixirs," I said, taking a wineglass and following him over to the couch.

"I've been all over the world chasing stories and have seen some pretty amazing things, Maya—people cured of terminal illnesses at Lourdes, children who can give detailed and verifiable accounts of past lives, psychics who help the police solve crimes. Could the philosopher's stone be real? Who the hell knows? But I'm open-minded enough to believe in the possibility that it could be."

"I can respect that. But until they come out with the Philosopher's Stone Anti-Aging Cream and the Philosopher's Stone Gold-Making Kit, I'm still a skeptic." I laughed when I said it, but I couldn't get that snapshot and Dr. Hewitt's voice out of my head. *Would you believe me if I told you my Agnes was almost forty years old?* And I didn't want to contemplate all the weirdness that had happened since I'd put on the posy ring.

"And I'm happy to contemplate the mysteries of life," Simon replied, interrupting my thoughts and clinking his wineglass against mine.

"Speaking of mysteries," I said, shaking my head to clear it. "I wonder what Monsieur Marcel meant about things not being as they seem." Simon scooted close to me on the couch and squeezed my thigh. I rested my head on his shoulder.

"It probably means we should have thought twice about coming here. How do we know that old man hasn't called the police and told them where to find us?"

"You honestly think he would have told us everything that he did if he thought we were murderers?"

"*Non.* But he might if he's the killer."

I sat up and looked at him. "Are you serious?"

"Look around you. Your Monsieur Marcel is hardly living like a king, is he? Oliver Renard could afford to go on sabbatical to write a book and Evalyn Hewitt was comfortably retired. They obviously had money, but not Marcel. He's earning a living as a tour guide. Maybe he needs the money the book can bring. And have you stopped to wonder why neither Renard nor Hewitt's homes were broken into? They knew whoever killed them. Marcel could have easily walked up behind both his unsuspecting old friends and slit their throats for them."

"No." I shook my head. "No one snuck up on Dr. Hewitt. She knew she was going to die or she wouldn't have pulled those books off the shelf."

"Marcel could have pulled those books off the shelf. He could have used Garland murdering Juliet as an opportunity to kill off the rest of the society so he wouldn't have to share the book, knowing their deaths would be blamed on someone else…us!"

"He doesn't even know where the book is. And he's the only one helping us. Besides he's an old man. I don't think he has it in him to kill anyone. We need all the help we can get. You insisted that I trust Francoise, Mr. Open-Minded. Can't you at least have some faith in Monsieur Marcel?"

"You're forgetting I know Francoise. I don't know Marcel and something is still off about all of this. All I'm saying is that we shouldn't be so quick to drink that man's cool ale." He leaned his head back against the couch and ran a hand over his face.

"Kool-Aid, Simon," I corrected, chuckling. "Once he gets here, Monsieur Marcel will be able to help us figure out what Juliet did with that crucifix. But right now," I said, yawning and laying my head in his lap, "I'm really tired."

THE APARTMENT WAS DARK when I woke up alone a few hours later. When I rolled over, I found myself looking into Marcel's cat's icy-blue eyes. I reached out my hand and the cat rubbed his head against my palm and then began to groom himself.

"Simon?" I called out and got no response other than the echo of my own voice. I stretched and called out again. "Monsieur Marcel?"

Suddenly I became aware of voices coming from the hallway just off the small foyer. I headed down the short hallway with the cat on my heels. Simon was watching a small TV in a dark office. Before I could say anything, Sylvie Renard's beautiful, smiling face filled the small TV screen. Then the picture disappeared, replaced by a shot of what I recognized as the guest parking lot of the American Hospital and a black Mini Cooper surrounded by a police barricade. The bottom dropped out of my stomach.

"She's dead, isn't she?"

"*Oui.* A parking attendant found a blood trail in the parking lot that led to Sylvie's car and called the police. Her body was in the trunk. They're looking for the couple that brought her to the hospital. Good thing I wiped our prints from her car."

"When did you do that?"

"While you were busy in the hospital about to be turned in by your upstanding friend," he replied sarcastically.

"Where's Monsieur Marcel?" My heart started to beat faster.

"He never showed up, Maya. Not so much as a phone call."

When Oliver Renard's picture flashed onto the TV screen next to his daughter's, I slid down the wall next to the office door. The cat jumped into my lap and curled up.

"But he was going to help us."

"I'm not so sure about that. I found these in his desk drawer." He handed me a pile of papers.

I riffled though the unpaid bills and letters from collection agencies. Monsieur Marcel was in a mountain of debt.

"He was being evicted from this apartment." Simon handed me another letter with the words *Notification D'expulsion* stamped across the top in bright red letters. "He must be desperate for cash. And desperate people are dangerous people. We have no idea what the extent of his connection to all of this is."

I tossed the bills on the floor in disgust. Could I have been wrong about Sebastian Marcel, too?

"Now what are we going to do?"

Simon just shook his head and continued to stare at the TV. Sylvie was dead and now Monsieur Marcel was missing and possibly dead, too. The only two people who could have helped us were gone. I would have cried if I had the strength. I didn't want to see any more. I took the cat with me and went back to the living room couch. Simon joined me a few minutes later.

"Are you hungry? Marcel's got some fruit and cold chicken or I could go out for food."

I shook my head no.

"You have to eat something. You haven't eaten all day."

"Hold me." He just stood there watching me with a worried frown.

"Please," I pleaded when he didn't move.

Simon knelt in front of me and pulled me into a tight embrace. My arms wrapped around him. My cheek rested against the top of his head. I could smell his hair and feel his warm breath against my skin. We stayed like that for a long time until his hands found their way under my sweater and unhooked my bra. I pulled the sweater over my head. Simon tugged at my pants. Thirty seconds later, I was completely naked and unfastening Simon's pants. He grabbed my hands, shook his head and smiled.

He pushed me down on the couch and kissed me long and deep. He cupped my breasts and squeezed gently as he kissed the valley between them. He began to leave a trail of kisses as he moved lower and briefly stopped at my belly button, showering it with attention. Then he lifted my legs over his shoulders and kissed and nibbled my inner thighs. Just when I couldn't stand it anymore, his tongue found me and I shuddered and gasped from the sheer pleasure as he slowly explored.

The roughness of his beard only added to the intensity. He kneaded my breasts, while he worked me with his tongue, until I was about to lose my mind. Simon held me in place as I came. He kept his mouth fastened on me until I stopped thrashing around. My moans turned to soft whimpers and then heavy breathing, then he laid his head on my stomach.

After I caught my breath, I pulled him all the way onto the couch. I pushed him onto his back, not taking my eyes off him as I slowly unfastened his pants. His eyes widened in surprise then quickly glazed over as I took him into my mouth. When I pulled him in deeper, I was rewarded by a sharp intake of breath as his head fell back and his fingers tangled in my hair. We spent the rest of the evening lost in each other. We were in big trouble and our options were growing limited with each passing hour, but at least for a little while, we could forget.

LOUISE-MARIE ENTERED the room and sat on the side of the couch where I lay with Simon. She took my hand and brought it to her lips. She kissed the posy ring.

Once again, I was the Black Nun and I was filled with the most overwhelming sense of heartache as I peered out of my rain-streaked window onto the ornamental gardens below.

I had been at Fontainebleau for a month and had yet to be presented at court. The royal family visited me whenever they came to the convent to fill their candy boxes, but I was not deemed fit to dine amongst them. I had been hidden away, again, in these rooms. And though lavish they may have been, they were nothing but a gilded cage. My only confidante, besides Philippe, was my young maid, Anne-Elise, and she was but a young girl of twelve.

It was never meant to be. It had been an impossibility all along. Of course the king refused our request to marry. I should have known better. Philippe was his nephew and who was I? An outcast. A mistake to be reviled. Philippe will marry his first cousin Mademoiselle de Blois. She was the king's daughter but she was not my sister. Her mother was not my mother, the queen, but Louis's mistress, Madame de Montespan. And she would be Philippe's wife, not me. According to

Anne-Elise, the mademoiselle had a two-million-livres dowry. And what could I bring to a marriage besides love? Books? Sugar candy?

"Vous devez manger, mademoiselle." *Anne-Elise sat the silver tray of food on the table by the window. I hadn't heard her come in.*

I had no appetite but I sat and allowed her to serve me a bowl of pea-and-leek soup. "Merci." *I spooned a bit of it into my mouth to satisfy the girl, and she left.*

Restless, I wandered over to the canopied bed where a white silk gown lay. It was beautiful with a tight bodice and low, broad neckline trimmed in lace. The dropped shoulders were of the latest fashion, or so I was told, along with paned sleeves lined in a pale blue the same shade as the bow-covered petticoat. Another gift from Phillip. It arrived this afternoon. But it was not a gown for a wife. This was a gown for a mistress, which I had now become. It was not made for me and I wondered if it was cast off from some other mistress.

Philippe insisted that this was the way of things and despite his upcoming marriage to a woman he did not love, we would still be together. All the men of the court had mistresses and provided for them quite well. I could not blame him for his way of thinking. This was the world he was born to. It was I who had been naïve. I looked down at the silver ring on my finger. Of his love I was sure. But a deep sorrow tugged at my heart. A loud knock followed by a voice at my bedchamber door startled me out of my thoughts.

"Louise-Marie…mon amour." *It was Philippe. I hesitated. But finally rose when he called my name again, knowing I could not deny him.*

"Maya! Maya! Wake up!" Simon shook me by the shoulders as the sound of police sirens disrupted the predawn silence.

"Get dressed. We've got to go." He tossed me my clothes from the floor. He was already half-dressed.

"Is that the police? Are they here for us?" I was suddenly as awake as if Simon had thrown cold water in my face. I quickly pulled on my underwear and pants. I forced the sweater down over my head. I stuffed my bra in my bag and slipped my sockless feet into my shoes.

"I don't know, but we're not taking any chances. Let's go."

I barely had time to grab my bag before Simon pulled me out the door. The sounds of running feet sounded on the stairs and floated up to where we were standing. Simon pulled me up three flights and paused on the landing to listen. A loud voice was calling out from below in French. It sounded like they were at Monsieur Marcel's door.

"Ouvrez, maintenez l'ordre!"

I looked at Simon questioningly for the translation.

"Open up, police," Simon whispered.

"Oh my G—" Simon clamped his hand over my mouth before I could utter another sound.

We ran up several more flights of stairs until we reached the door to the roof. It was locked. I could hear shouts from below. They were coming. Simon started kicking frantically at the door. *Wait! I still had Marcel's keys!* I fumbled around in my bag until I found them.

"Move!" I shoved him aside and tried first one key on Marcel's silver-and-garnet key fob without luck and then another. The second key worked and I opened the door just as three police officers arrived at the bottom of the stairs and drew their guns.

"Arrêt! Police!" yelled Thierry Bernier. Our eyes met and I could see the intensity in his.

"I don't want to harm you or Monsieur Girard, Madame Sinclair. We can get this all straightened out. Just give yourselves up and you won't be harmed. I cannot guarantee your safety if you keep running," he called out in his heavily accented English.

For a split second I considered it. I was tired. I wanted this to be over. I wanted to go home to Columbus and familiar surroundings. Dealing with demanding students and uppity professors at work was a piece of cake compared to this. I would never complain again. Bernier's eyes narrowed. Who the hell was I kidding? The only thing waiting for me was a French jail cell. Screw that!

A large trash barrel stood next to the door. I gave it a hard shove and it bumped down the stairs with a shocking amount of speed, knocking down Bernier and the other officers like bowling pins. Simon let out a whoop and pumped his fist.

"I knew there was a fat ass inside you just dying to get out!" he said.

*"Bad*ass!" I screamed. "I'm a badass," I insisted as he pushed me through the door out onto the roof. There was a soft click as the door locked behind us.

"Now what?"

"This way." Simon motioned for me to follow him.

I followed him to the edge of the roof. The street down below was filled with police cars. I jumped back, pulling Simon with me before we were seen. The door to the roof started to buckle outward in its frame. The police were using a battering ram. We ran to the other side of the roof. A large dump truck filled with dirt idled in the alley below.

"There's no other way but down, *cherie*." He grabbed my hand and pulled me onto the roof's narrow ledge.

"You've got to be kidding me!" We were at least six stories up. The pounding behind us grew louder.

The driver of the truck emerged from the building next door. He got behind the wheel and started the engine just as the door to the roof flew off its hinges. Officers dressed in riot gear flooded the roof like water in a basement after a heavy rain. Simon quickly pulled his cell phone out of his pocket and threw it to the far corner. A stack of metal chairs toppled over with a loud clatter. The officers rushed over and trained their guns on the pile.

"Come out with your hands up!" Bernier yelled.

Simon and I looked at each other. The truck below started to pull off. It was now or never. I closed my eyes and we jumped. For a few seconds, my entire body went rigid with terror. Then my arms flailed like a windmill and my feet pedaled in midair as gravity sucked me down. After what felt like an eternity in freefall, I landed with a hard, bone-rattling thud in the dirt. I was too stunned from the impact to do anything but lie there with my arms and legs splayed. And then I quickly found out that what I thought was dirt was actually fertilizer. Manure-rich fertilizer.

The sour stench slapped me in the face, threatening to knock me out. Simon, who landed next to me, frantically started covering us up with the foul-smelling fertilizer until we were buried. Between the horrible smell and the jolting movement of the truck as it sped off, I had to bite my lower lip to keep from retching. But the good news was that I couldn't hear any sirens following us and after a few long, tense minutes I dug myself out enough to breathe in some fresh air and to take a peak behind us. No police cars. We'd gotten away. Suddenly the fertilizer smelled as sweet as the finest French perfume.

ONZE

AN HOUR LATER, the truck made its next stop at a nursery and the driver went inside. Simon and I scrambled out of the back and shook the fertilizer out of our clothes and hair. We reeked. I smelled so bad I could hardly stand myself. Simon burst out laughing when he saw the look on my face.

"It's not so bad. I've smelled worse," he said.

"You've smelled worse or you've *smelled* worse?"

"Both, actually," he replied with mock seriousness. I couldn't help myself. I laughed. "Remind me to tell you about working undercover at a sewage treatment plant."

"Any idea where we are and what we do next? We seem to have worn out our welcome everyplace we've been so far. And we're still no closer to finding that crucifix."

"No thanks to your precious Monsieur Marcel. I knew we shouldn't have trusted that bastard! There was something pissy about him all along."

"Pissy?" I sighed. "What about him is *fishy*, Simon?"

"Something about Marcel stinks worse than we do, Maya. How else do you explain the police showing up at his place?"

"First of all, just because he's in debt doesn't automatically make him some kind of geriatric assassin. Secondly, how do you know the neighbors didn't call the cops on us with all the noise we were making last night? Thirdly, why call the cops this morning? We were there all night long. Why not call them last night if that was his intention? It doesn't make sense. Something must have happened to him."

"Makes perfect sense to me," Simon mumbled under his breath.

"Don't hold back on my account!"

"All I'm saying is that Garland could have offered Marcel a deal, a cut of the proceeds from the sale of the book, in exchange for getting rid of the remaining members of the society."

We glared at each other, neither of us giving an inch, until a woman out walking her dog glanced nervously at us and pulled her dog close.

"Look," I whispered. "I stink and I'm starving. What are you going to do about it? 'Cause we can't stand here all day. We've got a crucifix to find and a seven o'clock deadline to make!"

He gave me a sly smile that I didn't like one little bit. "Our luck hasn't run out just yet. There's still one more place we can go."

SIMON'S GODDAUGHTER, Phoebe Samuelson—a.k.a. Francoise the teenaged hacker—lived with her clothing-designer mother, Claire, in a luxury apartment just off the Boulevard Saint-Germain in the fashionable section of St-Germaine-des-Prés in the 6th *arrondissement*. When she opened the door and saw Simon, her face lit up with delight. That is, until she caught sight of me and caught a whiff of the both of us.

"Eew! You guys smell like you rolled in dog crap!" She clamped both hands over her nose and I could see each one of her short fingernails was painted a different color, as were her toenails. She was wearing plaid pajama bottoms and a white Abercrombie T-shirt.

"It's like 6:30 in the morning. What are you doing here?" She ran her fingers through her tangled wavy hair and shifted self-consciously from foot to foot.

"It's good to see you, too, Francoise." Simon ruffled the girl's hair and stepped inside without being invited. "Is your *maman* at home?"

The girl rolled her eyes. "Are you kidding? You know she's not here. Like when is she ever at home? She's in London 'til Sunday getting ready for the spring line, remember?"

"Fabulous." Simon rubbed his dirty hands together. "We are in desperate need of your help. How would you like to harbor a couple of fugitives?"

Francoise flushed with pleasure and grinned. I could see she was wearing a retainer. It was my turn to roll my eyes.

AFTER TAKING A LONG, hot shower and scrubbing my skin practically raw with the absent Claire Samuelson's Chanel body wash, I wrapped myself in her thick black velour robe and wandered through the ultramodern apartment. It was minimally decorated in blacks, tans and reds. Abstract art hung on the walls. The large floor-to-ceiling windows provided spectacular views of the Seine and the Eiffel Tower.

I followed laughter up a set of steps into a large open kitchen overlooking the living room. Francoise and Simon were sitting around a big, round, block-glass island, feasting on fruit, pastries, cheese, ham, baguettes and hot chocolate. Simon's hair was wet from his own shower. He was once again clean-shaven. He

had changed clothes and wore faded jeans and a black
T-shirt that fit him perfectly. Where had he gotten
them?

"You guys sure sound like you're having fun," I commented. There was a small plasma-screen TV turned to
MTV France mounted on the stainless steel refrigerator
door.

"And you sure smell a lot better," commented Simon.
He tossed me a pear and winked at Francoise who dis-
solved into a fit of giggling.

Their obvious ease with each other made me feel like
an intruder. Francoise filled in Simon on everything
from her lame school, to her recent vacation to Majorca
with her lame cousin Steffie and their upcoming concert date. She slid the cheese and ham in my direction—
with the distain only a teenaged girl could muster—in
one of the few acknowledgments of my presence that
I'd received from her so far. While she talked a mile a
minute, she unashamedly stuffed herself with grapes
and veggie chips.

The kid obviously loved spending time with Simon.
As I listened to them talk and joke, I couldn't help but
be impressed at how comfortable Simon was in his role
as surrogate father. I wished I could join in their fun.
But I was too worried about Monsieur Marcel. What
could have happened to him? Was he dead? Was he
the one who reported us to the police? Could Simon
be right? Was he a killer? The clock on the microwave
read 7:18. We had roughly thirteen hours left to find out
where Juliet hid the crucifix. And what would happen
if we couldn't find it? What would Garland do?

Thwack!

A grape bounced off my forehead. Francoise burst out laughing.

"I've been talking to you for two minutes. Where did you go?" Simon smiled and revealed a handful of grapes.

"What do you want?" I lobbed a strawberry at him and missed, eliciting more laughter from Francoise.

"What is it with you Americans and your guns?" He gestured toward the TV.

MTV news was on and from what I could deduce, since I understood very little of what was being said, some American athlete-turned-action-star named Chaz Chandler had been arrested at JFK Airport trying to get through security with a gun hidden in his clothing.

"How would I know? I don't own a gun and I'm not the spokesperson for America or idiot actors. And by the way, the only time I've ever been shot at in my life was right here in good old Paris, France."

"Not by a Frenchman. By one of your fellow gun-happy Americans."

"Then I suggest you ask Vincent Garland when we see him tonight."

"Asking that bastard anything is the last thing I'm planning to do." His voice dripped ice.

He'd told me that night in Luc's apartment about not being sure what he'd do when he found out who killed his brother. But I'd hoped he realized we needed Garland alive. I wasn't so sure now. And I didn't feel like talking about it in front of a thirteen-year-old. I grabbed a bunch of green grapes and went to sit on a chaise by the living room window. Minutes later, Francoise padded after me and sat.

"My mom's got gobs of clothes she's never worn.

You're welcome to them if you want. She'll never miss them."

"Thanks."

"They're on a rack in the back of her closet." She got up and headed back into the kitchen and seconds later was laughing with Simon.

Claire Samuelson's closet was bigger than my living room. It was filled with rack after rack of clothing and shoes, all organized by type, season and color. One hundred odd purses and evening bags hung on hooks on the walls. Stacks of sweaters filled the upper shelves. A 360-degree mirror and a vanity table occupied their own alcove. At the back of the closet I discovered a rack of clothes that still had their price tags. I picked out a pair of rich chocolate-brown suede jeans that cost more than I earn in a month and a clingy dark-gold V-neck sweater. My shoes were toast. So I helped myself to a pair of low-heeled ankle boots that were a little loose but fit fine with a pair of thick socks.

"You look nice." Francoise was leaning against the inside of the closet door, watching me intently.

"Your mom has great taste in clothes."

"If you want a scrunchy or a scarf for your hair, I've got some on my desk in my room. It's down the hall."

"Thanks." She left and I wondered why she was suddenly being so nice to me. In the end, I chalked it up to teenage moodiness.

As I began to close the closet door a flash of red caught my eye. I lifted up the hanger. It was a dress much like the one Juliet wore the day she died. Brian and Jarrod swore the dress was a designer knock-off. But Juliet had written in her journal about buying a new red Dior dress. Why would she have written that unless the dress had been a real Dior? People don't lie in their journals. If the dress was real, what had been up with the lopsided, clumsily sewn hem Brian and Jarrod had noticed? Then the image of Chaz Chandler, the actor arrested for trying to board a plane with a gun hidden in his clothes, flashed into my mind and I grinned. I knew where Juliet had hidden the crucifix. I had to tell Simon.

On my way back to the kitchen, I came across Francoise's bedroom. I glanced inside at the rumpled, unmade bed and posters of anime characters on the walls. I wasn't surprised by the massive state-of-the-art computer with a 27-inch computer screen but there was something sitting on the desk that made me stop dead in my tracks. Sitting on a shelf next to a collection of DVDs was a framed photo of Francoise, Simon and a gorgeous woman who looked like an older, blond version of Francoise. The woman's arms were wrapped around Simon's waist. Now I knew why a vegan's fridge had meat and cheese in it and the clothes Simon had on fit so well. The food was for him and the clothes were his. He must keep clothes and a razor here because he and Claire Samuelson were a couple.

"She's really beautiful, isn't she?" came Francoise's voice from behind me.

"Very." My throat was suddenly dry.

"They make a cute couple, huh?"

I finally understood. She'd wanted me to see this picture. Francoise thought I was infringing on her mother's territory. I was sick and it took everything in me to retain my composure. How could I be so stupid…again! Well, she and her mother had nothing to worry about from me. Simon and his wandering dick weren't my problem. After tonight, crucifix or no crucifix, I was getting the hell out of Paris and not looking back.

"When this is over, I'll make sure to get your mom's clothes back to her," I said as I walked passed her.

"No big deal. Like I said, she'll never wear them. Those are her fat clothes. She's a size two now."

I ignored the comment. Simon was still in the kitchen nursing an espresso. I sat across from him and could barely look him in the eyes. But there was no time to dwell on him and Claire. It was time to get it together.

"Guess where I think Juliet hid the crucifix?"

I explained about the dress and Simon grabbed me and bent to kiss me. I pushed him away. He looked bewildered but didn't comment.

"Where is the dress now?"

I shrugged. "She wasn't wearing it when I found her. I guess the police took it. It's probably with the rest of the stuff they took from our hotel room."

"You okay? You seem a little off. You know I was just teasing you about the guns, right?"

I gave him a tight, fake smile. "Yeah, I know. I'm just tired."

"I'm sorry. We didn't get a lot of sleep last night, did we?" he whispered conspiratorially.

I wanted to scream and slam my fist into his handsome, arrogant face. Not that I had a right to be upset. No promises had been made. No words of love had been spoken. He hadn't taken anything from me that I hadn't freely given. And, yeah, I'd done my share of taking, too. But I wouldn't have let things go so far if I had known he was involved.

"Maya?" Simon waved his hand in my face to get my attention.

"Sorry, what did you say?"

"I said if Juliet wasn't wearing the dress when she was killed, then her things were probably taken to the evidence room at the DCPJ."

"Can your police contact help us?"

Simon leaned against the counter and put his hands in his jeans pockets. "My contact is only a file clerk. She doesn't have access to the evidence room and if she got caught, she'd get fired."

She. I should have known it was woman. Otherwise, Simon wouldn't be able to work his considerable charm to get what he wanted. I bet all his contacts were women.

"How do we find out if the dress is even there if she can't help us?"

"You guys are so pathetic," came Francoise's voice from the living room. "Have you forgotten just who I am and what I can do?"

We went into the living room to find her sitting on the floor in front of the red leather couch with a black laptop perched on top of the frosted glass coffee table. By the time we joined her, her fingers were already flying across the keyboard as codes and symbols flashed up and down the screen. I recognized the DCPJ logo in the background. She was hacking onto their system. My hand involuntarily flew to my mouth. Simon gave me a look that told me now was not the time to get on my high horse. We needed to find that dress. I kept my mouth shut.

"Crap!" exclaimed Francoise. Her brow was creased in concentration.

"What?" Simon scooted forward to get a better look at the screen.

"They've put in a new security system since I was last in here."

"You've done this before?"

"Lots of times," said Simon proudly.

I bit my tongue.

"No biggie. I'll just go through the back door. It'll just take a little bit longer, that's all."

"And how do you do that?" I asked.

"Any site with a search feature has a back-end database to handle the queries. All I do is enter a bogus search in order to generate an error message. Then I use the error code to get the system information and take it from there. Don't worry," she said, glancing at me, "I'm strictly white hat."

"White what?"

"White hat. It means I'm a hacker with ethics. I only look. I'm no cyber terrorist."

"Good to know," I said dryly, thinking it sounded like breaking into someone's house and only *looking* at all their stuff.

We watched her do her thing for about fifteen minutes before she pumped a fist in the air in victory.

"Yes! I'm in!" She turned and gave Simon a high five. "What am I looking for?"

"Look for Juliet Rice's case file," instructed Simon. "We need a list of all the items collected from her crime scene."

Her fingers flew and it only took seconds for Juliet's name to pop up on the screen along with folder icons labeled: *dossier de cas, Notation d'évidence, photographies de scène du crime*.

"Try the second file folder," said Simon.

The folder labeled *Notation d'évidence* contained the

log of evidence taken from the hotel, as well as photos of each item. But as we searched through the list and the photos we discovered a big problem.

"I don't understand. I know she had that red dress in the hotel room. Why isn't it listed here?" I said. We'd gone through every item on the list and every picture that had been taken of each item from the scene. No red dress had been listed as having been taken from the hotel room. In fact, nothing red in color had been taken from the room.

"Let's look at the crime scene photos." Simon reached over Francoise's head, grabbing the laptop from the table and setting it on his lap.

"Hey! What are you doing?" the girl yelped, but Simon held the laptop out of her reach.

"Sorry, *cherie*. No way on earth am I letting you look at grisly crime scene photos. It'll stunt your growth and your *maman* would kill me."

"She'll only find out if I tell her," she protested before adding, "And why am I old enough to get you this info but not old enough to look?"

"Because life is not fair and it's time you got ready for school," Simon told her as he clicked through the crime scene photos.

"Hypocrite!" Francoise got up and stalked off in a huff, leaving us alone to look at the pictures.

Looking at the pictures of my hotel room was like a kick in the gut. They took me back to the night I'd found Juliet's body. Everything was the same as I'd remembered it, the crooked mattresses, clothes all over the floor, emptied suitcases. There was a shot of the open bathroom door that looked to have been taken from across the room that made me flinch at the memory of the sight and smell of Juliet's body stuffed into the shower. I turned away when he clicked on the photos of Juliet's body.

"*Merde,*" Simon exclaimed softly after opening the first picture. He looked at me, concerned, his finger poised on the touch pad.

"I'm okay. Go ahead."

Finally, after searching through two-thirds of the pictures, I spotted what looked like something red balled up on the floor and partially hidden under Juliet's bed.

"I think that might be it," I said, sitting up straight and pointing at the screen. I didn't bring anything red to Paris. That had to be the dress.

"Why isn't it in the evidence log? It was clearly at the scene. Unless…" Simon closed out the folder and went back to the folder with the evidence log. Jerome Hubert had logged and photographed the evidence.

"You think this Hubert guy would know what happened to the dress?" I asked.

"Jerome Hubert was in charge of the evidence, so I think he should know, don't you?"

"But why steal a dress from a crime scene?"

Simon shrugged. "Maybe he sold it or gave it to his wife."

Before I could reply, the image of a white silk gown flashed in my mind and the ghost who'd been haunting my dreams whispered in my ear with icy breath. *"It was not a gown for a wife. This was a gown for a mistress.…"*

Before I could process anything, Francoise emerged from her bedroom dressed in her school uniform, with her backpack slung over her shoulder. She tossed us a venomous look as she headed toward the front door. I'd bet money she was more pissed at being treated like a child in front of me than in not being allowed to look at the pictures.

"Arrêt!" commanded Simon. Francoise ignored him and kept walking. *"Arrêt, s'il vous plaît,"* he said a little more gently. Francoise stopped and shifted impatiently from foot to foot but didn't turn around.

Simon went over to the sulky girl and pulled her into a tight hug. Francoise resisted until Simon began tickling her.

"Jerk." She laughed and pushed him away. "And you owe me—again. Big-time." She pulled a set of keys on a Hello Kitty key chain from her backpack and handed them to Simon.

"I am forever in your debt, *mademoiselle.*" Simon bowed. Francoise rolled her eyes, but I could tell she was pleased.

Simon had been forgiven but the hard look she gave me before walking out the door told me that no amount of tickling would make her a fan of mine.

"She adores you, Simon. Where's her dad?"

"He died when she was three. A brain tumor." Simon shoved Francoise's keys into his pocket and rejoined me on the couch.

"Was he a good friend?"

"The best," he said, smiling softly. "I met Marty Samuelson at Columbia University when I did a study-abroad program in college. My English wasn't so good back then and Marty was my tutor. He was a funny guy and really smart. But we had a big fight about a month or so before it was time for me to return to Paris. We never spoke again. Then six years later I got a letter from his lawyer informing me he'd died. His last wish was for me to be Phoebe's godfather."

"That's so sweet, Simon. He must have thought a lot of you, too."

"I just wished he'd have asked me himself. I would have said yes in a heartbeat."

Simon's eyes held the same pain they had when he'd talked about his late wife. I had the urge to hug him but reminded myself about that photo with Francoise's mother and him. It was only natural that he and Claire had grown close. How would she feel knowing I'd slept with her man and was wearing her clothes? Probably exactly the way I had when I found out Ben was sleeping with his ex. And speaking of cheating…

"Look, I don't know if this Jerome Hubert is married. But if he is, I doubt he gave Juliet's dress to his wife," I said with certainty. "He's either got a girlfriend or a mistress he's trying to impress."

"What makes you think so?"

"He's an evidence tech, Simon. A wife would know he couldn't afford to buy her designer clothes. She'd figure out where it came from. But a mistress wouldn't care." This explanation was better than telling him about my dream.

Simon nodded in agreement. "It does make sense."

"But how are we going to talk to Jerome Hubert? We can't go to the DCPJ."

"If we're lucky we won't have to." Simon grabbed the cordless phone from the end table and started dialing. "Keep your fingers crossed," he told me, then asked whoever answered for Jerome Hubert.

I listened as he conducted a terse conversation in

French. After ten minutes, he hung up and rubbed his hands together in excitement.

"Monsieur Hubert is going to come to us."

THE SKY THREATENED TO ERUPT with rain at any moment. Simon and I sat in the back booth of an Indian restaurant about two blocks from Francoise's apartment. No one gave us a second glance when we walked in. The murders of Oliver and Sylvie Renard had bumped Simon and me from the front page of the papers. But I'd put on the red horn-rimmed glasses and piled my still-damp hair under one of Claire Samuelson's tweed hats just in case. Simon wore a black woolen scarf wrapped around his neck, partially obscuring the lower half of his face.

"What makes you so sure he's going to show up?"

"He'll show. He must be ready to crap his pants after what I told him on the phone."

To test my theory, Simon had called Jerome Hubert at work and told him he was a private eye hired by his wife and he would be willing to sell him the info he'd uncovered about his affair instead of turning it over to his wife.

"I can't believe he agreed to meet."

He laughed. "Trust me. He doesn't want his dirty little secret getting back to his wife. He'll do whatever it takes to keep living his double life."

It takes a cheat to know a cheat, I thought as I sipped my chai. A bell above the door chimed, announcing Monsieur Hubert's arrival. He was a chubby-cheeked man of about forty, with slightly bulging brown eyes that darted nervously around the room. Simon put up a hand and waved him over.

"Have a seat, *monsieur.*"

"Qui est ceci?" He gestured toward me instead of sitting. He wanted to know who I was; that much I understood.

"My partner, *monsieur.* Don't worry. She is the soul of discretion. And in deference to her we shall speak English, *d'accord?*"

I nodded and smiled. Hubert stuffed himself into the other side of the booth and looked around again. Sweat beaded his upper lip.

"What is this about? Did Jacqueline really hire you?" he asked in a hushed tone. His accent was so thick I could barely understand him.

"I'm afraid so, Monsieur Hubert," replied Simon with a grave seriousness that almost made me laugh.

"How did she find out? I've been so discreet."

"She's been suspicious for a while. But it was the red dress that was the final straw," I answered before Simon could.

"You see, she saw the dress and thought it was for her. When you didn't give it to her she must have realized what was going on," concluded Simon, not missing a beat.

Hubert looked confused. "But I never even brought the dress home. I took it straight from work to my girlfriend Dominique's. How could my wife have seen it?"

Simon, you idiot! Of course he wouldn't have taken the dress home. We'd be screwed if he realized we were lying.

"You gave your girlfriend a dress from your job? Aren't you a crime scene technician? You gave her a dead woman's dress?" I quickly asked to deflect any further suspicion, though my disgust was real.

Hubert started sweating even more profusely. He pulled at the neck of his too-tight sweater and let out a nervous laugh. "What does a dead woman need with a Dior dress? She'll never wear it again. Why not let someone else enjoy it? Where is the harm in it?"

"Because it could all come out in the divorce, *monsieur*. At the very least you could lose your job if anyone found out you've been stealing from crime scenes," said Simon.

"Divorce!" Hubert sputtered. "I—it—it was only just this one time. I've never taken anything before. What do I do?"

"You need to get that dress back," I said.

"I can't," he whispered. "Dominique loves that dress. She's wearing it to a party tonight. If I take it back, I could lose her." He looked close to tears. I wanted to slap him.

"You'll lose a lot more than your girlfriend if you don't get that dress back," I said. Simon looked over at me and I could tell by the look in his eye what he was about to do.

"Monsieur Hubert, as I mentioned on the phone, I'm willing to withhold the evidence I've compiled against you for a fee. I'd also be willing—for another fee—to get the dress back for you. That way neither your wife, your job, or your girlfriend will be any the wiser."

"I'm not a rich man. How much are we talking?"

"Why don't we talk price *after* I've retrieved the dress."

"And you won't say anything to Jacqueline?"

"Not a word," promised Simon.

Hubert pulled a large ring of keys out of his pants pocket and pulled off a key. He slid it across the table at

Simon. "She lives in the 10th at 40 Boulevard de Strasbourg. She's a beautician. She lives above her salon. But you already know that, don't you?"

Simon nodded and grabbed the key. "We'll meet back here tomorrow at the same time?"

Jerome Hubert nodded then got up. He to started to walk away but suddenly turned back looking much more relaxed and confident. "Make it look like a robbery, eh? I don't want her to know I've had anything to do with this."

"Don't worry, Monsieur Hubert," I told him with a smile. "We'll take care of everything."

DOUZE

"I BET THAT ass alone was enough to make Jerome Hubert lose his religion," mused Simon as we paused in the doorway of Gloire de Couronnement—Crowning Glory—Dominique's beauty shop. Jerome Hubert's mistress was petite and curvy with smooth, cocoa-brown skin and long, thin braids that fell to her waist like silken threads.

"Is that so?" I bristled. "Never trust a big butt and a smile, huh? Unbelievable. Men!" I shook my head in disgust. Simon had me so pissed off I was quoting song lyrics.

"Huh? That's not what I meant," protested Simon, managing to look both angry and confused. "What is with you? You've been moody all morning."

"Nothing!" I snapped. "What's the plan?"

"The plan is for one of us to watch Dominique while the other searches her apartment for the dress."

"And I guess I know who's going to be doing what?"

"Meaning?"

"Meaning, I'm the one who's going to be stuck down here keeping watch and risking being recognized, while you go look for a dress you've never seen before."

He took a deep breath like he was counting to ten. "You're forgetting that I, too, saw Juliet wearing that red dress the day she died. And wouldn't it be more reasonable for you to sit down here than me? No one is going to believe I need *my* hair done," he replied stiffly.

"Fine," I said, matching his tone. I knew I was being bitchy and unreasonable but couldn't help myself.

"I'm not sure if there is another entrance to the apartment from in here. So if you lose sight of her for longer than five minutes, call me, *d'accord?*"

"Yeah, right."

After handing me one of the two disposable cell phones he'd bought from a street vendor along the way, he left quickly without a backward glance. I walked up to the black lacquered reception desk. The receptionist, an African woman with thick braids wound round her head like a beehive, welcomed me with a gap-toothed smile.

"Bonjour, madame. Avez-vous un rendez-vous?"

"Parlez-vous Anglais?"

"But of course, *madame.* How may I assist you?"

"Do you take walk-ins?"

"Do you have a lot of hair, *madame?*"

Before I could answer, the receptionist pulled off my tweed hat. My hair sprang out as though I had stuck my finger in a light socket. She giggled—as did the other women in the waiting room.

"We do take walk-in appointments. But with so much hair I'm afraid it may be some time before we have a stylist with enough available time."

Perfect, I didn't really need an appointment. I had no money and Simon had used the last of his on the cell phones. I just needed to be able to keep an eye on Dominique.

"I can wait, *merci.*" After giving her a fake name, I put my hat back on and went to sit in the waiting room.

Ten minutes had passed since Simon left and I was getting antsy. How long could it take to find a red dress? Another ten minutes went by and I flipped through a copy of French *Vogue*.

"*Bonjour, madame*. I am Dominique Barbeau. What can we do for you today?" Jerome Hubert's girlfriend stood over me. She had a high-pitched singsong voice and a beautiful smile. There was a small diamond stud in her left nostril. She smelled of Shalimar perfume. I shook the hand she offered me.

"Uh…um…I'm…still deciding."

"You'll never find a style in there." She laughed and gestured to the magazine on my lap. "I've got some new hair magazines in my apartment. I'll just run up and get them for you."

"No!" I jumped up to block her path. Everyone in the waiting room stopped what they were doing. Dominique took a step back and laughed nervously.

"I mean I have decided what I'd like. I don't need to see any more magazines. I'm ready." My glasses slipped down my nose. I pushed them up and pulled down the hat farther on my forehead.

"*Bon*, take my chair, *s'il vous plaît*."

This wasn't the way this was supposed to go. When she found out I had no money to pay her, she was going to call the cops and I would be toast. Where the hell was Simon? I sat in a plush black leather stylist's chair in front of a station with a large gilded mirror. Dominique took off my hat and ran a large-toothed comb through my hair.

"Such nice, thick hair. Have you had it braided before?"

"No."

"Then I'm honored to be the first. How would you like it?"

"I don't want anything too elaborate."

"How about I cornrow the front halfway back and leave the rest loose, *d'accord?*"

"Fabulous." I was getting really worried and kept checking my phone every few minutes.

"Are you expecting a call?"

"My boyfriend. He was supposed to be meeting me here and he's late as usual. You know how men are. I could just kill him," I said through gritted teeth. Dominique laughed.

"My man is always late. He works two jobs. But he's so sweet to me, I hardly care. Just the other day, he gave me the most elegant Dior dress. He's always giving me things." I sat up straighter in the chair.

"Really? He sounds like a keeper." I tried to keep the sarcasm out of my voice. This poor woman must not have a clue that her man's other job was being married to someone else.

"*Oui.* And guess what I found hidden in the hem of the dress?"

I was too afraid to ask. Instead, I smiled and shrugged. Dominique put down the comb and pulled out a thin black silk cord from inside her suit jacket. I was expecting to see a gold crucifix dangling from it. It wasn't a crucifix. It was a small gold key. I leaned forward to get a better look.

"That's a key." Tears of frustration welled up in my eyes. "You found a key in the hem of the dress?"

"I thought it was strange, too. But when I asked Jerome—my boyfriend—guess what he told me?"

"I can't imagine," I replied miserably as I blinked the tears away.

"He said it was the key to his heart."

"How romantic." Shit! We weren't home free after all. Instead, we had another damned puzzle piece and we were running out of time.

Dominique excused herself to sign for a delivery when my phone finally rang.

"I found the dress but there was nothing in the hem," he said in a breathless rush.

"That's because she found it and is wearing it around her neck."

"She's wearing the crucifix?"

"The crucifix wasn't in the hem, Simon. It was a key." He swore.

"Are you sure?"

"I know a key when I see one."

"Can you get it from her?"

"Didn't you hear me? It's. Around. Her. Neck."

"Think of something. We need that key!" He hung up on me.

"Everything okay?" came Dominique's melodic voice from behind me. She put her fingers in my hair and began to lightly message my scalp.

"Just fine."

Forty-five minutes later, she was finished and I still had no idea how I was going to get the key or pay this woman for doing my hair.

"How do you like it? I think it suits you."

She handed me a large mirror and I had to agree. My hair looked fierce. It hung to my shoulders like a sleek, glossy curtain. Dominique had woven bits of shiny gold ribbon into the cornrows in front. It matched my sweater perfectly. I wasn't used to having my hair pulled back from my forehead. But it looked great.

"Wow. It's beautiful. *Merci!*" Simon was looking through the shop's large picture window, impatiently pointing at his watch while Dominique smiled at me. The key was hanging around her neck glinting under the fluorescent lighting a mere arm's length away.

What the hell? I was already a fugitive. What was one more offense? Mentally promising I'd mail the key back with money and an apology when we were done with it, I reached over and yanked it from around her neck and ran like hell.

"WHAT COULD THIS BE a key to?" I asked.

Simon and I were back in Francoise's mother's apartment. The key in question, small, round and stamped with the number 419, was lying in the center of the kitchen island, mocking us. It wasn't a car key or an apartment key and it was too big to be a luggage key.

"It sure as hell isn't the key to that bastard Jerome Hubert's heart," said Simon. I laughed.

We were silent for a long time, each lost in our own thoughts.

"You were the one who followed Juliet for two weeks. Do you remember seeing her go anyplace where she could use a key like this?"

"I only tracked her from hotel to hotel. I didn't follow her every move."

"That's a start. What hotels did she stay at?"

"She started out at the Ritz-Carlton then moved to the Westin, then the Sofitel, and finally the Bienvenue."

"Maybe this is a key to a safe deposit box at one of those hotels," I said excitedly. Simon shook his head.

"Wouldn't they have given her whatever she'd kept in the box and made her turn in the key when she checked out?"

"Well, yeah, *if* she checked out. She could have been so scared of Garland that she just took off without bothering to check out."

"And have the hotel confiscate the crucifix when she left without it, or risk some light-fingered hotel employee stealing it? I don't think so. I think this key is to a secure location that she'd be able to easily access."

He had a point, but before I could say anything we heard the front door open. Was Claire Samuelson home early from London? Before we could react, Francoise came flying up the kitchen steps and dumped her backpack on the floor by the fridge.

"Why are you looking at me like I'm a ghost?" she asked, then grabbed an apple from a basket on the counter, turned on MTV and plopped down next to Simon.

"What are you doing here? Why aren't you in school?" demanded Simon.

"Um, it's like almost three o'clock," Francoise said, looking at Simon like he was crazy. "School's over at 2:30."

It was now 2:47. While we'd been puzzling over the key, time slipped away from us. We now had little more than four hours to track down the crucifix.

"How'd you get in? You gave me your key."

The girl laughed around her mouthful of apple. "I've got at least ten keys to this place. I'm always losing them and having to get a new one made. It drives Mom crazy," she said, leaning forward in her chair. "Crap! Is that my locker key? Where'd you find it?" she asked excitedly, grabbing the small key from the middle of the island and examining it.

"Locker key?" we asked in unison.

"Yeah, I lost mine last week," she said then shook her head. "Oh, this isn't mine." She tossed it back on the table.

"A locker!" I said. "Of course, Simon! Didn't Juliet's journal say she gave a lecture at the Sorbonne back in April during the same trip she met Garland? Maybe she had access to a locker or something in that auditorium she gave her lecture at."

"Only one way to find out," Simon replied with a grin. We got up to go and Francoise grabbed her back-pack and followed us.

"And just where do you think you're going? Don't you have homework?" asked Simon when we got to the door.

"I did it all—and *hellooo!* You guys need me," insisted Francoise, looking at Simon like he was an idiot.

"How?" I asked. Francoise sighed and rolled her eyes.

"You do know the Sorbonne is actually the University of Paris and is divided into thirteen separate universities and that only three of them actually have Sorbonne in their name, right?" She was looking at me.

"No." I was embarrassed not to have known and Francoise knew it. The thirteen-year-old was way too smug for my liking.

"We don't have time for this. But I'm sure Maya appreciated that bit of trivia," said Simon.

"Do you have any idea at which of the three universities this Dr. Rice gave her lecture?" she persisted.

"The Richelieu Auditorium at Paris-Sorbonne University. It was in her journal," Simon replied with a thin smile as he opened the door.

Francoise shut the door and stood in front of it. The girl reached into her cavernous backpack, pulled out a student ID card for Paris-Sorbonne University and waved it at us with a big grin. "You think they're just gonna let you two fugitives wander around the buildings on campus looking for lockers? Besides, there could be lockers in other buildings and they aren't open to visitors. Let me help. If anyone catches me someplace I shouldn't be, all I have to do is say I got lost looking for my prof's office and I have an ID to prove I'm a student. If you two get caught, it's sirens and handcuffs."

She had a good point and at least she wouldn't be hacking into anything.

"Come on." I pushed between them to open the door. "We're wasting time. We'll figure it all out on the way."

The Sorbonne's campus was in the Latin Quarter, a short ten-minute walk from Francoise's apartment. As we walked on the Place de la Sorbonne, a cobblestoned, tree-lined street, that unique college campus vibe enveloped me. It was a mixture of carefree, youthful enthusiasm mingled with timeworn tradition and jaded weariness. It reminded me of home and my own job at Capital. A tidal wave of homesickness hit so hard it made my eyes water.

Francoise stopped at a fountain in front of a large blue domed building, the main entrance to the university.

"Wait here. I'll be right back," she commanded. We watched her disappear through the door. Anxiety gnawed at my stomach the second she was out of sight.

I sat on one of the low walls by the fountain and Simon joined me. I checked my watch. It was 3:27.

"Don't worry. We'll find it." Simon squeezed my shoulder reassuringly, though his wary eyes and tight worry lines etched around his mouth told a different story.

"Do you think it was a good idea to give her the key?" I asked after we'd been waiting for about fifteen minutes. "What if she loses this one, too?"

Simon sighed and stood. "I'll go check on her."

Five minutes passed, then ten with still no sign of either Simon or Francoise. After twenty minutes had gone by, the gnawing sensation in my stomach had turned into full-blown pain.

Where the hell were they? I became aware of a muted beeping sound coming from somewhere close. At first it sounded like an alarm on somebody's watch, but then there was a reddish glow coming from inside my bag. My *bag* was beeping or rather Monsieur Marcel's silver key fob was beeping. I examined the key fob more closely and for the first time noticed how heavy it was. On the back there was a compartment for a small battery.

The key fob beeped to help locate lost keys! Was Monsieur Marcel trying to get my attention? I stood to see if I could see him anywhere—and there, walking toward the main entrance was a short man with the collar of his blazer flipped up around his ears. A beret pulled down over his ears covered most of that distinctive white hair. Something silver glinted in his hand.

"Monsieur Marcel!" I called out. He stopped at the doorway and turned.

His deathly pale face and dark feverish eyes stopped

me in my tracks. He paused and put an index finger to his lips, indicating with a slight jerk of his head that he wanted me to follow him. Then he stepped through the doorway.

"Wait!" And just like Alice following the white rabbit, I hurried after him. I ran to catch up, but he didn't stop to acknowledge me until I grabbed his arm.

"Monsieur? Are you alright? I've been worried. Where the hell have you been?"

Instead of answering, he pulled me inside the building and ducked behind a large pillar.

"We cannot talk here, Madame Sinclair. We must not be seen," he whispered. There was a thin red cut just under his right ear. It looked as if someone had pressed a knife to his throat.

"Did Garland do that to you?" I demanded, pointing to his neck. His only answer was to pull the collar of his blazer up higher and steer me toward a nearby stairwell.

"I barely got away with my life. I've been hiding out down here in my old office since last night. I was too afraid to go back to my apartment for fear of leading my attacker to you and Monsieur Girard. You two are in grave danger."

"Did you tell the police where we were?"

"Please forgive me." He stopped abruptly at the bottom of the steps and gave me a remorseful look. "It was the only way I could think to keep you safe from that lunatic. Better in jail than dead."

"You could have just called to warn us," I pointed out.

He didn't reply. We'd arrived at an age-scarred office

door and he fumbled with the lock. Once it was unlocked, he held the door open.

"I didn't realize you taught here, *monsieur*."

"For nearly forty years. I retired just this past June," he said, unable to mask his pride.

He flipped a switch and the room was bathed in dim yellow light. The small office was filled with mismatched furniture. It smelled like a moldy basement. A blanket was balled up in a leather recliner behind his desk. He must have slept there the night before.

"They let you hold on to your office?"

"My replacement has a nice new office upstairs. Soon this office will be used for storage." He pulled out a handkerchief and took off his glasses, cleaning them with trembling fingers.

"What happened last night?" I sat on a hard wooden chair in front of the desk.

"I'd just left work and was heading home when I was grabbed from behind and pulled into an alley. Something sharp at my neck pressed into my skin. I knew I was about to die. Then I remembered the penknife in my pocket and plunged it into my attacker's thigh and ran. This was the safest place I could think to come."

"Why didn't you call us?"

"No phone." He pointed toward an empty phone jack in the wall. "I was in such a hurry to get home last night I forgot my cell phone at work. I was so worried that something terrible might happen to you, I called the police first thing this morning. I was too scared to look for a phone last night. Forgive me."

His red-rimmed eyes filled with tears and I reached out and grabbed his hand.

"There's nothing to forgive. I'm just glad you're

safe." He smiled at me and squeezed my hand. "Did you get a good look at Garland? Could you identify him in a police lineup?"

Monsieur Marcel looked confused and shook his head vigorously. "I have no idea who you are talking about, Madame Sinclair," he said stiffly. His face colored slightly. "I know who attacked me. It was *la petite nonne.*"

I didn't like the wild look in the old man's eyes one bit. He was about to board the train to Crazy Town. I needed to pull him back before the train left the station.

"*La petite nonne?* Who the hell is that?"

"Why the little nun, of course," he replied.

TREIZE

"A NUN ATTACKED you?" The train left the station.

"She's very angry about what was taken from her," replied Monsieur Marcel, leaning close to me. He was so close I could smell coffee on his stale breath and see the large pores in his nose.

"You mean the Moret Crucifix?" I assumed he was talking about the Black Nun of Moret.

He nodded. His eyes were as big as saucers.

Poor man. The death of his friends Drs. Hewitt and Renard must have pushed him right over the edge. If that were the case, he'd be no help at all to Simon and me when it came to reporting Garland's attack on him. And speaking of Simon, he was probably wondering where I was. I jumped up and checked my watch. It was 4:30.

"Where are you going? You can't leave now! She's out there…waiting! She'll kill us both!" The old man grabbed my arm. His face turned bright crimson and he started to gasp for breath.

"*Monsieur,* calm down! Take a breath. It's okay. There's no nun out there. I promise. You're coming with me. You'll be safe with us, with Simon and me."

"Where is Monsieur Girard?"

"Waiting for me in the Place de la Sorbonne. Come on. Let's go."

I guided him toward the office door, but he wheezed

loudly and sank to his knees. He clutched at this throat like he couldn't breathe.

"Oh my God! Are you okay?" I knelt down next to him.

He pointed frantically to something behind me. A blue-and-white plastic asthma inhaler sat on top of a filing cabinet. I ran to retrieve it. Monsieur Marcel jammed the mouthpiece into his mouth and pressed down on the canister. After a minute, his breathing slowed down and his color returned to normal. I helped him to his feet.

"I've had asthma since I was a boy working in my family's *boulangerie.* It went away when I stopped working there, but it came back a few years ago."

"Is there anything else I can get you, *monsieur,* because we really need to get out of here." A sense of urgency tugged at me. Simon must be panicked by now. He probably thought Garland had me.

"My briefcase is in the closet over there. Could you get it for me, *s'il vous plaît?*"

Anxious to get back to Simon, I rushed over to the small closet in the corner of the room and opened the door. The feel of hands on the small of my back made me realize my mistake. Monsieur Marcel pushed me into the closet and slammed the door shut. A key turned in the lock. The crazy old bastard had locked me in. I jiggled the handle and pounded on the door.

"What are you doing? Open this door! Monsieur Marcel! Are you out there? Let me out!"

I stopped pounding and pressed my ear to the door. I could hear the old man's breathing. It was pitch-black in the closet, but a strip of light shone from a gap at the bottom of the door. I got on the floor and looked through the gap. Marcel stood right outside the door.

"I know you're still there! Let me out right now!" I gave the door a savage kick and it rattled in its frame but didn't open.

"This is for your own good, Evalyn. I assure you *la petite nonne* is out there. Somebody has to stop her. Too many people have died already. But I can keep you safe."

Evalyn? He thought I was Dr. Hewitt. He'd truly lost his mind. "Monsieur Marcel," I said in a calmer voice that I hoped would appeal to what sense he may have left. "Please let me out. I'm not Evalyn. I'm Maya, re-member? Maya Sinclair? I promise not to leave this office but I need you to let me out. Let me out now!" I screamed.

"Please don't strain your vocal cords by yelling, Evalyn. No one will hear you. As I've already told you, all the new faculty offices are upstairs now. No one comes down here anymore."

"Monsieur Marcel!"

The only answer was the sound of the office door slamming shut. I checked under the door. The light was out. The office was dark and empty. I was alone. To make matters worse, my cell phone was ringing in my bag, which was—of course, on the other side of the door. It couldn't be anyone but Simon calling. Had he and Francoise found the locker and the crucifix? I had to get out.

I felt around on the wall for a light switch and came up empty. Feeling above my head, my fingers encoun-tered a string hanging from the ceiling. After pulling it, the small closet was illuminated with light from a single, naked bulb. The closet walls were lined with shelves of boxes and old books. An ancient manual typewriter sat on the top shelf alongside an old Hewlett Packer computer. I rifled through boxes filled with paper, notebooks and manila folders. There was nothing to use to pick the lock or to remove the hinges on the door. I spotted a grate big enough for me to climb through over the closet door.

I pulled off the boxes on the shelf and tentatively climbed up on the lowest shelf. It creaked ominously but held my weight. I climbed until I was eye level with the grate. There were no screws or nails holding it in place. But the tight latticework design left no opening for me to pull it out of the wall. I'd need something to wedge under it. I jumped down.

The cell phone started to ring again. I scrambled around the paper and books littering the floor, looking for anything I could use to pry open the grate. Finally, I found a wooden ruler. I shoved it in the back pocket of my pants and started to climb. But this time when I stepped on the lowest shelf, it buckled under my weight and broke in half.

"Shit!" I wiped sweat from my eyes with the sleeve of my sweater and jumped up to grab a higher shelf.

This shelf was sturdier and I was able to put my right knee on the shelf above the broken one and pull myself up. I pulled out the ruler and started digging around the edges of the grate to loosen the paint. The paint was like cement. I took me ten minutes of scraping and digging just to loosen a half-inch section. The shelf I was standing on started to groan in protest. The cell phone started ringing again. I wedged the ruler under the edge of the grate and pressed down. It budged ever so slightly before the ruler snapped in half. I used the jagged half of what was still in my hand to pry the grate another millimeter.

My shoulders ached, but I kept at it for what seemed like an eternity, until I could get a couple of fingers behind the grate. I pulled with all my might, breaking my fingernails to the quick in the process. There was a loud scraping noise as I gave the grate one last pull. It crashed to the floor in a shower of dust, plaster and paint flakes just as the shelf I was standing on broke. There was just enough time to leap and grab hold of the ledge. My feet scrabbled at the closet door until one foot found the doorknob. I used it to boost myself up and used what little upper body strength I had left to pull myself through the opening.

At that point, I didn't care if I broke every bone in my body. I wanted out of that closet. I pushed forward and landed hard on my back. Everything hurt, especially my head. I don't know how long I lay there unmoving, trying to assess if anything was broken. Tentatively, I moved my legs and then my arms.

I pulled myself into a sitting position against the desk and then used the handle of one of the top drawers to pull myself to my feet, and it slid open the in process. Among the debris inside the drawer was a black velvet drawstring pouch. A glint of gold showed through the opening. Curious, I picked up the pouch. Whatever was inside wasn't very big but it was heavy. I pulled out a gold crucifix with a stained-glass scene inlaid in the handle.

The Moret Crucifix was in my hands. It was beautiful. Remembering what Monsieur Marcel had said about the date, I flipped it over. Nothing. This was the forged crucifix Simon's brother, Luc, had made. It was smeared with dried blood, probably Oliver Renard's blood. Sebastian Marcel was either there when Dr. Renard was murdered or sometime afterward. Was Simon right? Did Marcel kill his old friend for Garland?

The cell phone rang again. "Where the hell did you go? I've been calling you for an hour!" Simon was highly aggravated.

I quickly explained, surprised to find myself near tears. Simon swore and his voice softened...but not much.

"I told you we should never have trusted that old man. Are you okay?"

"I'm fine, and you can shove the I-told-you-so's," I snapped. "Did you find the locker?"

"No. And to make matters worse, Claire is home early from London. She finally pulled her head out of her ass long enough to turn on the TV. She saw me on the news and rushed home. When she realized I'd been in her apartment and Francoise was gone, she freaked out and called the police. Francoise is back home with her *maman* being grilled by the cops."

"Now whose turn is it to say I told you so? We shouldn't have involved her."

"I know," he said, sounding tired and utterly defeated. Did he feel bad about his girlfriend calling the police on him? I told him about finding the fake crucifix, which lifted his spirits considerably.

"I don't think Garland would know how to tell the fake crucifix from the real one," I pointed out. "We can just give him the fake one."

"Do you really think he's going to live up to his end of the bargain?"

"I guess we'll find out soon enough. It's not like we have a choice."

"You need to get out of there before the old man comes back. Meet me at the big fountain at Luxembourg Palace in an hour."

TO KILL TIME, I wandered around the Latin Quarter and scraped enough change together to buy a *crème café* but felt too nauseous to drink it. I arrived at Luxembourg Palace and slowly walked around the large central fountain where people were lounging in chairs and kids were floating toy sailboats. We were supposed to meet Garland at the Medici Fountain. Where exactly was it? Was the psycho already there? Feeling antsy, I kept my hand in my bag, fingering the velvet pouch with the fake crucifix in it.

Simon found me and pulled me into an embrace. Needing a hug, I allowed myself to be pulled. Why were the things that felt so damned good so damned bad for you? A hard bulge in the front of his pants made me push away. Something stuck out of the waistband of his jeans, partially hidden by his leather bomber jacket.

"What's that?" I already knew what it was. I was just hoping I was wrong.

"Insurance," he replied, zipping up his jacket to hide the handle of the gun. "If you think we're going to this meeting without some backup, you're crazy. I don't trust Garland as far as the end of my face."

"Face? It's... Never mind," I said, gesturing to the gun instead. "Where'd you get that thing?"

"It's Max's. He gave it to me for protection before we left his place." Thinking back on Max's reluctance at going to jail, I highly doubted it.

"He gave it to you or you took it?"

"Same difference," he replied nonchalantly. "And don't get uptight on me. We don't have time for it."

"Just promise me you won't get us into any more trouble than we're already in. Don't let Garland turn you into someone you're not."

"You've known me for three days, Maya. You have no idea what I'm capable of."

Touché. "Fine. You're right." I threw up my hands in defeat. "Just make sure you don't shoot your balls off, Dirty Harry."

Simon winced. "Are you ready for this?" I pulled out the pouch with the crucifix in it and handed it to him. He gave me a hard kiss in return.

"What was that for?"

"For luck," he said, coloring slightly. We needed a hell of a lot more than kisses.

"Let's go."

The Medici Fountain was in a secluded corner of the Luxembourg Gardens. Surrounded by trees, the large baroque fountain showcased a pair of sleeping lovers. A menacing figure loomed over them. It seemed a fitting backdrop to our meeting with Garland. Under normal circumstances I'd have loved to have spent time reading a book in one of the chairs by the pond or eating lunch in the grass.

"So where is the bastard?" asked Simon once we'd arrived. Save for a lone tourist in sunglasses and a straw hat snapping pictures of the fountain, we were alone.

"I've got a weird feeling about this. It's after seven. Where is he? I thought he was so hot to get his damned hands on this crucifix."

The hairs stood up on the back of my neck. Something was wrong. I leaned against one of the large stone urns that lined the top of the fence while Simon paced. A loud, terrified scream shattered the quiet. The tourist stood pointing at the pond. Her face contorted in horror.

I followed her gaze to something—or rather someone—floating facedown in the pond. There was a small black hole in the man's left temple and his arms were outstretched. A small tattoo of a coiled snake was plainly visible on one arm. My hands flew to my mouth as the woman continued to scream. Several other people who'd been in the vicinity had run over to see what the trouble was.

"It's Garland," I whispered to Simon as I swayed on my feet.

"Come on." Simon grabbed my hand. "Let's get out of here."

Simon pulled me stumbling behind him as he pushed through the throng of people that had begun to gather at the pond. We'd only gotten a few feet when our path was suddenly blocked by two police officers with assault rifles aimed right at us. Simon stopped and put his hands in the air. Officers with guns drawn seemed to come out of nowhere. A familiar voice spoke loudly, first in French then heavily accented English.

"Police! Show us your hands and lie facedown on the ground!" Thierry Bernier screeched. He aimed a rifle at us.

Simon sank to his knees, laid down on the ground and put his hands behind his head like he knew the drill while I stood there with my mouth hanging open, catching flies.

"Now!" Bernier was aiming his rifle at my forehead. I fainted dead away.

I WAS AWARE OF the steady tap of rain against a window-pane. Were there windows in jail cells? I opened my eyes expecting to see concrete and iron bars. Instead, there was a white ceiling and fluorescent light fixtures. Straight ahead was a closed door. There was a rolling hospital tray with a plastic cup and pitcher on my right. I obviously wasn't in jail. When I tried to reach for the pitcher, I discovered my right wrist was handcuffed to the bed rail, meaning I obviously wasn't free, either. A glance through the narrow window of the door to my room revealed a uniformed police officer guarding it. I tugged uselessly at the handcuff as the sound of a flushing toilet made me sit up in bed. Captain Claude Bellange emerged, zipping his pants.

"Ah, Madame Sinclair, you are awake, *bon*."

"What's wrong with me?"

"You've got quite a nasty concussion."

"Where's Simon?" I demanded.

"In jail, of course." Bellange settled his bulk into a chair next to my bed and poured me some water.

"We didn't kill Vincent Garland or that man at Versailles!"

"I know you didn't."

"And Garland is the one who killed Juliet Rice. They were lovers!"

"I know."

"And I'm going to sue the city of Paris if you don't drop all charges!"

Bellange held up his hands. "Calm yourself, *madame,* calm yourself. You've not been charged with any crimes."

"Then why am I handcuffed?"

"Because you are as slippery as an eel and I wasn't

taking chances that you would run off again before giving us a statement." He pulled a small key out of his pocket and unlocked the handcuff.

"Where's your partner?"

"With his wife. It's their anniversary. I'll tell him you asked after him."

That gargoyle had a wife?

"Wait a minute." What he'd just told me had finally sunk in. "Did you just say you know we didn't kill anyone?"

"Were you not listening to a word I've said?" he asked, looking annoyed.

"But…I don't understand."

"The case is closed. Vincent Garland committed suicide. But not before sending a letter to his mother at the U.S. Embassy confessing to not only Juliet Rice's murder, but his girlfriend Shannon Davies, and Bruno Allard, the statue cleaner at Versailles."

"Why?"

Bellange shrugged his thick shoulders. "Dr. Rice discovered he'd killed the unfortunate Madame Davies. She threatened to report him. He killed her and mistakenly thought she'd confided his secret to you. Thinking you knew what he'd done, he set up you and your friend Girard to take the fall. That poor bastard Allard just got in the way. We even found your corkscrew on Garland's body. And the gun he used to kill himself is the same make and model as the one that killed Allard. Apparently, his conscience got the better of him. At least that's what the letter to his *maman* said. Both she and Ambassador Garland identified the handwriting as their son's. And if you don't close your mouth, you'll catch flies."

My mouth snapped shut. I hadn't realized it was open. Had I heard him right? This was all about the murder of Garland's girlfriend? What about the crucifix, the *Aurum Liber* and the Society of Moret? I told Bellange everything that had happened, starting with Garland's attack on me at Versailles. The words came tumbling out in a torrent while Bellange stared at me with one eyebrow raised like I was a nutty relative making a scene at the family reunion. When I was finished, he sat back in the chair and rubbed his chin.

"If I'm not mistaken, you are a librarian. Correct?"

"Yes, why?" I asked warily. If he made a crack about sensible shoes and glasses on a chain, I was going to punch him.

"Madame Sinclair, you have had quite a bump on the head. Perhaps you are confusing what happened to you with a book you read, no? Maybe *The Da Vinci Code?* I know symbols and codes and secret societies are popular with you Americans. I bet you think you-know-who is really buried under the pyramid at the Louvre." He laughed heartily but I wouldn't be distracted.

"Well, what about the other murders—Evalyn Hewitt, Oliver Renard and his daughter, Sylvie? They were all friends of Juliet Rice's. They belonged to the same society." He continued to stare at me blankly. "The Society of Moret," I added. "Didn't Garland confess to killing them as well?"

"Why would he do that, *madame?* They were no threat to Vincent Garland. Why kill them? There is no proof he even knew them. Besides, we've already taken into custody another of Dr. Rice's colleagues for those murders. A Dr. Sebastian Marcel. I believe you know him, as well?"

"He was my tour guide," I said, nodding slowly.

"Either you've a knack for attracting trouble, *madame*. Or you are the most unfortunate tourist I have ever met." Bellange was studying me intently like has was trying to figure out what made me tick.

"You've picked Monsieur Marcel up for murder? On what evidence?"

"You know I can't tell you that, Madame Sinclair. It's an ongoing investigation."

"Was it over money?" I asked, remembering the mountain of bills in Marcel's apartment. The narrowing of Bellange's eyes told me I was right.

"Let us just say friends and money do not mix. And when one friend has much less than the others, and is constantly borrowing money, the resentment and conflict can often build to a murderous level."

Monsieur Marcel was a murderer. I'd been wrong about yet another man! When Simon and I caught up with him at the Galeries Lafayette, he had no idea I'd figured out the symbol on his handkerchief and connected him to Dr. Hewitt and Dr. Renard. He hadn't given it to me on purpose hoping I'd figure it out and come find him. It was all bullshit. He must have been the one who pushed Sylvie Renard down the stairs then finished the job later at the hospital. I didn't want to believe it was true. But I'd seen the blood-smeared fake crucifix with my own eyes. Wait a minute. The crucifix!

"Where's my bag? I can prove what I just told you is true."

Bellange retrieved my bag from the closet and handed it to me. I dumped the entire contents on the bed. Everything that had been in my bag was present and accounted for except the velvet pouch with the forged crucifix. It, like my Eiffel Tower corkscrew before it, was gone. I was suddenly muzzy-headed and confused. It hurt to think. Had I imagined the whole thing? Bellange looked at me with pity. I avoided his eyes as I shoved everything back into the bag.

"Just give it time and I'm sure things will seem much clearer to you in a day or two."

"How did you know Simon and I were in the Luxembourg Gardens?"

"We didn't. Ambassador Garland's wife notified us that her son had a gun and planned to take his own life. We dispatched units to the Luxembourg Gardens on the suggestion of his mother. It was his favorite spot. You and Monsieur Girard were spotted in the vicinity by one of our officers. *Mission accomplie.*" He grinned.

"Okay. If you know we're innocent, then why is Simon in jail?"

"There is the matter of an illegal handgun found in Monsieur Girard's possession at the time of his arrest. Would you happen to know where he got it?"

I shook my head. Bellange laughed. A nurse appeared in the doorway. She gave the captain a hard look and he got to his feet.

"I'll leave you to your rest, Madame Sinclair. But you still need to give me a statement at your earliest convenience."

"Wait!"

He turned and gave me a quizzical look.

"Don't you owe me and Simon something?"

"Something like what?"

"Something like an apology, maybe?"

Bellange's face crinkled into an indulgent smile. "As

an officer of the law, I can only act upon the evidence as it presents itself to me. And that evidence initially pointed straight to you and Monsieur Girard. But if it's an apology you want then so be it. Please accept my sincere apology on behalf of the DCPJ." And with that he was gone.

BELLANGE WAS RIGHT. Everything seemed much clearer to me the next morning. And still nothing the captain told me the night before made a bit of sense. But Juliet's killer was dead and it was over and that's all that mattered to me. I was released from the hospital later that morning. The media had camped outside the hospital, so I ducked out a service entrance to avoid them. The suicide of an American diplomat's murderous son had made headlines all over the world. With no place else to go, I took a cab back to the Bienvenue Hotel. My room was paid through Sunday and though it seemed like a lifetime since I'd set out with Brian and Jarrod for Versailles, it was only Thursday, a mere four days later. Zalima, the manager, was manning the front desk when I arrived. She did a double take when she saw me.

"Madame Sinclair, you're back." She came out from behind the desk to greet me. I could see the intense curiosity burning in her dark eyes but I wasn't in the mood for chitchat.

"Is my room still available?"

"Of course, *madame*."

"Do I have any messages?" I was hoping a certain Frenchman might be out of jail and looking for me.

Zalima reached behind the desk and grabbed a stack of white message slips. I flipped through them but they were mostly from my BFF, Kelly, begging me to call her. A few were from members of the Associated Press wanting interviews, and amazingly one was from Ben. I stared at it for so long dots appeared before my eyes. I balled it up and tossed it in the trash. There was nothing from Simon.

"Is there anything else I can get for you? Lunch is being served in our restaurant and if I'm not mistaken, you have a complimentary meal coming to you."

"Maybe later. *Merci.*" I started up the steps and stopped. "Would you happen to know if Mr. Perlman and Mr. Mitchner are still in Paris?"

"I'm sorry, *madame.* Monsieur Mitchner suffered another heart attack while in the hospital and died on Tuesday. His friend, Mr. Perlman, left Paris with his body only this morning."

I hurried up the steps to my room so Zalima wouldn't see my tears.

QUATORZE

AFTER A LONG, hot shower and an even longer nap, I dressed in the only clean outfit I had, the khaki cargo pants and white shirt Brian and Jarrod had picked up for me at the Monoprix. While I dressed, I watched the news. An ashen-faced Ambassador Ernest Garland, who looked nothing like his son, came out of the coroner's office. He supported his weeping wife as he ushered her into a waiting limo. From the few words I could understand, they'd just come from identifying their son's body. Then another familiar face popped up on the screen.

Simon, in need of a shave and drooping from fatigue, was being mobbed by the press outside the DCPJ headquarters. Cameras and microphones were thrust into his face from all directions. He smiled graciously and said something in French that elicited laughter from the reporters. My heart did a happy little flip-flop. He walked toward a waiting Mercedes. The crowd parted enough for me to see Claire Samuelson by his side with her arm looped possessively through his. It was all size two of her in a cropped red jacket and skin-tight jeans with to-die-for black leather knee-length boots laced up the front. She must have bailed him out of jail. The least she could do considering she called the police on him. Francoise must be in heaven. Why had I been so happy to see him when he was another woman's man?

When would I learn? I turned off the TV and swore to myself that I'd hop a plane home tomorrow right after I made my statement.

Once downstairs I was happy to discover the hotel had started serving dinner. I ordered chicken and sausage *cassoulet* and practically buried my face in the large fragrant bowl when it arrived. I was mopping up the juices in the bottom of the bowl with a hunk of crusty bread when a painfully slim woman sat across from me.

Her face was expertly made up. Her glossy lipstick probably never smudged and her gray eyes were made wide by the artful use of smoky blue eyeliner. She smiled at me with blindingly white teeth and held out a business card in her manicured hand.

"Diana Hughes, Miss Sinclair, BBC World News. I was hoping you'd be willing to speak with me about being framed for murder by the son of the U.S. ambassador."

Her accent was what the Brits would call posh. But her measured, careful way of talking screamed elocution lessons. She'd probably revert back to her regional accent if she got enough liquor in her. I ignored her outstretched hand and took a weary sip of wine. She placed the card on the table and slid it over to me.

"I'd really just like to put this all behind me. I'm not interested in talking to the press."

"Not even to set the record straight?"

"About what?"

"Ernest Garland and his wife have made claims to the press that their son was murdered. They say he'd never have committed suicide and he must have been forced to write that letter. They're blaming you and Simon Girard for his death. Didn't you know?"

I slammed the wineglass down so hard on the table it shook, causing Diana Hughes to sit back in alarm.

"If that's the case, then why did his mother call the police and report that their son had a gun and was suicidal?"

"Well," she replied, crossing her thin arms and fixing me with a predatory gaze. Her eyes went suddenly hard. "I could tell you. But what would be in it for me?"

Idiot. I'd completely fallen into that trap. But I really wanted to know. "Fine. I'll give you a brief interview and I get to pick the questions."

"Fair enough." She scooted her chair close to mine. "Here's the thing, Miss Sinclair—there was a call made to the police by someone claiming to be Martha Garland. Only she denies she made the call. In fact, the Garlands claim they didn't even know what had happened to their son until they were notified by the police. It was only after getting that call that they found the suicide note. The Garlands say their son was framed for murder and was then killed."

"Of course they'd say that. What family would willing believe a loved one capable of murder and suicide? The Garlands are in shock, that's all. And shame on you for exploiting their grief and trying to make this a bigger story than it is. And just how do they think Simon and I were involved?"

"They don't. I just wanted to wind you up a bit." She actually grinned.

The urge to hurl my wine in her face was so strong I got up and started walking away.

"I guess you're not at all interested in the results of the preliminary toxicology report on Vincent Garland?"

Keep walking, Maya. It's not your problem. KEEP WALKING! screamed the voice in my head. Except I don't like being screamed at. I went back. "What about the toxicology report?"

"What about my interview? Tit for tat, remember?"

"Why should I talk to a woman who just lied to me?"

"Because I'll bloody well camp out in front of this hotel until you do," she replied sweetly.

The brief interview with Diana Hughes ended up taking over two hours. Unbeknownst to me, Hughes's camera crew was cooling its heels in a news van parked outside. Zalima allowed us to use an empty suite for the interview. The whole thing would have gone much faster if the rather vain Ms. Hughes didn't need her makeup retouched every five minutes and if she wouldn't have wasted so much time trying to find the right camera angles to capture the best side of her chinless face.

Even though she promised to stick to the questions we'd agreed on, she asked me plenty of questions I had no intention of answering, such as exactly how close I got to Simon while we were on the run. I gave her a blank stare and refused to answer until she moved on. Only she wouldn't move on.

"So, you're not denying things became physical between you and Simon Girard when the two of you were on the run?"

"Simon Girard and I were two innocent people thrown together by unusual circumstances. We came to rely heavily on each other and I'd like to think we became friends but that's all we are...friends," I stammered.

Hughes smirked, realizing she'd finally found my weak spot. I took off my microphone and stood. I'd had more than enough of her. I estimated that after editing out all my silent, blank stares, she probably had maybe two minutes of usable footage. I shoved my mic into her hand.

"Now, what about that toxicology report? You were saying...?"

It's amazing how the thin veneer of politeness wears off once insincere people get what they want. Diana Hughes didn't even bother looking at me when she replied. I was already old news.

"Vincent Garland had alcohol and muscle relaxers in his system. Not enough to render him unconscious, mind you, but enough to render him out of it to the point that loading, let alone pulling the trigger, on a gun would have been highly unlikely. There were also cotton fibers found in his bullet wound. Someone most likely held something against his head to muffle the sound of the gunshot."

"And you got this info from...?"

"I'd have thought you'd have learned from your *friend* Simon Girard that a reporter never reveals a source."

Vincent Garland's parents were partially right. Garland hadn't committed suicide. He had to have had a partner and his partner must have killed him. Could it have been Monsieur Marcel? Boy, was I glad this wasn't my problem anymore. Whoever killed Vincent Garland had done the world a favor. I was just happy to be going home.

LOUD POUNDING WOKE ME early the next morning. I felt a strange sense of déjà vu. Wasn't this the way Monday had started?

"Who is it?" I asked before looking out the peephole. A pair of intense green eyes stared back at me.

"It's your *friend*...Simon. Open up, sleepyhead."

I opened the door and Simon pushed past me and dumped a duffel bag on the floor, then stretched out on the bed with his hands behind his head.

"Don't I even get a kiss?" he teased.

I leaned against the door and studied him. He was clean-shaven again. He had on faded jeans and a black turtleneck. He still looked very tired. The reunion sex with Claire must have kept him up all night.

"I guess you heard about Monsieur Marcel?"

"I know how much you liked him, Maya. I didn't want to be right about him."

"Someone took the fake crucifix from my bag. It was gone when I woke up in the hospital."

"You gave it to me right before we walked back to the fountain, remember? And I dropped it when we ran after seeing Garland floating in the pond. It's probably in the bushes somewhere near the Medici Fountain. Seriously—you're really not going to give me a kiss?"

"Did you hear Garland had drugs and alcohol in his system and couldn't have shot himself?"

Simon shrugged, unconcerned.

"You don't care that he probably had a partner?"

"What I care about is that the man who killed my brother is dead. Whether by his own hand or someone else's makes no difference to me."

"And the crucifix, the Black Nun of Moret, the

Aurum Liber and all the rest of it? We didn't just imagine it all. It was real."

"It doesn't matter anymore. It's over, Maya. The police have a suicide note, one dead murderer and another in custody. And we're alive and off the hook. Can't you just be happy?"

He was right. And more important, he was here.

"What's that?" I nodded toward the duffel bag on the floor. I was trying not to let him see how happy I was to see him, and trying even harder not to be happy to see him.

"I need a place to hide out for a little while."

"And you couldn't go to Max's?"

"Max is pissed at me because of the gun."

"Serves you right. And if you're hiding out from the press, this is the last place you should have come."

"I'm not hiding from the press and don't worry, there're no news vans parked outside waiting to pounce on you. I watched that horrible interview you gave the BBC on TV last night. You've got a reputation now."

"What kind of reputation?" I asked, mildly amused.

"Of being a lousy interview subject with the personality of lint."

"Hmm." I sat on the edge of the bed. Dangerous territory but the only chair in the room was piled high with my crap. "Is that anything like being a lousy lay?"

"Come over here, *madame,* and I'll let you know." He sat up and reached for me. I jumped up, suddenly aware that I was only wearing a white cotton nightshirt. My nipples pebbled and pushed through the thin fabric. I crossed my arms to hide myself. Damn! The man hadn't even touched me and I was getting wet.

"If you're not hiding from the press then who are you hiding from?"

"Claire," he practically spat out.

"Claire? That's a nice way to treat the woman who bailed you out of jail."

Simon let out a harsh laugh. "Nothing that woman does is without ulterior motives. One minute she's bailing me out of jail, the next she's hired a publicist and is booking me on talk shows. She's trying to get me an agent and a book deal." He threw up his hands in disgust.

"I'm sure your girlfriend means well," I commented dryly.

Simon looked momentarily taken aback. He grinned, sitting up against the headboard. "So that's why you were so annoyed with me yesterday. You think Claire is my girlfriend?"

"Isn't she?"

"No. And if she were I'd be in a world of hurt because the only thing besides money and clothes Claire Samuelson loves is herself."

"What about her daughter?"

"Motherhood cramps Claire's style. Why do you think Francoise is alone so much?"

"If she's not your girlfriend then why is she trying to help you cash in?"

"Because she's a media whore who'll do anything for attention. The more famous she can make me, the better it looks for her to be seen with me. Were you really jealous?"

"No!" I grabbed my pants from the floor and started to put them on. Simon grabbed me and pulled me on top of him.

"Let me guess. Francoise told you we were a couple. Am I right?"

"She didn't have to tell me. That was a really cute picture of the three of you at Euro Disney in Francoise's room."

"Taken last month on her thirteenth birthday. She's been trying to push Claire and me together since I moved back from Hong Kong." He laughed.

"And you're not interested?"

"Do you want to know why Francoise's father and I stopped speaking?"

"I'm all ears."

"It was because of Claire. I dated her first, but when she found out about Marty's trust fund she dumped me for him. I tried to warn him about how calculating and high maintenance she was. He just thought I was jealous. After I returned to Paris, I found out he'd married her. In the letter I was sent after he died—the one in which he asked me to be there for his daughter, he also admitted that he had found out the hard way Claire was nothing but a gold-digger. I'm crazy about that kid. She's the apple in my pie. But she has to give up this fantasy about her *maman* and me. It's never going to happen."

"It's the apple of your *eye,* not pie." I tried to keep a straight face. Simon just looked confused.

"Eye? Why would I have an apple in my eye? That makes no sense."

"Never mind," I said with a laugh. "Okay. If Claire's not your girlfriend, then why is your stuff at her place?"

"Because Claire got stranded in Miami when a hurricane shut down the airports and she couldn't get home for days. Francoise begged me to come over to stay with her. I packed a bag and went over. I must have left some clothes over there. So stop thinking you're fooling around with a man with commitments. I'm free and single—just like you."

He kissed my neck. I could feel his arousal pressing against my stomach. His hands were under my nightshirt, caressing the warm flesh of my back. "Your skin is like silk," he murmured against my ear as he started to tug the shirt over my head.

My will started to drain away. My body wanted him so badly but my head knew I was just delaying the inevitable. I was going home and needed to be able to put him and Paris behind me and move on with my life.

"Tell me you want me," he commanded in a husky voice. He didn't wait for my response and kissed me hard. I squirmed, trying to get away. Not because I wasn't enjoying what he was doing, but because I'd yet to shower or brush my teeth. Simon didn't seem to care.

"Tell me," he commanded again, this time pulling my arms up and pinning them above my head with one hand.

"I can't, Simon. I've got to go give a statement to the police this morning and then I've got a plane—"

He covered my mouth with his and guided his free hand between my legs. I wasn't wearing panties and gasped when his cool fingers met my warm flesh. He stroked me, first slowly, then harder and faster as my breath quickened. I moved against his fingers and closed my eyes, losing myself to the sensation, until he abruptly stopped.

"Tell me you want me."

"I want you," I replied in a hoarse whisper. I pushed up against his fingers but they remained still.

"Say, 'I want you, *Simon.*'"

Tired of the game he was trying to play, I rolled over until I was on top. I took off the T-shirt I was wearing and quickly unfastened Simon's jeans and yanked them and his briefs down past his hips. He stripped off his turtleneck and gasped when I mounted him. His hands kneaded my breasts as I rode him hard. I bent down and kissed him.

"I...want...you...Simon," I whispered between kisses.

His only answer was a groan. As I came, he sat up and held me close. I was vaguely aware of him calling my name as his own orgasm hit. Afterward, he lay back against the pillows, breathing heavily with me nestled against his damp chest, fighting tears. This couldn't happen again. It was time to go home. I got up and turned away from him and put my T-shirt back on.

"You okay?"

"Never better."

"No one could accuse you of being a lousy lay. God, I needed that." He was sitting up against the headboard, looking relaxed and pleased with himself. I was flying home—*today*—and still he'd said nothing about ever wanting to see me again. All I was to Simon Girard was stress relief.

"Yeah, and that's what I'd call a great send-off. Thanks. Make sure you pull the door shut on your way out," I tossed over my shoulder as I walked into the bathroom.

I didn't mean for it to sound so harsh. But I couldn't help it. I was hurt and disappointed, and in all honesty, had no right to be. Simon had made me no promises. It was my own stupid fault for letting things go so far.

The stunned look his face that I glimpsed in the dresser mirror as I passed told me Simon wasn't used to being dismissed by any woman.

"I'm happy I could oblige," he replied through gritted teeth. He sat up and began to pull on his pants.

I thought about stopping him. But it was better this way. Better to end it now before I got even more attached. When I got out of the shower, Simon and his duffel bag were gone.

"So YOU TOLD THE MAN his money was on the dresser and not to let the doorknob hit him in the ass on the way out?" asked my friend Kelly.

I was on the metro having just come from giving my statement at DCPJ and was careful to leave out tales of nuns, crucifixes and priceless gold-bound books. They were sending my clothes and suitcase back to the hotel by police messenger, but I insisted they give me my cell phone. Unfortunately, it was dead. I had to use the cheap one Simon had bought. Forget about the murder, mayhem and being on the run. All Kelly wanted to hear about was Simon.

"I did not say that to him."

"You may as well have. You treated him like a two-dollar ho, Maya, and after he saved your sorry behind and everything. Poor Simon."

"Oh, please. Trust me. Simon Girard will never be short on female companionship. In a week he'll have forgotten all about me."

"And what about you?"

"I'm fine." It was a lie, of course, but it would be true in time.

I was about to tell Kelly about getting a message

from Ben, but the phone dropped the call and the train suddenly stopped. An announcement was made in French and everyone started to get off.

"What's going on?" I asked a lady loaded down with shopping bags.

"Bomb threat. We've got to get off."

Bomb threat! I jumped up and followed her off the train. It was a good ten-minute walk in the semi-darkness back to the previous stop, Champs-Elysées Clemenceau. The narrow platform was lighted, giving me plenty of opportunity to read the graffiti on the filthy, dank tunnel walls. Rats scurried somewhere below us. There were about thirty of us and everyone except me seemed calm and collected. I couldn't shake the thought of Simon's poor wife, Justine.

I took the stairs to the street above. I had been in such a hurry to get my statement over with at the DCPJ that I forgot the station was a mere stone's throw from the Arc de Triomphe and the Champs-Elysées, the widest street in Paris. My flight didn't leave until 7:00 p.m. I still had hours to kill and since I was no longer a fugitive, I figured I may as well enjoy what time I had left in the City of Light, doing a little shopping on the most beautiful avenue in the world.

I had a leisurely lunch of smoked salmon and crepes at a little corner bistro where I watched the chaos of cars, taxis and tour buses racing in and out of the enormous traffic circle around the Arc de Triomphe. Multiple boulevards converged upon the circle and as the vehicles battled with each other for the right of way, it was a wonder no one was killed.

After a decadent dessert of Grande Marnier chocolate mousse, I browsed the numerous designer shops and upscale boutiques, quickly discovering that the only shopping I'd be able to do was of the window variety. Then I spotted a Monoprix department store and made a beeline straight for it. I bought chocolates and cookies for my boss and coworkers back home, a silk scarf and scented bath oil for Kelly, and a bottle of champagne for my neighbor, whom I hoped was watering my plants. They wouldn't know it all came from the French equivalent of Walmart and what difference would it make? It was still from Paris, after all.

I was leery about getting back on the metro, so I took a cab back to the Bienvenue. I lugged my bags into the lobby. Georges was behind the desk.

"Madame Sinclair!"

"Oui?" I said with a smile to let him know I had no hard feelings about his mix-up with Juliet Rice and me. He smiled shyly back in return.

"The gentleman is here for you, *madame.*" He gestured toward the small seating area across from the front desk where a balding, middle-aged man sat in the lone recliner, talking animatedly on his cell phone.

He was dressed in a gray suit. The jacket pulled tightly across his belly. His trousers were threadbare at the knees. A coffee stain on his red tie made him look sloppy. When he spotted me, he stood. He was easily over six feet tall.

"Madame Sinclair?" he called out to me in a voice that was higher pitched than I expected from such a large man. "May I have a word with you, *s'il vous plaît?*"

"I'm sorry. I'm not giving anymore interviews." I headed toward the stairs.

"No. No," he said, reaching out a hand to stop me.

"I'm not with the press. My name is Paul Moyet. Sebastian Marcel is my client. I'm representing him." He handed me a business card, but I barely glanced at it before shoving it in my pocket.

"You're his lawyer?"

"Ah, *oui*." He smiled at me. His teeth were stained.

"Why do you need to talk to me?"

"Monsieur Marcel would like to see you. He's says it's very important."

"Why?"

"He would only say that it was a matter of life and death."

"There's already been enough death, Monsieur Moyet, and your client is responsible for much of it. He's in need of psychiatric help and I really hope he gets it."

"You are referring to his mental state from yesterday?"

"That and the fact that he killed three people."

"Madame, Sebastian Marcel is only guilty of suffering from the beginning stages of dementia. He didn't have access to his medication yesterday and was confused and disoriented. I can assure you that he's quite himself today."

"And what about the people he's accused of killing?"

"There is absolutely no proof he is a murderer. There is no motive," insisted Moyet.

"What about all the debt he's in and the money he owed the victims? That sounds like plenty of motive to me," I practically shouted.

"Please lower your voice, *madame*." He looked over at Georges, who was shuffling papers around and pretending not to listen. "If you just calm down, I can explain."

"You've got five minutes." I followed him over to the seating area and noticed a beat-up briefcase next to the recliner. He picked it up and sat it on his lap.

"There is no physical evidence linking Sebastian Marcel to these crimes," began Paul Moyet.

"What about the money motive?"

"There is *no* money motive, *madame*." Moyet pulled a sheaf of papers from his briefcase and started reading them aloud. "He did not owe either victim more than a few hundred euros. In his will, Oliver Renard left him an antique snuffbox collection worth perhaps ten thousand euros, which would hardly be worth killing for. And Evalyn Hewitt left her entire estate to her dog."

"Agnes?"

"*Oui.* I believe that is the animal's name. Sebastian Marcel was merely named its caretaker. Once the dog dies, all of the money and property are to be given to charity. The police are bending the facts to fit their case. I would think you of all people would understand this, given what you've just been through."

I certainly could but that still didn't mean I wanted to get involved or that I trusted this lawyer, whose job it was to stretch the truth on his client's behalf, any more than I did the French police.

"I'm really sorry, Monsieur Moyet. I'm leaving Paris in a few hours. Even if I wanted to, I can't see Monsieur Marcel. There just isn't enough time."

Moyet sighed heavily and nodded solemnly. "I understand, Madame Sinclair," he said, though he looked anything but understanding. "You have my card if you change your mind."

He pulled a tweed cap from his briefcase and put it on, then walked to the door where he paused before leaving.

"You know," he said, turning to face me, "Sebastian Marcel is a sick old man who could spend the rest of his life in prison for crimes he did not commit. And his only concern is for others. Maybe that is his real crime, eh, *madame?*"

The slow, cold ooze of guilt seeped into my brain, wormed its way into my consciousness and flooded my senses. Was it so wrong for me to want to put this nightmare behind me?

ONCE I WAS BACK in my room, I dumped the Monoprix bags on my bed. The police had delivered my suitcase, and it sat just inside the doorway wrapped in clear plastic. I tore off the plastic and sifted through my things. All the new clothes I'd bought for the trip had been balled up and stuffed inside the suitcase. Everything was there along with an extra piece of clothing, a black Calvin Klein bikini top, size 8.

"This isn't mine," I said aloud. I held it up to inspect it and then dropped it like a hot rock when I recognized it as Juliet's. I'd gotten my feet tangled up in it when I'd come back to our room the night I found her body. I had identified all of my things at the station; the bikini top hadn't been there. Then I remembered I had run into Jerome Hubert while I was there. He had given me the evil eye but hadn't said anything. What could he say? This must have been his idea of a joke.

I picked the top up and tossed it in the trash. The quiet in the room was too much for me. Thoughts of both Simon and Sebastian Marcel tempered my joy over going home. I switched on the TV and clicked through the channels until I found an English-speaking one. Unfortunately it was BBC World News. I'd avoided watching my own interview last night.

But I wasn't going to get away from Diana Hughes that easily. She was on the screen interviewing a couple of young women who were identified as Danielle Savard and Brigitte Mathieu, school friends of Sylvie Renard. A picture of Sylvie and her father, Oliver, were in the background. The words *Father Daughter Double Murder Rocks Paris* were under the pictures. It made me mad they were ignoring Evalyn Hewitt's murder. But I wasn't surprised that the murder of an elderly woman who lived alone with her dog wasn't an interesting enough story to the media. And who was taking care of Agnes now?

"What was she like?" Diana asked the women.

"Quiet," said the woman identified as Brigitte. She had short red hair and blushed as soon as the word was out her mouth.

"But not shy," added the other woman, Danielle, who seemed the more assertive of the two and had a slightly thicker accent. "You never knew what she was thinking. It was a little creepy at times."

"Sylvie was a very serious girl," said Brigitte, cutting Danielle a look. "She kept to herself mostly. Dani and I were her only friends."

"She was a good girl," said Danielle like *good* was a dirty word. "No parties, or drinking, or smoking, or sneaking out. We used to call her *la petite nonne.*"

"What does that mean?" asked Diana Hughes in her cool, modulated tone.

"The little nun," I said aloud along with Brigitte and

Danielle. I dropped the shirt I was folding and sank down on the edge of the bed.

Monsieur Marcel had said *la petite nonne* was the one who'd attacked him. He hadn't been talking about the Black Nun of Moret. Had he been talking about Sylvie Renard? It wasn't possible. But as the memories of what had happened these past few days flashed through my mind, it all made perfect sense. When Dr. Hewitt had pulled those books from the shelf as a warning to Monsieur Marcel, she wasn't warning him about Vincent Garland. She didn't know Garland. But she knew Sylvie Renard, her friend and colleague's daughter. She'd have let Sylvie into her home not knowing she was in any danger. When did she realize the young woman was there to kill her?

King Lear had been pulled from the shelf because it is a tale of scheming daughters who betray their father. Sylvie killed her father, too. Simon had said it smelled like Oliver Renard had been dead for days. Had Sylvie killed him before leaving on her trip? Or had she lied about being in Spain and had been in the house all weekend with her father's body rotting in his study?

Sylvie Renard knew Vincent Garland from working at the U.S. Embassy. She must have been his partner. She already knew about the Society of Moret from her father. Sylvie and Garland had been working together to get their hands on the *Aurum Liber* and Juliet was the weak link they'd exploited. Sylvie killed Garland and made it look like a suicide. She was probably close by, watching when we'd found his body in the pond and saw Simon drop the pouch with the crucifix.

But how had she faked her own death? Her body had been identified. If it wasn't her body in the morgue, then whose was it? I thought long and hard about everyone connected to Garland and had a sudden sick feeling I knew.

I hurried downstairs and asked for the internet access code from Georges for the public-use laptop in the lobby. I logged on and pulled up a search engine. My fingers lingered over the keyboard momentarily before I hunt-and-pecked out the name *Shannon Davies* in the search box. I clicked on the first link in the results list, a news report about her disappearance. I stared at the picture that accompanied the story. Though Shannon Davies's face was a bit fuller and her hair a shade lighter, she could have been Sylvie Renard's twin. My fingers trembled as I pulled Paul Moyet's business card from my pocket.

QUINZE

ABOUT THE TIME I should have been picked up by the airport shuttle, I was sitting on the other side of a Plexiglas window opposite Sebastian Marcel. He looked frail and so much older than when I'd seen him last, right before he locked me in that closet. But as soon as he saw me, a smile creased his thin lips, and he eagerly picked up the phone on his side. I'd almost gone home and left him in this mess and still he was happy to see me. I was so ashamed. I picked up the phone on my side of the window.

"I'm so sorry, *monsieur*. I understand now what you were trying to tell me yesterday. It's Sylvie Renard who's *la petite nonne,* right?"

He nodded. "*Oui.* I knew as soon as you told me about the books you'd found at Evalyn's house. And she must be stopped, Madame Sinclair. Sylvie is a very sick and dangerous young woman."

"She wants the *Aurum Liber.*"

Marcel shook his head sadly. "I'm afraid this was never solely about the *Aurum Liber,* though I'm sure Oliver's obsession over the years with finding it must have made Sylvie want it just to spite him. No, Madame Sinclair, for Sylvie this is also about revenge. Revenge against the mother who abandoned her and for the child that was taken from her."

"The mother who abandoned her?" My hand flew to my mouth. "Juliet? Juliet was Sylvie's mother?"

"The product of her ill-fated affair with Oliver Renard. Oliver was in love with Juliet. He wanted to marry her. His wife, Camille, was Catholic and wouldn't give him a divorce. Even if she had, Juliet didn't love Oliver. She was just using him to make Bernard jealous."

"Dr. Fouquet?"

He nodded. "Bernard was a magnet for women. They loved him. He was handsome and brilliant, arrogant and charming—but kind."

That picture I'd seen in Monsieur Marcel's apartment certainly proved Fouquet had been a very handsome man. He had probably gotten more distinguished-looking as he'd gotten older. He must have been in his early fifties when he was Juliet's advisor.

"And did she make him jealous?"

"*Non.* Bernard may have desired Juliet but he never crossed the line with a student of his. Never. Oliver was a different story. I loved him like a brother but he was weak when it came to women. He met his match in Juliet. When she ended the affair, he tried to keep her from joining our society. But he was outvoted. Every time she came to France for our yearly society meetings in Moret-sur-Loing, Oliver would beg her to meet him in Paris. She always told him no, but relented just once when she needed a professional reference from him. That was the meeting in which Sylvie was conceived."

"She didn't seem like the maternal type to me."

"She wasn't. Juliet wasn't heartless, just very ambitious. She knew she wasn't cut out for motherhood when the only thing that mattered to her was her career.

Oliver wouldn't hear of her aborting the child. His wife longed to be a mother and could never carry a child to term. So Oliver and Camille raised Sylvie."

"Dr. Renard's wife raised Oliver's and Juliet's child?"

"*Oui.* It meant she could finally be a mother and there was no love left in that marriage. Camille didn't care what Oliver did as long as he was discreet."

"And Sylvie never knew?"

"That was the agreement. Juliet was to have no contact with the girl. At Camille's insistence, she had to legally sign away all her parental rights. Camille loved Sylvie like she was her own. And then it all went wrong." He sighed heavily.

I waited for him to continue.

"Sylvie was such a beautiful child, like a little angel. And for the first few years of her life she was an angel. It wasn't until she was maybe five that Oliver noticed something was wrong. They gave her a kitten for her fifth birthday which somehow ended up drowned in the toilet. Sylvie cried and cried and neither Oliver nor Camille suspected anything other than an accident. But every pet they gave her ended up dead within a month or two. Oliver knew it had to be Sylvie, but Camille would hear none of it. Sylvie was always so quiet. No one ever suspected her of any wrongdoing. But she was very sly. Few of the other kids would play with her. Most were scared of her. Then there were the nannies."

"She hurt them, too?"

He nodded. "And drove them mad with her lies. She would steal from them. She would break expensive antiques and blame them. Oliver even suspected she shoved one off a ladder. They could never keep anyone for more than a few months. It wasn't until she was ten that Camille finally realized what Oliver had been trying to tell her for years. Camille was coming from her bedroom one day when she saw Sylvie arguing over a doll with another child. When the child refused to give it to Sylvie, Camille watched as the daughter she adored calmly threw herself down a flight of stairs and broke her arm. She claimed the other child pushed her."

"And did they get her help?"

"There was no help for the child, though Camille tried everything, including special blessings from priests. If she were schizophrenic, bi-polar or obsessive compulsive, there would have been treatments and medications. But how do you treat someone who was born without a conscience, without a sense of right or wrong, without a soul? There is no treatment for such people."

"She's a sociopath," I said.

"That is one name for it," he replied sadly. "I call it pure evil. And when Sylvie ended up pregnant at sixteen after seducing one of her teachers at school, Camille and Oliver were beside themselves. Abortion was out of the question, but Sylvie couldn't be trusted with a pet, let alone an infant. They were terrified she'd kill it."

"They took the baby from her?"

"It was a boy. They told her the baby died, and they placed him with an English couple in a private adoption."

A stone-faced guard appeared and barked something to Monsieur Marcel. He nodded solemnly.

"I've only a few more minutes," he said to me.

"How did Sylvie find out about everything?"

"Camille told her eight months ago on her death bed.

She'd become a broken and bitter woman. The burden of raising Sylvie took a hard toll on her and she felt Juliet had gotten off easy. She wanted her to suffer, too. So Camille confessed all to Sylvie before she died, knowing Sylvie would seek out Juliet like an avenging angel. She also harbored a hope that motherhood might change Sylvie, so she told her that her child was alive. But all Sylvie cares about is punishing everyone who's lied to her all these years and getting her hands on the *Aurum Liber* in the process. I shudder to think what she'll do if she decides to find her son. The boy would be about ten now."

"Did you know Sylvie had connected with Juliet?"

He sighed heavily. "Evalyn and I tried to warn her. But Juliet had come to regret her decision of giving up her baby and didn't want to hear the truth about Sylvie. What woman would?"

"Do you have any idea where Sylvie could be hiding?"

"Oliver's sister, Annette, spends half the year in South Africa with her children. You might check her house here in Paris."

He gave me the address and I wrote it on the back of the picture of Shannon Davies I printed from the internet. Then I asked him the one question I really needed answered.

"*Monsieur,* I found the fake Moret Crucifix in your old office at the Sorbonne. It had blood on it. Were you there when Dr. Renard was murdered?"

"Heavens no," he replied, looking hurt. "Oliver gave me the crucifix the day he discovered it was a fake. I still had it in my coat pocket when Sylvie attacked me. I assure you the blood on it is mine, Madame Sinclair."

"You have to tell the police what you just told me."

Suddenly, Monsieur Marcel's face went blank. He seemed to disappear before my eyes. He looked around clearly confused. He was staring at me like he didn't know me.

"Where am I? What is this place?" he asked, looking lost, helpless, old.

"*Monsieur,* are you okay?" But I knew he was gone, at least for now. I'd get no more out of him. And he was in no shape to tell the police anything.

He started to cry, and the guard gently took the phone out of his hand, hung it up then led the frightened old Frenchman away.

Paul Moyet was waiting for me in the lobby when I emerged and stood abruptly when he spotted me.

"I need your help, Monsieur Moyet."

"Anything for my client." His eyes were shining with excitement. "How can I help you?"

"I need you to help me track down a dead woman."

"WHEN WILL HE BE BACK?" I asked the officer manning the front desk at the DCPJ headquarters, who'd just informed me that Captain Bellange was away on another case.

"I have no idea, *madame.*"

"Do you know what kind of case it is or where he went?"

"I cannot give you that information," she replied wearily.

"It's very important that I see him. I'll just wait for a while."

The officer gave me a dismissive nod and I went to sit on a hard wooden bench. I'd told Paul Moyet everything Monsieur Marcel had told me and he'd gone off to find out who had positively identified the bodies of Oliver and Sylvie Renard.

The more I thought about Marcel's story, the more sense it all made. Juliet's journal had mentioned meeting the one she'd been waiting for so many years at the embassy reception. I'd thought she was talking about finally finding love with the man of her dreams, Vincent Garland. But she'd been referring to Sylvie, the daughter she'd given up years before and wasn't allowed contact with. She must have been waiting for her child to contact her. And Juliet must have also come to realize something wasn't right about her daughter when she'd made mention in the journal of seeing a side she didn't know existed, which is why she hid the real crucifix.

A young woman pushing a cart loaded down with files walked passed me and stopped at the elevator down the hall. Although she wore a uniform with a drab blue sweater and her curly blond hair was pulled into a demure ponytail, her long bright orange fingernails and large silver hoop earrings belied a more flamboyant style. A pink iPod Nano hung around her neck and her head bobbed to techno music so loud that even I could hear it. On a hunch, I followed her onto the elevator when the doors slid open.

"Excusez-moi, madame."

She didn't hear me, so I tapped her lightly on the shoulder. She scowled at me as she pulled the earbuds from her ears.

"Do you know Simon Girard? Are you a friend of his?" Simon had told me his contact at the DCPJ was a file clerk. I'd bet my passport this was her.

"Who wants to know?" She looked me up and down suspiciously with bloodshot eyes.

"Maya Sinclair. The fugitive from the news." Recognition washed over her face and she smiled.

"Ah, *oui!* I know your face now. Too much club hopping last night. Makes me grouchy. I'm Valerie Lebrun."

"Nice to meet you, Valerie. So, are you a friend of Simon's then?"

She gave me a sly smile and shrugged. "*Oui.* We are friends. We help each other." She put an extra emphasis on the word *help*.

I didn't even want to know what that meant but it somehow it made me feel a little less guilty about how I'd treated Simon. Was there a woman in Paris he hadn't slept with?

"What would I have to give you to get you to help me?"

Valerie's overly plucked eyebrows shot up and disappeared into her hairline. She took a step backward and put up her hands. "Hey. I'm not like that. You've got the wrong idea."

"No. No." I burst out laughing. "I just need information, Valerie, just information."

She let out her breath and smiled sheepishly. The elevator doors opened and Valerie got off. I followed her.

"Depends on what kind of info you need."

"I need to know where Captain Bellange went. I really need to talk to him. It's important." I pressed two twenty-euro notes into her hand and she looked around quickly before stuffing them into her bra.

"He's in St-Germain-des-Prés. Some hotshot American fashion designer's daughter is missing. Never showed up at school this morning. You could have found that out for free. It's all over the news by now. And just so you know, Simon never pays me in money. He takes care of my poodle, Zsa Zsa, when I'm out of town." Valerie laughed as she pushed her cart down the hall.

I'd stopped listening as soon as the words *fashion designer's daughter* left her lips. My blood ran cold. Francoise was missing.

I NURSED A COFFEE in a café across from Claire Samuelson's apartment building. Police cars were parked out front. I really wanted to believe Francoise had simply had an argument with her mother and had run off to sulk at a friend's house, but I knew better than that. The press camped out, waiting to pounce on whoever walked out of the building. From what Simon had told me, I bet Claire was enjoying all the attention.

I'd tried calling Simon several times but he wouldn't answer the phone. In the meantime, Paul Moyet had called and informed me that Oliver's and Sylvie Renard's bodies had been positively identified by Oliver Renard's sister, meaning she was in town and not in South Africa.

Simon emerged from the building and was surrounded immediately by the press. He pushed his way through the crush of people and then headed off down the street and hailed a cab. I ran across the street calling for Simon and narrowly missed being creamed by a florist's van in the process. A cab pulled up. We both jumped in at the same time as cameras flashed all around us. The driver looked at us expectantly.

"Just drive! I'll tell you when to stop," Simon barked.

The driver floored it, and I was thrown back against the seat.

"I've been calling you for two hours. Why haven't you answered your phone?"

"I've got other things on my mind. And besides, I thought you had a plane to catch." He wouldn't even look at me.

"My plane left an hour ago. I found out about Francoise at the police station. I think I know who has her."

Simon scowled and abruptly told the driver to stop the cab. He tossed money at him and dragged me out of the barely stopped vehicle after him. We were in the Latin Quarter about a block from the Sorbonne's campus.

"You want to know why I haven't answered your calls?" He flipped open his cell phone and thrust it at me.

On the display screen was a picture of a bound and gagged Francoise sitting in a chair. The picture wasn't the best quality but I could see she was wearing her school uniform and her eyes were wide and frightened. Her face was tear-streaked and her nose was running. A cut on her lip had dripped blood on her chin.

"Oh my God! Did you show this to Bellange?"

"Read the message."

I scrolled down farther and saw the brief text message. *No Police or she DIES. I'll B in touch.*

"I got that an hour ago. I couldn't call you back. I had to keep the line free."

"It's Sylvie Renard, Simon. She's the one who has Francoise."

Simon grabbed me by the shoulders and shook me. "She's dead!" The more upset he became the thicker his accent got. "This has nothing to do with you. Go home where you belong."

He shoved me and then walked away. I chased after him. When I caught up, I pulled the picture of Shannon Davies from my bag and pushed it in his face. The resemblance to Sylvie stopped him in his tracks.

"*This* is who they found in Sylvie's trunk. Shannon Davies, Vincent Garland's girlfriend. Sylvie played us all. She was behind everything. I'm not even sure Juliet Rice knew Vincent Garland."

He snatched the picture from me and stared at it.

"Come on." I took his hand and led him over to a table at sidewalk café. "I'll explain everything."

SIMON GULPED TWO GLASSES of wine as I broke everything down, nodding periodically when I stopped to see if he was following along.

"If she's taken Francoise that could only mean one thing." He looked up from his wineglass.

"She knows the crucifix you dropped at the Medici Fountain is the fake one," I said, looking at the cell phone image of the terrified teen.

"And we're back to that damned crucifix again." Simon started to pour himself another and I put my hand over his glass.

"This won't help. Trust me. I should know. We need to stay sharp."

Simon's cell phone rang in my hand. I was so startled I almost dropped it. So much for staying sharp. The caller's number was blocked. I quickly handed it to him and he took a deep breath before answering it.

"Allo." He listened for a minute then looked at me and put the cell phone on the table between us and

pressed the speaker button. "We're listening," he told the caller.

"Did you enjoy my little performance at the Medici Fountain? I think it was my best one yet," came the disembodied voice of Sylvie Renard.

I was confused, but Simon's eyes narrowed. "You were the screaming tourist in the hat with the camera. You shot Garland and shoved him in the pond before we got there. You killed your own partner."

"He'd already served his purpose," she replied without a trace of emotion.

"How were you planning to get the crucifix from us at the fountain with Garland dead?" asked Simon.

"Oh that was simple. I just needed you to show up. The pickpocket I hired would have relieved you of the crucifix had you not dropped it when the cops showed up."

"And Juliet? Had she served her purpose, as well?" I asked.

"All she had to do was tell him where the crucifix was. Vincent never responded well to the word *no*. And don't change the subject. I'm so disappointed in the two of you." She sounded like she was chastising two children. "All you were asked to do was find the damned crucifix. And what did you do, instead? Tried to fool me with that fake piece of shit."

Unlike the terrified and weeping young woman we'd found at the bottom of the staircase at her father's house, this Sylvie sounded ice cold.

"We have no idea where the crucifix is," insisted Simon.

"Where's Fran— I mean Phoebe Samuelson? We want to talk to her," I blurted out. There was silence on the other end. "Put her on the phone now or we're hanging up."

Another agonizing minute of silence passed before we heard a small voice come on the line.

"Simon? Are you there?" It was Francoise. Her voice was thick with tears.

"I'm here, *cherie.*" Simon snatched the phone from the table. "Are you, okay? Has she hurt you?"

"I'm okay. Just give her what she wants so I can come home. You, Mom and me being together is all that matters. Remember Disney? It's the key to…" We heard a muffled cry like something was being pushed into her mouth and Francoise was silenced before she could finish her sentence.

"It's all so touching but I don't have time for this nonsense. You know what I want and you know what I'm capable of. Taking another life means nothing to me."

"And how do we know if we find you the crucifix that you'll let her go?"

"Crucifix? No, I'm afraid you're going to have to do much better than that to get back into my good graces. I want the book. I want the *Aurum Liber.* And you two are going to find it for me."

"If we couldn't find the crucifix, how do you expect us to find the *Aurum Liber?*" asked an incredulous Simon.

"Your father's society has been searching for that book for forty years. What makes you think we can find it?" I added.

"Because you have more incentive than they did. If you don't meet me at noon tomorrow with the book, for every hour that you're late, this little bitch will lose a body part. I think I'll start with the fingers first."

Simon buried his face in his hands.

"You're asking the impossible," I said. "Isn't there anything else we can do?"

Sylvie laughed and a chill went down my spine. "Okay. I'm a reasonable person. I'll give you a choice. You can either get me ten million euros by midnight tonight. Or the *Aurum Liber* by noon tomorrow. It's your choice."

How the hell were we supposed to get ten million euros? I nudged Simon and mouthed the word *Claire?* He shook his head no.

"She spends it as fast as she earns it and if she tries to get that much from Marty's trust, the police will know," he whispered.

There was no doubt that Sylvie would kill Francoise. We needed to buy as much time as we could.

"We'll get you the *Aurum Liber,*" I said.

Simon's face turned bright red with outrage. He put his hand over the receiver.

"Are you crazy?" he hissed. "You're going to get her killed. We have no idea how to find that book."

I pulled the phone away from him. "Are you there, Sylvie? Did you hear what I said? We'll get you the—"

"I heard you," she replied. "Tomorrow. Noon at Notre Dame. Don't keep me waiting."

"Wait!" shouted Simon. Sylvie didn't speak but she hadn't hung up yet. "I swear if you don't have Phoebe with you tomorrow, alive and well and without a hair on her head harmed, then the deal is off and I'll throw that damned book into the Seine before I let you get your hands on it." The light on the phone went out indicating that she'd finally hung up.

I could tell Simon didn't know whether to kiss me or kill me. "You wouldn't happen to still have that key, would you?" I ventured.

"No. I forgot to get it back from Francoise but I'm pretty sure I know where it is," he replied, finally smiling.

"You do?"

"Didn't you hear what Francoise was trying to tell us on the phone just now? Remember Disney. It's the key."

Disney is the key? It took me a minute to get it. "She hid the key in that picture of the three of you at Euro Disney!"

"I told you she was a smart kid." He beamed as proudly as a father.

I THOUGHT SIMON WOULD just zip back to Claire Samuelson's apartment to get the key while I waited at the café for him. But since we had a bad habit of getting separated, he insisted I come with him. I was not pleased, and neither was Claire, who alternated between glaring at me when no one was watching and sobbing on Simon's shoulder.

We'd already been there an hour and Simon had been unable to tear himself away from Claire to retrieve the key from Francoise's room. I tried to get it but Thierry Bernier, who had taken over the shift for Bellange, was watching me like a hawk. The police had already confiscated all the computers in the house, thinking Francoise may have met up with someone she'd met online.

"I'd have thought you'd be in a hurry to get back

home, Madame Sinclair. I'm surprised you're still lingering in Paris," said Bernier coolly after cornering
me in the kitchen. He was dressed in a black suit that
emphasized his lanky build and made him look like a
funeral home director.

"You make me sound like a rash that won't go away,
Lieutenant. Am I bothering you?"

"Madame Samuelson doesn't need the distraction of
your presence here with her daughter missing. Unless
you know something about this case you aren't telling
me, you are only in the way. Or are you just trying to
get more media attention for yourself?"

"I don't know anything. The media is overrated. And
whether or not I'm a distraction is not for you to say."

I left him in the kitchen and went to the living room
where Claire was sitting on the couch with Simon, staring at a phone that wasn't going to ring. She may not
win an award for mother of the year, but Claire Samuelson looked like she'd aged ten years since I'd seen her
on TV yesterday. I handed her the glass of bourbon I'd
poured for her in the kitchen and she snatched it out of
my hand and drained it. It was her third.

"Why doesn't that damned phone ring? Where is she,
Simon? Why is she doing this to me?" Claire wailed.
Her face was blotchy with tears. She was dressed in a
pale blue silk kimono that washed her out. Her long
blond hair was pulled into a sloppy ponytail.

I rolled my eyes and had to clasp my hands together
in my lap to keep from giving this self-centered woman
something to really cry about. I'd wondered the whole
way over to the apartment whether we should tell Claire
where her daughter really was. She deserved to know.
Simon vetoed the idea. And he'd been right.

"She'll be home soon. I promise," said Simon. I could tell he'd had enough, too. "I need to go to the bathroom, Claire. Maya will sit with you. I'll just be a minute." Simon eased out of Claire's grasp and kissed her cheek before looking over at Bernier, who was on his cell phone with his back to us, and heading off down the hall.

"You're fucking him, aren't you?" asked Claire, casually swirling the ice at the bottom of her glass. My face grew hot.

"Don't you have more important things to be worrying about than my sex life?"

"It's no big deal, honey. I've already had my turn. There's nothing wrong with having a little fun with Simon Girard as long as you don't get attached. You see," she said, leaning so close to me I could smell the bourbon on her breath, "Simon's still hurting over his dead wife and he'll stick his dick in every woman in Paris if he has to just to make himself feel better."

So, this was where Francoise got her cattiness. She'd certainly learned at the feet of a master. I glared at her.

"Did you think he loved you? Oh, you poor thing." Claire laughed and my face burned hotter.

The doorbell rang and Bernier answered it at the same time Simon reappeared in the living room, patting his pocket to let me know he had the key. I stood as none other than Diana Hughes of BBC World News arrived with her camera crew in tow to tape a public appeal for information and the safe return of Phoebe Samuelson. Thankfully, she barely glanced my way. Simon and I were able to slip out the door unnoticed as a stylist went to work on Claire to get her ready for her close-up.

SEIZE

"ANYTHING YET?" asked Simon from across the tiny hotel room.

"Not since you asked me two minutes ago," I snapped. I was rereading Juliet's journal for any clue as to where she could have hidden the crucifix.

After leaving my room earlier, and not wanting Claire showing up at his brother, Luc's, Simon had checked into the Timhotel in the Latin Quarter. I didn't think it was possible to have a room smaller than the one I'd had at the Bienvenue. I was wrong. There was hardly enough room to turn around let alone think.

"Are you sure there was no locker at the Sorbonne that that key could have fit?"

"For the thousandth time, *non.* I already told you Francoise had searched the Richelieu and tried the key everywhere in the building she could get to before Claire called and demanded she come home."

"Maybe there's some other campus facility she used while she was there."

"Anything is possible, Maya. The problem is we have no idea whether she even visited the same places she did when she was here back in April."

"Yeah, but she hid her flash drive in my camera for a reason. Something in her journal must be a clue, otherwise why bother?"

I continued to reread the entries made during and

after Juliet's stay in Paris back in April. My tired eyes were starting to burn when something I hadn't paid much attention to before jumped out at me.

"Maybe this person she visited when she was last here might know something."

"Who?" Simon came and leaned over my shoulder.

"Jean Taris. See." I pointed to the journal entry dated April 5, the day of the embassy reception where she met Sylvie. "It says, *Spent an hour at Jean Taris's.* Maybe that's one of her colleagues."

Simon chuckled. "Jean Taris was a French Olympic swimmer in the thirties."

"Maybe they were friends."

"He died years ago. There's a public pool named after him not far…" His voice trailed off as the answer hit us both at the same time.

"Juliet brought a bikini with her. I tripped over the top the night I found her body!" I shouted, jumping up.

"If she swam at Jean Taris, then she would have used a locker for her clothes. Let's go."

I grabbed my coat and followed Simon out the door.

PISCINE IS THE FRENCH WORD for pool. And Piscine Jean Taris was on rue Thouin behind the college Henri-IV, a five-minute walk from the Timhotel. It was dark outside as we hurried down the crowded streets, bumping into people out on the town for dinner or some Friday night fun. It was already well past nine o'clock and the cafés and bistros were filled to bursting. I was afraid the pool would be closed. But a quick call by Simon confirmed they were open until eleven o'clock.

"I can't believe I didn't think of it before," I said, practically running to keep up with Simon's long strides. "I didn't give that bikini top much thought. I just figured she swam at one of the hotels she was staying at."

"Jean Taris is popular with academics from the Sorbonne. She may have even had her own personal locker."

It was quiet and pretty deserted when we arrived. A muscular young man was the only attendant in sight as we searched the halls for the locker room.

"Peux-je vous aider?" inquired the attendant. I assumed by the inflection of his tone that he was asking if we needed help.

"Oui," Simon replied and pulled out the small key. He rattled off something in French. The young man took the key and recognition flashed across his face. He nodded.

"Un moment," he said and walked away.

"Where's he going?"

"I told him I forgot and left my things behind in a locker here last week. He's going to check locker 419."

We smiled at each other. The anticipation made it hard for me to stand still. Then Simon swore out loud. The attendant walked toward us empty-handed.

"It was empty?" I asked.

"Items left behind in lockers for more than a week get moved to our equipment office and have to be claimed in thirty days or they are discarded," replied the young man in English. "Please follow me."

We followed him through to the pool area where a few people were having a quiet night swim. The smell of chlorine was thick and the water in the pool cast lazy undulating shadows on the tiled walls. In the distance, through the wall of windows, I could see the dome of the Pantheon. No wonder Juliet had liked to swim here. It was beautiful. The attendant had reached the office before us and was dragging a large cardboard box out from inside the door.

"When you're done looking, just leave the box here and let me know before you leave." With a smile he was gone and Simon and I got on our knees to hunt through the large box.

The box was crammed with everything imaginable, T-shirts, swim trunks, swimming caps, goggles, towels, a half a dozen flip-flops with no mates, lighters, watches, glasses, jeans, a man's suit jacket, a pair of size-ten stilettos that made Simon laugh.

"Maybe I should give these to Max as a peace offering, eh?"

"Keep looking," I said as I pulled a dog-eared copy of Italian *Vogue,* a metro map and a leather-bound book out of the box.

The more we looked, the less likely it seemed that we were going to find the crucifix. Finally, we got to the bottom and had only succeeded in making a mess. The floor around us was strewn with the contents of the box.

"It was made of gold. Someone probably took it. Shit!" I threw the book back into the box and it landed faceup and the front cover fell open. Inside was a bookplate that read in fancy scroll lettering, "From the library of Evalyn Hewitt."

The book was *Rappacini's Daughter & Other Stories* by Nathanial Hawthorne. "Rappacini's Daughter" was the story of a botanist who had a beautiful daughter who was as toxic and deadly as the plants in his garden. Granted, Rappacini's daughter, Beatrice, wasn't a psycho like Sylvie Renard. Though her touch was deadly, she was a good person. Still, the connection between Beatrice and Sylvie's beauty and their lethal natures had not been lost on Evalyn Hewitt. Had she given the book to Juliet to warn her about her own child?

"What is it?" asked Simon.

"I think this may have been Juliet's." My voice was barely a whisper as I was afraid speaking louder would somehow make what I'd just said not true.

I flipped through the pages, and when I got to the center, I discovered the book had been hollowed out. A gold crucifix and a folded piece of parchment paper, yellowed and faded with age, lay in the secret compartment.

I held the Moret Crucifix in the palm of my hand and the gold glistened and shimmered in the light. Simon let out a whoop of joy. We hugged and kissed each other and then we quickly stuffed everything back into the box and rushed back to the hotel.

"THINK SHE'LL SETTLE FOR just the crucifix?" I asked as I lay across the bed that night, or rather early that next morning.

"Not when you promised her the book." Simon was stretched out next to me. He stroked my hair, twirling one long strand around his finger.

It was four in the morning and we were exhausted from racking our brains studying the crucifix and trying to figure out how to decipher it and find the *Aurum Liber*. The parchment paper that was with the crucifix was no help, either. It was just an old faded genealogy chart. I was staring up at the ceiling, trying to blink sleep away. Neither of us said anything for a while.

"What are you thinking about?" asked Simon.

"About two daughters born hundreds of years apart, both as the result of an affair," I said, rolling onto my back. "One daughter was shut away and hidden in a convent, denied a family and a life of her own, but ultimately accepted her fate thinking she was doing something noble, while the other daughter was accepted, loved, cherished and despite all that, has caused nothing but death and destruction."

"There's really no way to know what makes us who we are, Maya. But you can't compare Louise-Marie and Sylvie. They were born in different worlds."

"Hmm. Maybe." I was also thinking about the circumstances of my own birth and how it had shaped me. What kind of person would I have been if my mother had kept me? Simon nudged me.

"Come on. We need to focus. I think we should forget about meeting Sylvie and try and find where she's holding Francoise. If I can enhance that cell phone picture, maybe we can tell where Sylvie's keeping her."

"How much time would that take?"

"Not much time at all if I send it to a photographer I know at *Le Monde*. I know one who owes me a favor."

"We can't risk your friend running that picture in the paper. Sylvie will cut her losses and take off." By cutting her losses I meant Francoise's throat.

"He was a friend of Justine's. He'll be discreet."

"No. We can't risk it," I said. "And how will Claire feel knowing we knew where her daughter was all along and didn't say anything?" I could just see Thierry Bernier's amused expression as he slapped cuffs on us for obstruction.

"What do you suggest then?"

"We keep trying." I sat up and walked over to the table where the crucifix and the parchment lay. "Why would Juliet have hidden this genealogy chart with the crucifix if it didn't mean something? There must be a clue on here somewhere, if we could only read the damned thing."

The only word on the chart we could read clearly was the word *Father* underlined with a large exclamation point written in the upper left-hand corner. It was newer, fresher ink and must have been added by Juliet. The names on the chart were faded. The dim lighting in the hotel room didn't help. Simon and I had deduced that this must be the same genealogy chart Bernard Fouquet made to trace the family tree of Sister Cecile, whom the dying Sister Louise-Marie had entrusted with the crucifix and the *Aurum Liber,* on her deathbed.

"You know there was a copy machine in the office behind the front desk. I bet we could make a copy and make the writing on it as dark as possible. It might help."

"I guess it's worth a try. But…" I smacked my hand against my forehead. "Man, I must really be tired." I started laughing hysterically and couldn't stop.

"But what?" asked Simon. "What were you going to say?" He grabbed me and shook me.

"I can't believe I forgot!"

"You are starting to freak me out, Maya. What are you babbling about?"

"When I was in library school I took a class on doc-

ument preservation. We learned some old-school tech-
niques to restore faded ink!"

"How?" Simon asked, looking excited.

"Liver of sulphur."

"Come again?"

"It's used in jewelry making to oxidize silver and
bronze. If we apply it to this parchment, it will turn the
faded writing black."

"Just where do you suggest we get this stuff?"

"A jewelry store. I've seen tons of them around."

"And they won't be open for a few hours yet. Time
we can't afford to waste. Are you sure we can't use
something else?"

"Okay. Okay. Let me think."

"I still don't see why we can't just use a copier," said
Simon, holding the parchment paper under the desk
lamp.

"Because it will just make what's already visible on
the paper darker. It won't restore what's faded."

He made a disgusted noise and I rethought his idea
to enhance the cell phone picture of Francoise.

"You know, you might be on to something. If we had
a scanner, we could scan the parchment, save the image,
and open it in Photoshop. Then we can adjust the con-
trast, which might make the writing more legible."

"Luc has a scanner at his place," said Simon. "And
I have Photoshop on this laptop."

ONCE BACK AT LUC'S PLACE, we hooked up the scanner
to Simon's laptop and we were in business. It only took
a few minutes to scan the parchment and save it as
a JPEG. After we opened it in Photoshop we experi-
mented and reversed the background color making it

black and the words a lighter color, which made the names on the chart finally come into full focus.

"Sister Cecile was a twin," I pointed out. As I read over the rest of the chart, a familiar name jumped out at me, Anne-Elise.

Cecile Lambert and her sister Marguerite were the youngest of five children born to Didier and Anne-Elise Lambert in 1715. Could this be the same Anne-Elise from my dream? The young maid who was Louise-Marie's only friend at Fontainebleau Castle? Is that why she entrusted the crucifix and *Aurum Liber* to Sister Cecile, her old friend's daughter? Could this be possible?

"What is it?" asked Simon.

"Nothing," I lied and continued reading.

Cecile Lambert died in 1734. While her twin sister was in a convent preparing to marry God, Marguerite married a man named Alphonse DeRose. The rest of the chart was made up of the marriages and offspring of Marguerite's four children. It ended with Albertine Dumaire, who was ninety-six when she died in 1970. It was all very interesting but not at all helpful. We were at another dead end.

"Now what? We can read the damned thing and still can't figure out what we're supposed to see." Simon pushed back from the computer.

"We're just tired. Why don't I make us some coffee?" I offered.

"No amount of coffee is going to change the fact that this is all my fault. You were right. I never should have involved Francoise. Sylvie must have seen her with us on the Sorbonne's campus and followed her home."

"That's impossible, Simon. Sylvie was too busy killing Vincent Garland and making it look like a suicide to have seen Francoise with us."

"Then she saw me on TV with Claire and followed us back to her place. It doesn't matter how she made the connection. Francoise's life is in danger because of me." His voice was raw with emotion.

"Simon." I grabbed his hand and he pulled away from me.

"I'm going to take a shower." He walked out of the living room and the bathroom door slammed.

I went to sit on the couch and stared at the Moret Crucifix, which was sitting on the coffee table, propped against a wineglass. What were we missing? My head was aching and I lay back against the cushions and closed my eyes. I could hear the sound of the shower in the bathroom and resisted the urge to join Simon. He needed to be alone and I needed to figure out how to find the book, since, after all, it had been my idea. It was already 5:30 in the morning. Time was running out, yet exhaustion weighed my eyelids down and soon I was dreaming.

THE CONVENT WAS in a state of excitement over the arrival of Père Lachaise. In the entire time I had lived here, King Louis's chief confessor had never graced us with a visit. While the other sisters found excuses to linger in the halls near Mother Elizabeth's chamber, hoping to get a glimpse of the elderly Jesuit priest or perhaps overhear what they were discussing, I chose to bury myself amongst the books in the library. There was much work to be done as it had been all but neglected while I had been away.

I left the convent prepared to become Philippe's

*bride and returned resigned to becoming a bride of
Christ. Today was Philippe's wedding day. In the weeks
since my return I had received no messages from him.
The decision to leave Fontainebleau was my own and
made against his wishes. It had not been easy to leave.
Becoming his mistress held the threat of becoming a
hell I could not have endured nor inflicted upon any
children borne of our union. What if his love for me
soured? Where would I be then? Anne-Elise told me
that had been the fate of so many royal mistresses.
Madame de Montespan had suffered such a fall from
grace. King Louis had cast her aside. She was not even
invited to the wedding of their daughter to Philippe.*

*I tied an apron over my habit and got to work sweep-
ing the floors and took care not to breathe in the co-
pious dust dislodged by my broom. The sound of the
heavy library door opening and closing did not distract
me from my task. I imagined it was one of the sisters
and did not look up.*

"Excusez-moi, Louise-Marie." *An elderly man
dressed in a black cassock and skullcap stood before
me. A long white cloak was draped around his stooped
shoulder. Père Lachaise.*

*I instantly dropped my broom and knelt before him,
causing him to chuckle softly and gesture for me to rise.
With him was a young priest with pockmarked skin carrying a large leather-bound book tied shut with a red
silk ribbon.*

"Une donation pour la bibliothèque, Père?" *I asked,
hopeful that he had brought a wonderful new illuminated manuscript for our collection. So excited was I
at the prospect that I had failed to notice he had addressed me by name.*

"Non," *he replied, gesturing for the young priest to set the mysterious book on the table in front of me.*

Once the ribbon was untied, the young priest removed a false covering and revealed the book to be bound not in leather as I had originally thought but in solid gold. The front was covered in jewels set in a figure eight. I gasped and looked at Père questioningly.

"Le Roi Louis a une tâche importante pour vous," *he said, suddenly serious.*

King Louis had an important task for me? What did he mean?

THE SHRILL SOUND OF my cell phone startled me awake. A glance at the clock confirmed it was 6:50 in the morning. Why had Simon let me sleep? Where was he? I didn't recognize the number but answered anyway.

"Madame Sinclair?" came the voice of Monsieur Marcel's lawyer, Paul Moyet.

"Yes."

"I hope I've not disturbed you at this early hour."

"No," I said, shaking my head to clear the cobwebs. "It's okay. Have you found anything about Sylvie Renard?"

"Not much, I'm afraid. I'm outside the home of her aunt, Annette Renard, as we speak and I have bad news."

"What is it?"

"Annette Renard is dead. Her cleaning lady found her this morning. It appears she slipped and hit her head on her coffee table."

"Slipped or was pushed?"

"We've no way of knowing that at this point."

"And we've no way of knowing whether or not she

was really the one who identified the bodies of her brother and niece or if Sylvie impersonated her aunt." Deep down inside I knew Annette Renard's death was Sylvie's way of covering her tracks.

"All is not lost, *madame*. The parents of Shannon Davies are due to arrive here in Paris later this morning. I've arranged for them to view the body to see if it is indeed their daughter."

"You'll let me know what happens, right?"

"But of course," he replied and hung up.

"Simon?" I called out as I headed toward the bedroom. It was empty. The bed was still made. The bathroom was empty, too. There was a note taped to the bathroom mirror.

Maya,
Can't sit around doing nothing. We need a plan B. Went to see Justine's photographer friend Alain about enhancing cell phone pic. I will be back soon.
Simon

Damn it, Simon. I need you here, not chasing after dead ends, I thought as I balled up the note and threw it at the mirror.

I rooted through the kitchen cabinets until I found a lone bag of tea and boiled some water. I took my mug back into the living room and pulled open the blinds to let sunlight into the dark room. At the same time, the door opened, announcing Simon's return.

"Couldn't you at least have woken me up before you ran off?" I asked, not bothering to turn around.

Simon didn't answer. Instead, his sharp intake of breath made me look up. He was staring at the wall across from the windows. I rushed forward to get a better look. And when I saw what he was looking at I dropped my mug, splashing my pants with the hot liquid. The sun streaming through the windows had hit the crucifix propped up on the coffee table and was projecting the image of the stained-glass scene against the wall like a movie projector. Simon ran over and grabbed the crucifix.

"What are you doing? Put it back!"

"Flipping it."

He turned the crucifix so it was lying lengthwise and then had to maneuver it so the stained glass would catch the sun again. The result was like a giant stained-glass window in a cathedral. The colors were so vivid and the image was so clear that the nun's brown skin glowed, and she was actually smiling.

"Wait a minute." I walked over to get an even closer look. "Is this a different scene? I don't remember being able to see the nun's face before. This looks a lot like the Moret Tapestry."

"And the book the angel is holding wasn't open before, either, was it?" asked Simon.

"Do you still have Luc's sketches?"

Simon got Luc's sketchpad out of the cabinet and we confirmed that it was indeed a different scene. The nun's face wasn't visible and the book in the angel's hand was closed. Simon picked up the Moret Crucifix and studied it closely, putting his hand behind the handle so light couldn't shine through.

"Now it looks just like Luc's sketch again." He propped the crucifix back up on the coffee table.

"It's the sun. Remember what Dr. Hewitt said? The sun is the key to finding the book."

"That's amazing," whispered Simon. "It must be some kind of artist's technique to make it reflect something different when sunlight hits it."

"I can't believe all this time no one in the Society of Moret discovered this."

"They were stuffy old academics. They probably only studied the crucifix in their dark little faculty offices or behind closed curtains. Regular light wouldn't have this kind of effect."

"It still seems weird to me that in forty years no one would have discovered what sunlight did to the crucifix when Dr. Fouquet thought the sun was the key to finding the book."

"We can hardly ask him, Maya," replied Simon sarcastically, still clearly mesmerized by the scene on the wall. I went and stood next to him.

"Look, there's even writing inside the book the angel is holding? What's it say?" I asked.

"*'Dans le siège de la connaissance. Sous les yeux de tous les dieux. Sous la protection bénie du saint de Lutetia.'*"

I swatted his arm irritably. "In English, smart-ass!"

"'In the seat of knowledge. In view of all the gods. Under the blessed protection of the saint of Lutetia.'"

"Saint Lutetia? Who is Saint Lutetia?"

"Not Saint Lutetia, saint of Lutetia," Simon corrected.

"But what is Lutetia?"

"I've no idea. But it sounds familiar. Instead of obsessing about what we don't know, why don't we write down what we do know?"

I handed him Luc's sketchpad and sat next to him on the couch.

"Okay. We know the crucifix is the key to finding the *Aurum Liber*," I began.

"I thought the sun was the key to finding the *Aurum Liber*," said Simon, gesturing to the scene on the wall.

"Just write them both down."

"What else?"

"We know Sister Louise-Marie gave the crucifix and the *Aurum Liber* to Sister Cecile on her deathbed and someone in Sister Cecile's family hid…" I stopped mid-sentence when the answer to my earlier question suddenly hit me.

"What is it?"

"Of course!" I ran and got the copy of the genealogy chart we'd printed. "The sun, Simon! Don't you get it? The reason the Society of Moret never discovered what the sun did to the crucifix was because when Fouquet theorized that the sun was the key to finding the *Aurum Liber* he didn't mean *s-u-n*. He meant *s-o-n*. He was talking about one of Sister Cecile's descendants."

"Maybe," said Simon, looking skeptical. "But it's different in French—*s-o-n* in French is *fils,* and *s-u-n* is *soleil,*" said Simon.

"Evalyn Hewitt and Juliet Rice weren't French, so let's just say for the sake of argument Fouquet was speaking English when he made that statement."

"D'accord," he replied like he still wasn't convinced.

"Remember Monsieur Marcel said the stained-glass scene was older than the rest of the crucifix and was added a hundred years or more after Sister Louise-Marie's death?"

"By the person who must have hid it," said Simon, nodding his head.

"Exactly."

"But who?"

I spread the genealogy chart out on the coffee table. "Sister Cecile died a couple years after Sister Louise-Marie in 1734, right? So if we go forward by one hundred years and add an extra twenty years to be safe, that would leave us descendants who were alive between 1834 and 1854." I circled the names within the time frame.

"Make sure to narrow it down to only males."

"Yeah, that's usually what son means, Simon," I replied, cutting him a look.

"How many names fall into that time frame?"

"Seventeen," I said after recounting.

Simon let out a low whistle. "So many. We won't have time to look them all up."

"If we're looking for someone in the family who was a master glazier capable of doing the intricate stained-glass work on the crucifix, that would narrow it down, right?"

"Not necessarily. Back then tradesmen usually handed down such skills from generation to generation. Sister Cecile's male descendants could have all been glaziers."

"I forgot about that," I said, feeling deflated.

"Think we'll be able to find them all online?"

"Only one way to find out. And you can do the typing." I pulled out the computer chair for him.

LUCKY FOR US, France had started taking census records in 1836. Many of these records were available online in various databases. Twelve of the seventeen names were for male descendants living in and around the village of Fontainebleau where Sister Cecile had been born.

And Simon had been right. A skill had been handed down from the male descendants of Sister Cecile's family. But they weren't glaziers. With the exception of a barber, an innkeeper and a couple of butchers, the rest were bakers. We still had five names to account for and weren't having much luck finding anything other than their dates of birth and death.

"Dr. Fouquet tracked Albertine Dumaire to Paris. According to the chart she never married or had children. Maybe her obituary would give names of her relatives," I said. Simon wasn't listening. He was staring at the clock. It was a little after eight. I touched his cheek.

"Sorry, what did you say?"

"We need to find Albertine Dumaire's obit from 1970."

"Now, *that* I can do. I've got a friend who writes obits for *Le Monde* who could look it up in the archives." He pulled out his cell phone, dialed a number and asked for Etienne.

The conversation was in French and I couldn't follow along but after about fifteen minutes, Simon grinned, said *merci* and hung up.

"He's emailing it to me."

The obit was brief. Albertine Dumaire was born in Paris in 1874 the only daughter of Gillaume and Colette Dumaire. She worked her entire life in her family's bakery, Boulangerie Dumaire, taking it over in 1920. She was a lifelong member of Saint Severin church and was preceded in death by her parents and beloved fiancé, Yves Messier.

Next, I had Simon do an internet search for Boulangerie Dumaire and discovered a mention of it on a website dedicated to the gastronomic history of Paris.

Boulangerie Dumaire was listed as the place to get the best *pain au chocolat* in Paris from 1812 to 1955, when it was taken over by another family and renamed. The names of the Dumaire family were also listed and included all five of the names we'd been looking for.

"So they all came to Paris and worked in the family bakery. This is useless!" he said, waving the genealogy chart in the air. "We'll never find that damned book."

"Juliet figured it out. The answer has to be here, Simon."

"We don't have time to figure it out, Maya. Francoise's life is at stake!"

He was right. It was 9:00 and we were no closer to finding the book. Francoise was going to die and there was nothing we could do. It was on the tip of my tongue to suggest we call the police when Simon spoke up.

"I thought you said you got all the men's names between 1834 and 1854?"

"What?" I said as he handed me the genealogy chart.

"You missed this one." He was pointing to the name Hilaire-Marion Dumaire.

"That's a man's name? I thought it was a woman."

"It can be both. I had a friend in high school named Hilaire. It was a family name and all the firstborn sons got saddled with it but they all went by their middle names."

"If this is man's name, then why wasn't he listed as having worked in the family bakery?" I wondered aloud.

A quick look at the chart showed Hilaire-Marion Dumaire was born in 1822 the elder half sibling of Albertine Dumaire's father, Gillaume, and had also never married. His date of death wasn't listed.

Simon shrugged. "Every family has members who go their own way and don't follow in the family business. Sounds like he could be our guy." He typed the name into the census database.

"If he really is a guy."

And if he was, we couldn't find a single trace of him in any city in France with census records posted online. I studied the chart and noticed the word *Father* that Juliet had written in the upper left-hand corner was written with a capital *F*. And then it hit me. Hilaire-Marion Dumaire was born into a Catholic family, had never married or worked in the family bakery business.

"I think he was a priest, Simon."

Simon's head jerked up from the computer screen. I went over and joined him.

"That's why they couldn't find him. If he became a priest and changed his name, that would pretty much take him off the radar, right? This must be what Juliet figured out."

"But it's only nuns who take new names."

"It wouldn't hurt to look," I said, prodding him.

Simon's fingers reluctantly flew across the keyboard. He did a new search for Father Dumaire and came up with a solitary hit.

A Father Jean Dumaire was listed on a site about religious orders in France. He'd been a Eudist, a member of the Catholic Society of Jesus and Mary, and had left a promising career as an architect in Paris to join the priesthood. He moved to Columbia in 1855 to start a string of Eudist seminaries. Next, we looked up the Eudists and discovered their founder was Saint Jean Eudes.

"He took the name of Jean when he became a priest." I squeezed Simon's shoulders.

"And who better to hide a secret book than an architect," replied a grinning Simon.

"Okay. We know who hid the book. Now we need to find out where, because if he was an architect it could be hidden in any building he worked on." My heart was beating fast with excitement.

"That must be what that passage in the book the angel was holding is referring to, clues to where the book is."

We looked again at the words from the book the angel was holding that Simon had scribbled in Luc's sketchpad.

In the seat of knowledge. In view of all the gods. Under the blessed protection of the Saint of Lutetia.

"In view of all the gods? That's seems like a strange thing for a Catholic to write. For a Christian there would only be one God," I pointed out.

"Remember these are clues, Maya."

"I'm wondering if the seat of knowledge refers to a college." I mused.

"I hope not. Do you have any idea how many colleges are here in Paris?"

"I got it!" I had a eureka moment. "Ancient Greeks and Romans worshipped more than one God!" I started typing or rather hunting and pecking.

"We have buildings here in Paris modeled after Roman ones," added Simon.

When I found what I was looking for, I turned the laptop to face him. *"Voilà!"* I said. On the screen was a picture of the Pantheon in Paris. "The word *pantheon* in Greek means *temple of all the gods,*" I concluded triumphantly.

He hugged me.

"The book is hidden in the Pantheon! Let's go." He rushed past me for his coat and I caught him by his shirt and pulled him back.

"Not the Pantheon. It says in *view* of all the gods. Meaning wherever the book is hidden is in view of the Pantheon."

"That could be anywhere! You can see the Pantheon for miles," he said, throwing up his hands.

"Hold on. There's still this Saint of Lutetia thing to figure out. Maybe it's a church near there."

"The passage says the seat of knowledge. Wouldn't a church be considered a seat of spiritual enlightenment?"

"Yeah, okay, you've got a point. Is there a college named after this Lutetia person?"

"Not that I know of, but like I said that name sounds familiar." He did another internet search. "There's no Saint of Lutetia but there's a Hotel Lutetia," he said. "Now I remember. It's in St-Germain-des-Prés. I remember Justine took photographs of it for a travel article. It would certainly be in view of the Pantheon and maybe the saint is referring to St-Germain-des-Prés."

"But unless it used to be a college or something, a hotel isn't a seat of knowledge. What else came up in the search results?" I asked, leaning over his shoulder.

There were several links to the history of Paris and I reached down to click on one. Simon and I both read it and then looked at each other.

"Paris used to be a Roman settlement called Lutetia!" I exclaimed.

"I remember the Roman settlement part from my school history lessons, but who the hell is the Saint of Lutetia?"

More searching turned up no such person and it was 9:40. It was time to start thinking like a librarian. I stood and started pacing. If I were back home at work helping a student do research on this topic, how would I help them? I would tell them to look at the passage and take all the words into account that could be used in a key word search. Eliminate the unnecessary words, and add the one word we hadn't paid any attention to. The word *protection*.

"Under the blessed protection of the Saint of Lutetia. Okay, Paris used to be called Lutetia. So assuming the passage is referring to Paris, we'll leave Lutetia out of the search. And if something is under a saint's protection, what is that saint called?" I asked more to myself than Simon.

He shrugged, not in the mood to play guessing games.

"A patron saint!"

"I should have paid more attention in school," Simon grumbled and quickly did another search for *patron saint* and *Paris, France.*

"Of course, Saint Genevieve!" he exclaimed. "Saint Genevieve is the patron saint of Paris!"

"Is there a college or university named for this person?"

Simon didn't answer. He was having his own eureka moment. He jumped up and grabbed me.

"What is it? Tell me!"

"A seat of knowledge, Maya! You really don't know what that is besides a university? *You* of all people?"

"What—" I began and then I knew. "A library! It's a library!"

"Bibliothèque St. Genevieve to be exact. Located in the Place du Pantheon!"

"In view of all the gods," I whispered.

"Let's go get that book!"

DIX-SEPT

"THIS PLACE IS huge. Where the hell are we supposed to find the damned thing?" griped Simon as he looked down on the Bibliothèque St. Genevieve's massive reading room.

The dimly lit room was long and narrow. The high, vaulted ceilings supported by iron arches gave the room a cathedral-like feeling. Tables were arranged lengthwise in the center of the room between two rows of massive iron columns that supported the roof. The reading room was crowded, with few places to sit, yet it was so quiet you could hear a pin drop. Now, *this* was a library.

"Maybe it's on the shelf," I whispered. I didn't mean to whisper. My voice had automatically adjusted to library volume all on its own.

"You're kidding, right?" Unlike mine, Simon's voice pierced the silence and a couple of people looked up and gave him the evil eye.

I was only half joking. Hiding a book in a library was pretty damned smart, like hiding a grain of sand on a beach. And it wasn't just the librarian in me that thought so, either. The only problem would be making sure no one ever checked it out, which meant the book was hidden someplace where none of the library staff would have knowledge of it, or someone working here knew about the book and made sure no one had access to it.

Before Simon and I left the apartment, we printed out info about the library. It had been designed by French architect Henri Labrouste and built between 1845 and 1851, which was within the time frame for the stained-glass scene to have been added to the handle. Hilaire-Marion Dumaire, the future Father Jean Dumaire, would have had access to the talents of a master glazier in his line of work who could have altered the original crucifix for him. Four years after its construction, Dumaire had joined the priesthood and gone to Columbia where he most likely died. Sometime either during the construction or after, the *Aurum Liber* had been hidden in the library. Now we just had to figure out where. *Think, Maya.* My last dream ran through my head like a movie on fast-forward but suddenly stopped at the point when the young priest removed the leather covering from the gold book. I had a sudden revelation.

"You know, if Dumaire went to the trouble of having the crucifix altered, maybe he had the book itself altered in order to hide it here more easily," I said.

"Altered in what way?"

"The only way I can think of hiding a gold-and-jewel-encrusted book would be to cover it in cloth or leather."

"And he could have easily changed the title on the book, making it look like another book," said Simon, getting excited.

"Exactly."

I went over to an empty computer station and pulled up the online catalog. Luckily, the catalog allowed searches in English. I instantly felt at ease. I was on familiar ground. Simon pulled up a chair and sat next to me.

"What are you looking for?"

"Dumaire was an educated man. He'd have known how libraries work. I can't imagine he'd have meant for the book to be looked at by the public. I'm betting it's here hidden as a title connected to Dumaire that no one would ever check out or in a rare book collection no one would have access to."

I did a search on Saint Jean Eudes, the founder of the Eudists, and discovered the library had numerous books on the man, most of them located in the reserve room, which meant they were still accessible. I did searches on Saint Genevieve and architect Henri Labrouste with similar results. Labrouste actually had an entire collection devoted to him.

"Do a search for Jean Dumaire," said Simon. I gave him a quizzical look. "Just a hunch," he replied.

The search for Jean Dumaire pulled up no results. But a search on Hilaire-Marion Dumaire turned up a record for a single book about baking entitled *Cuisson de la Manière de Dumaire.* The copyright was 1851, the year the library's construction was complete.

Simon chuckled. "*Baking the Dumaire Way.* I bet the demand for that book is through the roof."

I smiled. "Sounds like a dust catcher alright."

"Does it say what the page count is? Dr. Hewitt said the *Aurum Liber* had more than five hundred pages of text."

"No, it doesn't."

"Where is the book?"

"It's just a brief record with just the title and author. We'll have to ask."

"ACCORDING TO OUR RECORDS, this book has never been on the shelf. It was a donation and has been in permanent storage for years," explained the librarian behind the circulation desk after consulting his computer.

"Is there any way we can take a look at it?" I asked.

"Non," he replied, shaking his head apologetically. "I'm afraid it is fragile and in a state of disrepair, though I'm surprised it wasn't completely withdrawn. It has a partial record as if they were planning to put it out here on the shelf when we automated the collection and never got around to it."

"Can we talk to one of the catalogers then? Maybe the book is about to be withdrawn and they'd be willing to sell it to us," I asked.

"I'm afraid they'll just tell you the same thing I just did," he replied a little stiffly. "None of them has been here long enough to know any more than I do. Our catalogers are currently undertaking a massive project to clean up our online holdings records and it may be many months before this book's status is updated. If you leave me your contact information, I would be glad to contact you once I have more information."

"But—" I began until Simon cut me off.

"Merci," he said, pulling me by the hand. He didn't let go until we were clear of the circulation desk.

"What are you doing? We can't give up. The book is here."

"I know. It's down there."

He was pointing down into the reading room where I could see a bank of doors beyond the stacks along the opposite wall. Most of them looked like offices. One of them was labeled *Stockage.* He headed down the stairs into the reading room with me on his heels.

"I noticed it when we first got here," he whispered when we arrived in front of the gray metal door. It was locked, of course.

"How are we going to get in?"

"Do you have a hairpin?"

"No. But how about this?" I pulled a paperclip from my bag.

"Excellent."

Simon turned so his back was to the door and got busy picking the lock. A middle-aged librarian with an armload of books came out of an office two doors down and I grabbed Simon around the waist and started passionately kissing him and pressing him against the door. I figured if we were going to get caught doing something we shouldn't be doing in a library, better it be locking lips than picking locks. However, the librarian just gave us a bemused look and walked the other way. I guess as long as we were quiet she didn't care. You just gotta love Paris.

"Hurry *up,*" I whispered in his ear. "What's taking so long?"

"Don't be so pushy. You're not the one performing under pressure."

"Do I even want to know where you learned how to do this?"

"I was an alter boy. You'd be surprised at what I learned in church."

At the sound of another person coming down the hall, I stuck my tongue in Simon's ear and he let out a low groan. At the same time there was a soft click. The door was unlocked. A quick peek around to make sure no one was watching and we were through the door and found ourselves at the top of a landing looking down two narrow flights of stairs. It was a basement.

"I hope if anyone saw us come in here they'll just think we're horny and not thieves," I said as I followed Simon slowly down the steps.

I felt along the wall on the way down for a light switch but couldn't find one. It was pitch-black and smelled like dust and long-forgotten things. I sneezed and Simon shushed me. He finally located a light switch and flooded the room with light. The basement was cavernous with painted concrete walls and linoleum on the floor. Metal shelving units filled the middle of the room and held books, boxes of books and old equipment. Numerous book carts loaded down with books were shoved into every corner. There were outdated wooden desks along one wall with old newspapers stacked on top.

"You look on the carts and I'll search the shelves," I told him.

It was 10:15 and we needed to hurry. The shelves toward the back of the basement looked the oldest and I got busy searching. I made quick work of the metal shelves because the majority of the books were from the '60s and '70s. I didn't find a single book older than fifty years. In my haste to move on to the next set of shelving, my shoulder knocked a dusty folder from its perch atop a file cabinet onto the floor. I bent to pick up the papers and pictures that spilled out. They were old sepia photos of a construction site from the 1800s.

They were photos of the construction of the Bibliothèque St. Genevieve from 1847. There were four photos in all showing the construction at various stages. Only one picture had people in it. Two solemn-looking men posing inside what I recognized as the partially constructed reading room. The room was bare save for the iron columns supporting the roof. The floor hadn't even been laid yet. I recognized Henri Labrouste from the internet research. Bearded and dressed in a suit, Labrouste stared directly at the camera with what looked like rolled-up building plans in one hand. The man next to him was shorter by several inches and also in a suit with a mustache, a goatee and thick, dark, wavy hair. The man appeared to be about twenty years younger than Labrouste. But his eyes looked so familiar that I held the photo up to the light to get a better look. The face of someone I knew stared back at me. It couldn't be him! It was impossible.

"Maya, any luck?" called out Simon, startling me so badly I dropped the photo. I let it lie where it fell, too afraid to touch it, and hurried off to join Simon.

"None of these books are the right date. Looks like there're more shelves farther back," I told him and hoped my voice didn't sound as shaky as I felt.

The deeper into the basement we got, the lower the ceilings became, the older the shelving and the dustier the books, but still no *Baking the Dumaire Way.* I spied a set of shelves against a brick wall and went over to search it while Simon rooted through boxes on the floor. I was halfway down the shelf when a glint of gold caught my eye. It was a red leather-bound book with a gold infinity symbol raised on the spine. I pulled it out and the title *Cuisson de la Manière de Dumaire* glinted up at me in flaking gilt lettering. It was Hilarie-Marion Dumaire's book.

"Simon! I found it!"

He rushed over and stumbled over a box of books

in his haste, but I'd noticed a big problem before he even reached me. The book was only one hundred and thirty pages. Not nearly long enough to be the *Aurum Liber*. And once we flipped though it, we quickly discovered it truly was a cookbook. It was now 11:57 and too late to search elsewhere. Tears of defeat filled my eyes and Simon punched the wall, bloodying his fingers and swearing.

"She's a good as dead," he said in a flat voice.

My only response was to slam the book hard back into its slot and in doing so the palm of my hand pressed against the raised infinity symbol. It depressed. We heard a loud creak and a scraping sound as the entire shelf swung out from the wall with a groan and a cloud of dust. I had to jump out of the way before it hit me. Behind the shelf was a long, dark, narrow passageway.

"Oh my God. Is that what I think it is?" I said between coughs. The dust was thick and settled in my nose and throat.

Simon walked into the opening of the passage. After pulling down thick cobwebs he held his hand out to me. I took it and he flinched. It was the hand he'd punched the wall with.

"Hold on." I rooted around in my bag until I found a silk scarf to wrap around his bloody fingers.

The passageway was too narrow for us to walk side by side. So I followed behind. It was dark, but yellowed candles sitting inside grime-coated sconces on the wall were visible. I pulled matches from my bag and lit the first two on either side of the entrance. Once the sconces were lit, we could see the path beneath our feet was dirty mosaic tile in swirling patterns of gold, greens, blues and purples.

As we walked deeper into the tunnel, we lit the candles along the walls to light our way. We were both silent. The passageway wound around for about a hundred feet. It finally opened up on a small circular room with a high domed ceiling. Simon quickly lit the large freestanding candelabras inside the room and revealed the robin's-egg-blue ceiling adorned with painted scenes of angels blowing trumpets.

"Dumaire must have built this when the library was being constructed," said Simon.

Even in the dim lighting a marble pedestal in the center of the room was visible. A large faded and worn tapestry hung from a rod in the ceiling. It was the stolen Moret Tapestry, missing since 1959. That meant that though this room was built one hundred and sixty years ago, someone had been in here sometime in the last fifty years. And as impossible as it still seemed to me, I knew who that someone was.

"So this is what this has all been about," breathed Simon in an awestruck whisper.

Sitting on the marble pedestal in front of the tapestry was a large dust-covered gold book, the *Aurum Liber*... at last. Emeralds, diamonds, amethysts and rubies were set free-form into the large infinity symbol on the cover. The pages were edged in gold. The jewels and gold glinted in the candlelight. Simon and I both grinned. I reached out to touch it and my hand froze as a cold voice came from the passageway behind us.

"I'll take that."

Francoise came stumbling out of the passageway first, followed by a limping Sylvie Renard holding a gun to the back of the girl's head. When Francoise saw

Simon, she launched herself at him, burying her face against his chest and sobbing.

"Are you alright? Has she harmed you?" Simon held the girl at arm's length to examine her.

"I'm okay," she replied.

Sylvie kept the gun trained on us but let her eyes wander around the room before resting on the *Aurum Liber.*

"Surprised to see me?"

"How did you…?" Simon began.

"I've been following you two ever since you left the fashion designer's apartment last night, Girard." Sylvie then turned to me. "And I can't believe you never noticed. I could have killed you when you ran across the street to jump in that cab," she said to me.

She must have been the one driving that florist van that almost ran me down.

"You didn't think I really wanted you to meet me in a public place, did you? Surely you realize I can't allow the three of you live. And what a fitting final resting place for a librarian.

Francoise gasped and I looked at Simon. He looked ready to tear her to pieces. Sylvie waved me aside with the gun to get closer to the book. Her hand stroked the cover, smearing years of built-up dust and grime in the process.

"I've waited my entire life to see this book. Endured my father's endless bedtime stories as a child about the magic gold book and the power it possesses, the power of eternal life and wealth beyond belief. And now it's mine. Do you hear me, Father?" she shouted. Her voice echoed off the walls. "You took everything from me, but I have your precious book and I'm going to live forever and be rich."

"You don't think what's in that book is real, do you?" Simon asked. "The book was just an expensive prop used to keep an unwanted, and unloved child in her place and out of sight. The book is a lie, Sylvie!"

"If it's a lie, why has it been hidden from the world all these years! Someone must have found out what was in it was real! Otherwise, why keep it hidden?"

"You're crazy!" I said, though I knew now that someone had discovered what was in the book was real.

Sylvie hit me in the temple with the gun. Pain exploded in my head and little balls of light swam in front of my eyes as I struggled to keep my wits about me. Simon clenched his fists and took a step forward until I gave him a warning look.

"Don't ever call me crazy," said Sylvie. "All my life I've been made to think there was something wrong with me. It's all of you hypocrites who have the problem with all of your fears and jealousies and inadequacies, such useless emotions. How do think I got Juliet to betray the Society of Moret and steal the crucifix?"

"I'm sure you're just dying to tell us," I said, rubbing my temple where a small knot had formed.

"I told her about how my son was taken from me and put up for adoption without my knowledge. I'd found out who adopted him and wanted him back but I needed a lot of money for a good lawyer. His adoptive parents were very wealthy and planning to put up a fight. My father cut me off financially. It was Juliet's idea to steal the crucifix and put a fake in its place. She was convinced she could find the book and we could sell it, get my son back and run away and live happily ever after like one big happy family. I had Garland trash her hotel room so she'd think the society had found out what she'd done and go into hiding. I played on all her emotions." She laughed.

"And her guilt and regret over giving you up? When did she figure out you were just using her?" I asked.

"Right after she finally figured out where the book was and I have him to thank for that," she said, training the gun on Simon. "Juliet had no idea your brother was dead. She didn't find out until the day you confronted her demanding answers. That's when she realized I killed him and she hid the crucifix from me."

Simon looked like he'd been punched. His eyes narrowed.

"That's right. I killed your brother. Juliet was sloppy. She gave him our real names. He was a liability I couldn't afford."

"You soulless monster!" Simon shook off Francoise and lunged for Sylvie.

Sylvie didn't hesitate. Before I could stop her, she fired the gun and the sound was deafening as it reverberated off the walls like thunder. The bullet struck Simon in his side and sent him crumpling to the floor.

Sylvie kept the gun pointed and pulled her finger to fire again. "No!" screamed Francoise and she threw herself on top of Simon to shield him.

I grabbed the heavy gold book from its pedestal and swung it at her, hitting her in the shoulder and knocking her sideways as the gun fired. The bullet whizzed past Francoise's head and hit the wall. I dropped the book and tackled Sylvie, knocking her down and grabbing the hand with the gun, pinning her to the floor. She bucked and kicked like a wild horse. Simon groaned and clutched his side. Blood seeped from between his fingers.

"Get up to the library and get help, Francoise! Now! Hurry!" I yelled at the weeping girl who gave Simon an anguished look before taking off like a shot through the passageway.

"I should have killed the two of you when you came to my father's house. I should have put you in the freezer with Shannon Davies," she said as she panted and struggled beneath me.

"So you killed her, too, you crazy bitch!"

"Vincent killed her for me when I realized how I could use our resemblance to my advantage. He would have done anything for me. I did all the kinky things his beauty queen wouldn't do. Sylvie Renard died and I'm going to disappear with the book and start a new life."

"How could you let him kill Juliet…your own mother?"

"She was never my mother!" Sylvie shrieked, spittle flying. "She spent her whole life studying the life of a secret princess, an abandoned, unwanted child. And what did she do when she had a child of her own? Abandoned me!"

"And what about your son, Sylvie? How will he feel when he finds out his real mother is a murderer?"

"My son is dead! Hit by a car two years ago like a dog in the road! That English couple they thought was so much better for him than me weren't even watching him!"

We continued to struggle and rolled across the floor, knocking over the marble pedestal. Sylvie rolled on top of me and pressed the barrel of the gun to my forehead.

"You're going to die just like my father and the rest of those old fools. They all knew about my real mother and they all lied to me! They all knew about my son and they all lied to me!"

"Careful, Sylvie. Your emotions are showing. All this anger isn't useful."

Enraged, Sylvie balled up her fist to punch me and I moved my head causing her to punch the floor. She screamed in pain and I managed to knock the gun out of her hand. It skittered across the marble floor and we both scrambled after it. Sylvie reached it first. She spun around and fired. But the shot went wide and missed me by a mile, taking out a candelabrum, instead.

I kicked her injured thigh, knocking her off balance. Simon wasn't moving. I couldn't tell whether he was breathing. He was as pale as a ghost. Blood pooled underneath him. I ran toward him. I could hear voices coming down the passageway. Sylvie aimed at me. I slipped in Simon's blood and fell. I frantically grabbed for the nearest thing to me, which turned out to be the *Aurum Liber*. Sylvie fired and I held the book up like a shield.

The bullet must have struck one of the jewels on the cover because it ricocheted, hitting the marble ceiling, then the floor, then bouncing upward and striking Sylvie Renard right between the eyes. Her mouth formed an *O* of surprise as she sank to her knees. A single trickle of blood ran down the side of her nose and she fell on her face just as Francoise, the librarian from the circulation desk and a security guard came running out of the passageway. I crawled through the blood over to Simon and cradled him. He was still breathing but just barely.

"Don't you dare die on me, Simon Girard. Not after everything we've been through! Stay with me. Please hold on. Don't let go," I whispered as hot tears streamed down my face.

Simon's eyelids fluttered open and he squeezed my hand. "I won't let go if you don't." His voice was a hoarse whisper.

"I won't," I assured him as I squeezed his hand in return.

"Promise?"

The look in his eyes told me he meant more than letting go of his hand. I kissed his cold forehead. "I promise."

He gave me a weak smile and then passed out.

ÉPILOGUE

Five days later

"THESE SUTURES are driving me mad! And where the hell is that doctor? I'm ready to go," Simon exclaimed irritably.

"Oh, quit your bitching. Better sutures than that bullet. And you could be a little more grateful, you know. The man did save your life." I was sitting in the chair next to his bed, reading a magazine.

It was my last visit. Simon was being discharged from the hospital and I was flying home that afternoon. I'd promised to help him get settled in at his new apartment, which was his brother Luc's old place. Max had gotten past his anger at Simon and agreed to serve as his nurse, and had even bought a nurse's uniform and cap for the occasion. It had helped matters considerably that the gun charge against Simon had been dropped when he'd insisted he'd found the gun on the ground at the Medici Fountain and that it must have belonged to Sylvie Renard. With Sylvie dead, there was no way of proving otherwise. Everyone was more than happy to forget the whole thing.

"I've got enough gratefulness to spare. It's patience I'm in short supply of. I don't know how anyone gets any rest in a hospital when they come in every hour on the hour poking and prodding you. The food is a joke.

The only thing I've enjoyed were those sponge baths of yours." He gave me a devilish grin.

I swatted him with my magazine. The door swung open and I expected to see Simon's doctor come in but it was Francoise.

"So, is it true? Are you really getting sprung from this joint today?" Francoise plopped down on the edge of the bed.

Claire Samuelson had a brief flash of maternal instinct and tried to keep her daughter away from Simon, blaming him for her kidnapping—though she didn't mind milking the experience for all it was worth in the media. However, one invitation to dinner by a Russian billionaire who saw her crying on TV, and she was jetting off to Moscow. Francoise was left all alone again, free to do whatever she wanted.

"Oui," replied Simon. "And I'm tempted to just leave. You didn't see Dr. Babineaux lurking around out there, did you? Knowing that horny old bastard, he's got some poor nurse cornered in a supply closet."

Francoise laughed and then looked over at me and gave me a smile. Ever since that day in the basement of the Bibliothèque St. Genevieve, she'd been grudgingly nice to me. But that was probably because she knew I was going home. What she didn't know was that I'd be coming back...and soon. It seems Paris isn't done with me yet. I didn't know what the future held for Simon and me but I knew it wouldn't be boring and I wanted us to get to know each other without the threat of death and prison hanging over our heads.

Not interested in hearing all about the latest teen drama from Francoise's school, I got up to give them some time alone.

"You don't have to leave, Maya," said the girl. I was shocked. Usually when I said I was leaving, she practically held the door open for me.

"Oh, no, it's okay. I've got some phone calls to make. I'll be right back," I said and started to go. As I walked past Simon, he grabbed my hand and gave me a questioning look. "I'll be right back. I promise," I assured him. He gave me a dazzling smile and brought my fingers to his lips.

"You'd better," he said softly. "I'm not letting you go too far." I gave him a quick peck on the lips and caught a glimpse of Francoise rolling her eyes.

There was a small garden next to the hospital and I sat on one of the benches to people-watch. Minutes later, a Bichon Frise ran up to me and started barking. I bent down to pet Agnes's wriggling back and her new owner sat next to me on the bench.

"You've not been returning my calls, Madame Sinclair. You're not avoiding me, are you?" asked Sebastian Marcel.

He looked a little thinner than when I'd last seen him. But his eyes were alert behind his wire-rimmed glasses. He'd been released from jail last week and I'd yet to see him. I was too overwhelmed.

"I haven't meant to. I've just had a lot going on," I replied and it wasn't a lie.

Between keeping vigil at the hospital, dodging reporters and answering endless questions from the police, I'd had little time to really process what had happened in the library. And I still wasn't sure I truly believed what had happened.

"And Monsieur Girard? Will he be alright?"

"He's being released today."

"I'll be eternally grateful to the two of you for saving the *Aurum Liber* from Sylvie's clutches."

"Where is the book now?"

The old man shrugged. "It seems to have vanished from the police evidence room," he replied with a twinkle in his eye. I was getting mad.

"You know, you could have just told us where the damned thing was instead of putting us through all that drama. We could have all been killed. Simon almost was!"

"Madame Sinclair, I'm sorry. I don't understand..."

I pulled out the picture I'd found at the library and smuggled out during the chaos that ensued after the arrival of the police, and tossed it on his lap.

"Cut the act. Either that man is a relative of yours, or that's *you* in 1847. I need the truth, *monsieur*. I deserve the truth. And I want it now."

His shoulders slumped and he gave me a look of resignation. He picked up the picture and smiled. "Ah, I remember taking this picture like it was yesterday. I was so proud to be working with Labrouste, even though I was just a lowly assistant."

"How is this possible? How can you be close to two hundred years old?"

"I'm afraid you know the answer to that already."

"The *Aurum Liber?*"

He nodded. "I was such a sickly child, Madame Sinclair. My asthma was so bad I couldn't work in my family's *boulangerie*. My *maman* died in childbirth and I was never close to my father. He all but forgot about me when he remarried and had children with his new wife. The Boulangerie Dumaire was his life and that of my uncles, stepmother and eventually my half siblings.

I was always different from them. I loved to read and draw. I wasn't interested in being a baker. One day, when I was home sick and everyone else was at work, my *grand-mère* showed me the crucifix and the *Aurum Liber*. It had been in our family for decades, though not everyone in the family knew. She told me she was sharing the family secret with me because I was special. She told me all about the Black Nun of Moret and how she entrusted the book and crucifix to my great-great-great *tante,* Sister Cecile. She told me when she died, the book would be mine and I must swear to keep it secret and hidden away."

"But you used it instead?"

"Oui. I was still just a boy when my *grand-mère* died, barely sixteen. I did not know any better. I was bored and lonely and saw no harm in experimenting with the formulas in the book. It took me a few years to gather everything to make the philosopher's stone."

"But it worked," I pointed out.

"Oui," he said with a mirthless laugh. "But only as long as I took the elixir."

"You must have lived an amazing life, *monsieur.* You must have seen and done so much."

"I have, indeed. But it came with a price. I was very lonely for most of my life, watching everyone I loved grow old and die. I couldn't stay in one place for very long. I didn't have the vision or the ambition to become a great architect. After I commissioned the stained-glass work on the crucifix to mark its hiding place, and did my duty and hid the book away as I promised my *grand-mère,* I was called to the priesthood. I lived in South America for many years, many of them quite happy. I didn't return to Paris until after World War II when the only one left in my family was my niece, Albertine. She was born after I left Paris and didn't know me. I got to know her in my work at her church, Saint Severin."

"And you gave her the crucifix?"

He nodded. "She was elderly and had never married or had children. I couldn't burden her with knowledge of the book. But I did give her the crucifix before I left Saint Severin. But not before doing something vain and silly."

"What?"

"It was around this time that I left the priesthood. I was feeling quite invincible and I'm afraid my ego got the best of me. I had the initials of my new identity, Sebastian Marcel, added to the stained glass scene in the crucifix's handle before I gave it to Albertine."

"So that's why the *S* and the *M* aren't on the book or in the Moret Tapestry. I wondered why."

"I did it as a way of marking something that I'd come to believe was mine and mine alone. The crucifix was the only constant in my life, the only link to my past. I told myself after Albertine died I'd retrieve it but I never did. I enrolled in the Sorbonne where I met Bernard, Evalyn, Oliver and Anna, the best friends I could have ever hoped to have. I finally felt appreciated for the person I was."

"You were in love with Dr. Hewitt, weren't you?" I couldn't shake the image of the adoration on his face in that picture in his apartment.

"Very much so. I had hoped that one day she might fall for me, too. But," he said, sighing heavily, "she only had eyes for Bernard. Still, I was happy and honored to have been her friend."

"And Bernard was in love with Louise-Marie, a woman who died more than two hundred years ago. A woman he'd never have."

"*Obsessed* would be the better word. He and Evalyn were briefly engaged. But Evalyn couldn't compete with a dead woman. She ended the engagement but loved Bernard for the rest of her life and always wore his engagement ring on a chain around her neck."

"*Her* engagement ring? You mean the silver posy ring?" The September sun was warm but I was suddenly cold. Goose bumps had broken out on my arms.

"*Oui.* Bernard had it designed himself. It was an exact replica of a seventeenth-century posy ring Evalyn had admired in a museum while on holiday. What is it?" he asked, concerned when he saw my face.

Now that the dam had been breached I could hold it in no longer. Everything came pouring out. I told him about what Dr. Hewitt had told me about the ring and what happened when I'd put it on. I told him about the dreams where I was the Black Nun of Moret and the things in the dreams that had been real. When I stopped I expected him to be shocked. Instead, he squeezed my hand and smiled.

"As I've already told you, Madame Sinclair, Evalyn had a wonderful sense of humor."

"I don't think it was very funny," I said softly, pulling my hand away.

"Forgive me, my dear. I don't mean to make light of all you've experienced. I sit here beside you living proof that the impossible is indeed possible. I cannot explain what happened to you. But I will say that the power of suggestion is a very powerful thing, indeed. Perhaps Evalyn's story about the posy ring tapped into the connection you were already feeling to Louise-Marie, making you more susceptible for her spirit to guide you."

"Maybe." I still didn't know what I believed. I was just happy the ring was off my finger. Somewhere between the library and the hospital, while my hands were slick with Simon's blood, the ring had slipped off my finger. I had no idea where I'd lost it.

"You know, it was after I met Evalyn that I stopped taking the elixir. I was tired of moving around. Paris is my home. I want to die here and I finally realized everyone was moving on but me. I was trapped in time."

"But you never really wanted the Society of Moret to find the book, did you?"

"Sadly, no one paid much attention to Bernard's research and I wasn't worried about the book being found until he found the crucifix. Then I did everything in my power to prevent the discovery of the *Aurum Liber*. Each time it was my year to study the crucifix, I would come up with the most outlandish theories to try and steer them in the wrong direction. I even warned them that direct sunlight would fade the colors of the stained glass," he said, chuckling.

"Would it have been so wrong to let them find the book?"

He sighed. "I made a promise to my *grand-mère* to guard the book. And I've kept my promise. My friends told themselves they were seeking the book purely for academic purposes. But I knew if they found it they would do as I did and try the formulas. No one should live forever, Madame Sinclair. What value does life have if there is no death?"

"Well what about Agnes?" I asked, looking down at

the little dog sitting at her new master's feet. Monsieur Marcel smiled sadly.

"I'm afraid love makes us do foolish things. And when you're in love with a woman who is distraught because her beloved dog is dying of old age, you'll do anything to make her happy, to see her smile again, even if it risks exposing a secret you've been hiding all your life."

"But she looks so…healthy. Are you still giving her the elixir?" I reached down to pet Agnes and she licked my fingers.

"I gave her exactly one dose…twenty-five years ago. But animal physiology is different from that of humans. I have no way of knowing how long she'll live."

"Did Dr. Hewitt know what you'd done?"

"I suspect she may have. But anytime she brought the subject up, I always told her it was the power of her love that was keeping Agnes alive for so long. After a while, it no longer mattered to her."

"But why steal the Moret Tapestry?"

"I always felt it belonged with the book. And even after it was gone, Bernard was still undeterred in his quest. He was brilliant and determined. He always used to say that history is not lily-white but multicolored. He wanted Louise-Marie's story to be told—as well it should. I couldn't believe it when he managed to track down the crucifix. I'd lost track of Albertine in the thirty years after I'd given her the crucifix. I figured once she passed away it would simply disappear thus breaking the link between it and the book."

"Well, I hope it's in a safe place now. And you can put this with it." I pulled the Moret Crucifix from my bag and handed it to him.

He stared at it and smiled like he was seeing an old friend. Tears filled his eyes. "I would have told you where to find the *Aurum Liber* had I remembered at the time where I hid it. The stress of being in jail was hard on me. In all my one hundred and eighty-five years on this earth, I've never once been arrested. And I'm afraid after so many years my memory is failing me. Some days I'm unsure of my own name or where I live. But today is a good day." He smiled.

"Yes, *monsieur,*" I said, patting his hand and thinking of Simon and a future full of possibilities. "Today is a very good day."

* * * * *

REQUEST YOUR FREE BOOKS!

2 FREE NOVELS
PLUS 2 FREE GIFTS!

MYSTERY **WORLDWIDE LIBRARY®**
Your Partner in Crime

YES! Please send me 2 FREE novels from the Worldwide Library® series and my 2 FREE gifts (gifts are worth about $10). After receiving them, if I don't wish to receive any more books, I can return the shipping statement marked "cancel." If I don't cancel, I will receive 4 brand-new novels every month and be billed just $5.24 per book in the U.S. or $6.24 per book in Canada. That's a saving of at least 34% off the cover price. It's quite a bargain! Shipping and handling is just 50¢ per book in the U.S. and 75¢ per book in Canada.* I understand that accepting the 2 free books and gifts places me under no obligation to buy anything. I can always return a shipment and cancel at any time. Even if I never buy another book, the two free books and gifts are mine to keep forever.

414/424 WDN FEJ3

Name	(PLEASE PRINT)	

Address		Apt. #

City	State/Prov.	Zip/Postal Code

Signature (if under 18, a parent or guardian must sign)

Mail to the **Reader Service:**
IN U.S.A.: P.O. Box 1867, Buffalo, NY 14240-1867
IN CANADA: P.O. Box 609, Fort Erie, Ontario L2A 5X3

Not valid for current subscribers to the Worldwide Library series.

Want to try two free books from another line?
Call 1-800-873-8635 or visit www.ReaderService.com.

* Terms and prices subject to change without notice. Prices do not include applicable taxes. Sales tax applicable in N.Y. Canadian residents will be charged applicable taxes. Offer not valid in Quebec. This offer is limited to one order per household. All orders subject to credit approval. Credit or debit balances in a customer's account(s) may be offset by any other outstanding balance owed by or to the customer. Please allow 4 to 6 weeks for delivery. Offer available while quantities last.

Your Privacy—The Reader Service is committed to protecting your privacy. Our Privacy Policy is available online at www.ReaderService.com or upon request from the Reader Service.

We make a portion of our mailing list available to reputable third parties that offer products we believe may interest you. If you prefer that we not exchange your name with third parties, or if you wish to clarify or modify your communication preferences, please visit us at www.ReaderService.com/consumerchoice or write to us at Reader Service Preference Service, P.O. Box 9062, Buffalo, NY 14269. Include your complete name and address.

WWLI1B